She's Not You

Judi Getch Brodman

Publisher's Note:

This is a work of fiction. All names, characters, places, and events are the work of the author's imagination.

Any resemblance to real persons, places, or events is coincidental.

Solstice Publishing - www.solsticepublishing.com

She's Not You

By Judi Getch Brodman

Chapter One

A male figure crouched on the damp shoreline, silhouetted in the fading sunset. He straddled a woman on the sandy beach and licked her salty breasts. Her nervous giggle bounced off the water and evaporated into the night air. Her body lifted to join the man, the waves providing his rhythm. When he had satisfied himself, he kissed her lips, fondled her breasts and then, with one quick move, covered her face with his T-shirt, forcing her under the dark water, her long golden hair swirling around his large tanned hands. As soon as her thrashing stopped, he picked her up, tossed her limp body into a small boat, and paddled out against the incoming tide.

***

Lacing up her running shoes, Jamie Janson stretched and took off down the sandy path that led out to Great Island. The cool April morning air hung heavy with fog and a taste of salt. Jamie loved this time of day—just before sunrise when the world belonged to her, rosy in color signifying a new beginning and another chance to make things right. She loved the first, but struggled with the second. Every time she seemingly found herself in a good place, life kicked her in the butt and scattered the pieces of her being to the four winds.

Last night she had driven down from Boston alone. Friday night, and even in early spring, the traffic heading to the Cape was brutal. And of course there had been an accident. As she crept along Route 3 and came around a corner, there it stood above the trees. "I see the bridge," she whispered, still playing the game that her father had invented when she was young. He would remind her that he and Mom would be looking for the bridge, so she would sit glued to the window trying to catch the first glimpse of the glistening erector set structure. Mom and Dad would clap as if she had really seen it first.

Only another hour to Pita's magical cottage where the family—when there had been a family—spent their summer vacations. Some summers her parents would let her stay for weeks and weeks with Pita and Uncle Frank. The summers seemed endless then....

When she returned yesterday, it was sunset, the most beautiful time here on the hill. The bright reds and oranges and purples spread across the sky heralding the end of another day, another one without her parents, and now, without Pita.

The house, dark and abandoned, offered no outside light to greet her. Weeds poked through the cracked white shells in the driveway with Pita not there to yank them out before they took hold. Her bike, basket empty, leaned against the shed. She'd never have left it outside during the winter like that. All summer she could be seen riding around town, her grey hair pulled up in a bun, a bright colored shirt blowing in the breeze, wearing her denim "pedal pushers" as she had called them.

Jamie reconnected the drain pipe that fed Pita's oak barrel with water that she used for her plants. New crocuses pushed up through the dead dried stalks that Pita would have cleared away last fall.

She'd thought that, with the passage of time, the task of cleaning out Pita's belongings would become easier, the hurt less, but she was wrong, very wrong.

Her vision blurred from building tears. Her heavy breathing muffled the sound of the lapping waves as she pushed herself harder and harder. This house on the hill had always been her anchor, her happy spot, and her healing place.

Her foot caught on a yellow streamer that her tears had obscured.

"Ouch!" she cried, falling across the stake attached to the ribbon. "Can anything else go wrong?" The mingled sweat and tears stung her eyes. Taking a deep breath, Jamie stood, brushed the sand off her hands and knees, and wiped her brow with her T-shirt. At least she wasn't bleeding.

A sudden movement to her right came from a silhouetted group huddled around something by the water. A stranded dolphin? Maybe she could help carry the creature back into the water. She hurried forward when her phone screeched, breaking the silence of the morning.

"Hi Kate. Can I call back?" Jamie watched the dark scene in front of her.

"Sure. What's up?"

"I'm fine... are you okay? You're not usually up this early." Kate Kavanagh Ronan had been Jamie's college roommate years ago. Jamie had been Kate's maid of honor when she married Eddie Ronan. Eddie thought that he was doing Kate a favor by fixing Jamie up with his friend Aiden. When Aiden turned out to be snake, Eddie didn't know how to make it up to Kate and Jamie. He never knew Aiden to be a cheater and felt awful about fixing Jamie up with him. He ended his friendship with Aiden. In spite of all the drama, Kate, Jamie and Eddie remained close friends throughout the years.

Kate and Jamie couldn't be more different—Kate came from a close Irish Catholic family of three girls and two boys while Jamie, an only child with no other family, had given up on God years ago. Kate was tiny, with curly black hair and bright blue eyes, while Jamie was a tall blonde with green eyes reflecting her Lithuanian heritage. In spite of all their differences, they always referred to themselves as 'sisters by choice.'

"Well, I have some news and a question," Kate responded.

"Ma'am? Ma'am, please stop," an insistent male voice called from Jamie's left.

"Kate, I'll call you back when I can," Jamie shut Kate down in mid-sentence. Another damn interruption in her run.

"Ma'am, you'll have to turn around."

"If you call me Ma'am one more time," she emphasized each and every word. "What's your problem? I run here all the time." At five feet nine inches tall, Jamie matched the height of the baby-faced young man who approached her. The rising sun glittered off something pinned to his shirt...a badge.

"Scott, I'll handle this," a voice came from the huddled group.

Jamie's anger shifted to a male crouched over the pile of sandy debris, attempting to cover... hair, blond hair? A hand?

"Oh my God, is that a woman? Is she ...."

"Miss?" The unshaven male rose up standing a good foot taller than her. His dark thick hair fell over his forehead, and in the back curled over his T-shirt collar. A gun rested in the waistband of a pair of well-worn jeans, the knees wet and covered in sand from kneeling on the damp beach.

"Jamie, Jamie Janson," she uttered as she stared down at the seaweed entangled body.

"Miss Janson, I'm Chief Hereford." He flashed his badge and then slid it into his jean's pocket. "I'm sorry you had to see this. Somehow you missed the tape. No matter, you'll have to head back the way you came. This is a secure area and as you can see, we're a little busy right now." Visibly annoyed with her interruption, he shifted his large frame to block her view of the activities behind him.

"Tape? I'm not sure.... Is she dead?" Hadn't she read about another drowning here not long ago?

"Let's walk back," the Chief stated, making it clear that she had no choice. "Scott, keep checking the beach, will you?" he yelled back over his shoulder. "I'll take care of this. Phil, I'll be right back," he called to the small bald man with glasses who crouched next to the dead woman, barking orders to the young man beside him.

"Miss Janson, I'd appreciate it if you didn't discuss what you saw here this morning with anyone." It was not a question but an order. He struggled through the deep loose sand in his scuffed brown loafers.

"Jamie," she repeated as they stepped around the crime tape that had tripped her up earlier.

"The yellow tape?" he said as he hung his glasses from the neck of his T-shirt and rubbed his eyes. "Are you okay?"

She nodded. "I tripped over it and have the bruise to prove it." She rubbed the black and blue bump on her knee.

"Sorry, but we needed to keep people away from the scene. Obviously it didn't work." He brushed his hair back. "You look a bit shaken. Anything I can do?"

"No, but thank you." Death seemed to follow her these days.

"Is this your first time on this beach?"

"God no, I grew up down here. I bet my footprints are still on some of those dunes. I run this beach every day I can."

"Same time?" he asked.

"Pretty much—around dawn. Me and the hermit crabs." She hated hermit crabs. The bizarre little creatures with pinchers walked at strange angles and hid at low tide in depressions in the sand. When she approached them, they would gather into a giant multi-legged black monster out of a Stephen King novel and scurry away.

"Are you sure you're okay?"

"Perfect," she answered, more confidently than she felt.

"Did you happen to notice anything different this morning? Someone else on the beach? A boat on the water? A car in the parking lot when you arrived? Did you pass anyone on the road driving here? Anything odd? Out of place?"

"Nothing I can think of." She remembered dark fingers reaching for the water as the clouds marched across the bay. "I picked up my pace when I saw the rain clouds coming in. The top on my car was down and I wanted to get back to put it up."

He continued walking.

"There was no one else on the beach, no one on the road or in the parking lot," she stated. "I'm sorry." She hesitated and then added, "The sand felt looser than usual, but I saw no footprints—nothing but a bit of seaweed being pushed around by the waves. If someone was here, it must have been before the tide came in." She looked up at him. "How could two women drown right here?"

He scanned the water. "That's my job, to find out how and why. I haven't seen you before?"

"I'm staying on Milton Hill. At the top?"

His face registered nothing.

"Across from the Wharf? The Dalton place?"

"Pat Dalton's place? You're her grand—?"

"Grandniece," she filled in. "And you must be the Chief Shane Hereford that Pita often talked about?" She noticed a slight curve to his lips. "You don't go by Shane?"

"My mother wrote it on the birth certificate to appease my father and then called me Jack, my middle name." He slowed as they approached the parking lot. "I'm really sorry about Pat. The entire town misses her. A great lady. We were all wondering if someone would come or if the place would just be sold. Are you living there now?"

"'Til I sell it." She paused and then added, "I know that you watched over her, thank you."

"I liked her a lot. She was a good friend."

Jamie couldn't talk about Pita anymore. "That's my car over there," she said, pointing to a red Mustang convertible. "So, will I have to buy a newspaper to find out what happened back there?" He cast a long shadow over her, making her feel a chill all of a sudden.

He leaned against her car and emptied the sand from his loafers. He wore no socks. "I should probably take your statement later even though you don't think you saw anything."

"I'll be home." It felt strange to call Pita's cottage home.

"Do me a favor, please? Don't leave your car unprotected like this, even in your driveway. And lock your doors at home."

"That's two favors," she chided him as she climbed into the car. Then, in a more serious tone, she asked, "Are you trying to frighten me?"

He shut the door after her, placed both hands on the door frame. "I'm telling you to be careful. You saw what I saw back there."

His eyes stayed locked on hers. There was something in his tone.

"See you later." She put the car in gear and left him standing there.

***

Jack watched Jamie head out of the parking lot, her blond ponytail blowing in the wind. He had made a deathbed promise to Pat that he would look after her should they ever meet up, but now, having locked horns with her, he knew that it wouldn't be an easy promise to keep.

Chapter Two

The mid-morning sun shone through the skylight, hitting the brilliant hand-painted glass plates that sat on the shelves, turning them into prisms. The colors bounced off the white kitchen walls and cabinets, creating a kaleidoscope of colored patterns around Jamie as she washed her breakfast dishes.

But Jamie's mood reflected none of the brightness surrounding her. As she rinsed the cereal dish for the fourth time, all she could see was the woman lying in the lapping waves, her blond stringy hair floating in seaweed, a white shriveled hand lying open on the sand.

She had almost drowned once. Floating on an old inner tube, she slipped through the center. Down she went under the water, fighting to reach the surface. She struggled and struggled, but couldn't get to the sunlight above. Suddenly a strong pair of hands grabbed her and lifted her out of the water as she gulped for air. Coughing and sputtering, she rubbed her stinging eyes. Her Dad hugged her and whispered that she was safe. She had drowning nightmares for years, even as recently as last night when she had dreamt that she was being held under the water.

Rinsing the bowl again, she placed it on the rack to dry. Time to do some research. At her computer, her fingers flew across the keys searching for "drownings in Oyster Point." She thought about hacking into the police records, something she could easily do, but decided to wait and see what the Chief would share later.

The screen refreshed, producing 100-plus results. The word "drowning" triggered names of plays at the Oyster Theater, the story of a man drowning at Carter pond, the drowning of a middle-aged man off the Island about a year ago. And five years before that, an older woman had drowned off of the Neck. Jamie scanned pages until a unique story about a great white shark appeared. It washed up on Whitney's beach. That's what made this place special— people saved everyone and everything, including a great white. Yet, two women drowned just months apart.

Jamie's father always cautioned her about the fickleness of the ocean. "Beware of the undertow," he would say. She missed him.

Her parents had walked into her bedroom on a cold December night. She was struggling to complete her English paper, due the next week. Her Catholic high school English class required a five page paper on one of the "great" saints. To her, all saints were great. She reached high and chose Saint Peter…the head of the Church. As she wrote, he laid flat, dead, and uninspiring on her computer screen. She tried Saint Patrick writing about green beer and snakes. This effort read like a comedy. Finally, she searched and found a woman who made her writing come alive— Joan of Arc.

"How's it coming?" Mom asked, standing in the doorway dressed in a dark wool dress with a full skirt and black heels, showing off her tiny feet and skinny ankles. She smelled of lilacs.

"Slow. All the words are streaming through my head, but my fingers are so slow that the words just fade away. What comes out is stilted and stale."

"Relax and let it flow," Dad said as he kissed her on the forehead. He smelled of Old Spice. "We won't be gone long. Dinner with the Collin's and you know how they love to be in bed early."

Jamie pulled back the curtain above her desk. She had been so intent in finding her saint that she hadn't noticed that it had been snowing. The front lantern covered in Christmas lights showed through the snow that had turned to 'snice' as her parents called it.

"Looks nasty out there. Please be careful," she said as her Mom hugged her.

"We'll be home before you know it, honey." And then they were gone.

The next thing that Jamie remembered was a knock on her bedroom door.

"Come in Mom," Jamie said, without looking up from her computer. Mom always checked on her before Dad.

"Honey?"

Jamie swung around to see Aunt Patrice in the doorway. Aunt Patrice, her mother's aunt, had driven up from the Cape to spend the holidays with them as she always did. Jamie's real grandmothers had died before she was born, so Patrice, or Pita as Jamie called her, functioned as her grandmother. Pita's eyes glistened from within a pale and drawn face.

"What, Pita? Is it Dancer?" Dancer, Pita's ancient dog, followed her everywhere.

Just as she said that, Dancer pushed by Pita and attempted to jump on Jamie's lap, falling backwards and rolling over.

"Are you alright, you silly girl?" Dancer licked her hand.

Jamie looked back at Pita and saw the same sadness etched on her face that had been there when Uncle Frank had died.

"What? Tell me, what happened?" Jamie's heart pounded. The ice? "Where's Mom and Dad?"

Pita broke down sobbing, her face in her hands.

Jamie ran past Pita yelling, "Mom, Dad?" She turned at the top of the stairs, "No... no.... nooooooo."

Pita held out her arms to her.

She didn't want Pita's arms; she wanted her parents. She bolted down the stairs yelling, "Mom? Dad? Please, please answer."

She halted on the landing. Two policemen stood in the downstairs doorway, framed by the Christmas lights on the porch. Jamie's hands shook. "No... please tell me they're okay."

Pita touched her shoulders. When she turned, Pita shook her head, tears streaming down her lined face.

"Take me to them, please Pita. I have to be with them," she begged.

Jamie tore away from Pita, stumbled down the remaining stairs, and grabbed her heavy red plaid jacket hanging alone near the door. "Please take me," she asked the policemen. She knew him. Joe, a friend of her father's.

"It was icy, Jamie," he said. "I'm so, so sorry, honey."

"No... I won't listen to this," she cried, searching for the armholes in her jacket.

"A car hit them head on. There was nothing they could do. Your father still held your mother's hand," the other policeman added.

"No... no... stop saying it, it's not true. I won't listen," Jamie sobbed, covering her ears. "It's not them. You've made a mistake. They're coming back to help me with my paper." Then, as the realization of what had happened hit her, she slid to the floor, filling the house with a terrifying primal scream. Pita grabbed her up and held her close.

An apparition, surrounded by the glow of red and green lights, appeared behind the police officers. His face shown pale with deep crags etched into his cheeks, his dark squinty eyes bore into Jamie and his stringy sparse grey hairs stuck to his head from the snow. His black overcoat, sprinkled with snow, covered a long black cassock and allowed his dingy white collar to show below his hanging jowls. He stepped closer to Jamie and extended his hand.

She shrank further into Pita arms.

"The police called Father Jerome to be with your parents," Pita's voice cracked.

"My dear little one, this is God's will," the priest spouted as he waved his limp hand in a motion depicting a cross.

Jamie stared at him in horror and disbelief. "What kind of a God does this?"

"I understand your anger, child. But we have to accept it. He knows best."

"No, I don't. I won't accept it," she stated defiantly, tears streaming down her face. "No good God would do this."

Pita shushed her and pulled her close.

The apparition murmured something like "God forgive you child," turned and disappeared into the darkness. She heard him mumble, "It's her grief talking."

The rest of that night was a blur. She stood at the police station as unknown faces discussed her life. She heard the words "orphan now" and "underage." She shook in a corner knowing nothing would ever be the same. Pita looked over, nodded, and signed some papers and they had gone home to begin their new life together.

That day had changed Jamie forever. She had lost her parents, her God, and her protection. At sixteen years old, she was alone, an orphan. She felt her heart become hard as a rock as the molten rage that coursed through her cooled and solidified.

In the haze of the funeral, she walked behind the metal caskets, holding on to Pita's arm. She heard Pita's quiet sobs, yet she felt nothing. She was empty. Drapes were handed to her by the priest and she covered each casket, hearing his words, "It's the last act that you will do for them."

The ghoul of a priest's eyes bored into her as he chanted Latin words and swung a container of smoking incense over her parents to cleanse them. Her parents didn't need cleansing. The smell nauseated her and would for the rest of her life.

After that day, Jamie returned to church once when she was Kate's maid-of-honor. Jamie listened to the music that sang praise to a God who had abandoned her and stood at the church altar but never looked up at the cross. He had suffered for a valid reason; she had never understood why she had to. It was a standoff. And then, when Pita died, Jamie sat like a stone, Kate's arm around her, enduring the chants and music to a deaf God. Following the Mass, she left Pita with Uncle Frank, knowing that she would never again sit in God's house.

Angry for allowing those hurtful memories to creep into her mind, she blew her nose, wiped her face, and dialed Kate.

"For heaven's sake, I thought you had been absconded with," Kate answered in her usual dramatic fashion. Most times it made Jamie laugh, but not today.

"I'm fine," she responded reaching for another tissue. "Sorry I cut you off earlier, but I stumbled on"— she remembered what Jack had asked— "the Chief of Police. He was scouring the beach for something and didn't like me messing up their search." She felt guilty lying to Kate.

"You sound awful. What's going on? It's that house, isn't it? I knew it. Close it up and come home." Kate rapid fired her questions.

"Allergies," she lied again. "And I didn't sleep very well." When she entered the pitch dark house last night, she cried, watching visions of her Dad whirling her around the room as her mother pumped the pedals on the player piano; she and Pita out on the deck, rebuilding the castle dollhouse that Dad had rescued from the flea market. The old dollhouse still sat in the attic.

"Please don't stay there alone—it's too much for you. Clean it out later."

"It's already later, Kate. I don't have a choice. Anyway, tell me what's going on with you?" Jamie switched subjects, feeling a headache coming on.

"Well, maybe this isn't the right time to tell you this, but maybe it's the perfect time." She hesitated. "How do you feel about being an auntie?"

Jamie processed what Kate said. "Oh my God, oh my God, you're pregnant? I can't believe it. I want to hug you." A new life... she needed a new beginning to concentrate on. "You and Eddie are going to be the best parents."

"Well, we just found out and I had to let you know right away. I hope everything goes well."

"Stop it. Nothing's going to happen." Kate would bog her and Eddie down with all her family superstitions. No baby things in the house before the baby is born, bad luck. No nursery, bad luck. Baby's sex would wait till she or he was born. Kate's mother would make sure all the superstitions were followed to the nth degree.

Jamie's job would be to make sure that nothing harmed this baby, nothing. "You sound like there's more? Are you okay?"

"I'm fine... more than fine. I... you... I know you aren't much of a church goer, but I'd... Eddie and I would like you to be the baby's Godmother? Would you... could you do that for us? That way, we'll know that if anything happens to us, you'll take care of the baby." This was Kate's way of trying to lure Jamie back to the church.

"Don't be silly. No negativity, it'll affect the baby. Nothing's going to happen to you or Eddie or the baby. Do you hear me? Nothing."

"Oh Jamie. I'm so excited, scared, and overwhelmed."

Tears were coming again or maybe they had never stopped. "I just can't believe it—we're having a baby." She blew her nose. "You rescued me today, Kate. Thank you so much."

"Oh honey, don't thank me yet. I'll be leaning on you for years. I'll need all the help I can get to raise this kid of ours."

"I'll be right there." Jamie needed to go to the knitting store for yarn. Kate needn't know. "Our baby's going to be the smartest, cutest, most adorable kid ever born," she laughed as more tears came. She couldn't stop them.

"Are you okay?"

"Sure, why?"

"Well, remember how we used to talk about raising our babies together?"

Jamie smiled, "Young girls' dreams."

"I'm...." Kate's voice broke.

"It still may happen, who knows what lies around the corner."

"If you say so." After a few seconds, she asked, "So who were you yelling at earlier?"

The news of the dead women had to be kept from Kate. She didn't need to worry. "I bumped into the Police Chief searching for something, that's all. He's the man who was friends with Pita?" The conversation had to be taken down a different path.

"I remember. He watched over her?"

"He did." Jamie had assumed that Jack was older, like Pita. "So give me a date for the arrival of this little bundle."

"Late September or early October. Will you be ready?" Kate asked.

"I'm ready now." How wonderful it would be to hold Kate's baby in her arms.

"Okay, Eddie's calling. We're off to see my parents and tell them in person."

"Give them hugs from me as well. Bye, love you and talk later. You take good care of our baby, right? And call if you need anything."

"I will. And if you need me for something down there, you call too. Love you, Auntie."

Jamie went back to the kitchen, shook an aspirin from the bottle on the windowsill, and gulped it down with a mouthful of coffee. What a day it had been already, and it wasn't even ten o'clock.

Chapter Three

Jack slid a packet of spearmint gum from his jean's pocket. It took all his mental toughness and a vow that he had made to his mother to resist bumming a cigarette from Phil. He shook his head. He had to stop making these deathbed promises, they were killing him. He popped the gum into his mouth.

Phil wrapped the pale empty shell with unfocused sea green eyes and shriveled folded hands in a clear plastic sheet. With his helper, they placed the body into the ominous black bag. As they zipped it up, the bright pink fingernails mixed with the ancient seaweed validated the existence of a previous life.

Over the years, Jack had wondered if he had chosen this place, or if this town had chosen him. He had taken this position as an escape from Boston. His plans were to stay a few years and then move on. He assumed that he would be bored, maybe even lonely in an isolated town like Oyster Point, but he was neither.

He scanned the harbor as Phil finished securing the body. The moored boats swayed in the outgoing tide and sweet grey and white clapboard cottages tinted pink from the morning sun snuggled in the grassy dunes. The sandy beach was pristine—except for the body bag and a bit of seaweed that had come in with the morning tide. There were no footprints, no stranded boats— nothing. Another woman, tall, blonde with green eyes, dressed in a top and no underwear, had washed up a few feet away about a month ago.

The first woman could have fallen overboard and hit her head, except Phil found no bruises to prove that theory. In fact, there were no marks on her at all. Jack was beginning to think that he had been a Boston cop too long, but his gut was telling him serial killer.

"Anything, Phil?" Jack removed his baseball cap and pushed back his thick dark hair. It was starting to curl. He'd have to find time for a haircut.

"Nothing I can see, Jack. Come by the office later after I have done my examination."

"Call me if you find something." Jack started to walk away and then turned. "Doesn't feel right, Phil."

Phil looked over his rimless glasses. "Sure doesn't. Too similar to the last one."

Jack slogged through the sand, heading back to his car. He had been called the "Case Buster" in Boston because he could sniff out the smallest clue, follow it up and down trees, across rivers until he found the sign post pointing to the killer. He had to dig for that tiny clue with these women. He knew it was there.

As he drove the dirt road up to the Dalton cottage, he remembered all the nights that he showed up at Pat's door with dinner, a couple of beers, and a pint of black raspberry chocolate chip ice cream, her favorite. In summer, they ate out on the back porch; in winter, they hunkered down in the summery feeling living room away from the cutting wind off the water. With feet up on the driftwood coffee table, fireplace going, they debated the day's news.

Pat's quintessential gray-shingled Cape Cod cottage with snow white trim was perched high up on Shirttail Point. Part of Pat's love of the property was the story that her house along with five others had been moved to Oyster Point around 1900. The cottages were called "the Lemon Pie cottages" because of their yellow color and distinctive high peaked roofs resembling a wedge of pie.

Pat and Frank had purchased and rebuilt one of the Lemon Pies soon after they had been toppled and damaged by a hurricane.

"Thanks, Pat. For some reason I'm thinking Jamie's going to be a handful and you knew it," he said aloud as he walked up the white broken shell coated walk that led to the house. Now that was something he never understood, why would someone use broken seashells for a walk? The entire purpose of being here in summer was walking barefoot.

Jack tapped softly on the door. He fumbled in his pocket for the key that Pat had given him. The door swung open and Jamie appeared. He cleared his throat. "Morning again. Am I interrupting? I can come back if you want?" He stumbled over his words. "We got off to a rocky start this morning. Sorry, I hadn't had my coffee. Actually still haven't."

"Well come in, I have a fresh pot brewing."

Just the smell of the coffee cleared his head as he followed Jamie into the kitchen.

"And please, no apologies. I wasn't watching where I was going. That's what happens when you answer the phone while you're running." She smiled. "Hope I didn't scare your deputy too much. I was pretty cranky myself. I hate it when my run is interrupted, and your deputy was the second interruption this morning."

"Scott wasn't too scarred."

Her smile reached the huge green eyes that had been hidden behind sunglasses this morning. She wasn't gorgeous, but there was something special, maybe even vulnerable about her. From what Pat had said, she held a pretty good job and from what he had seen on the beach, she seemed pretty confident in her own skin. He couldn't say that about many of the woman he had come across. And those large eyes and that genuine smile sure held a man's attention.

"I'm glad you had a chance to stop by. So quiet here now."

He nodded, "I realize it's not the same which is another reason I stopped by, to see how you're doing here— alone."

"Well... she was all I had." She scanned the room. "I know I should've been here sooner, but I couldn't. I dreaded walking through that door last night alone. It must be hard for you as well."

He wanted to hug her like he did his niece when she thought her world was falling apart. Instead, he stood there and did nothing. "Certainly not like you."

She adjusted the oversized sweatshirt that hung over her shorts. "As I washed the dishes, I couldn't get that woman out of my mind." The loose curly strands of light hair that she tucked into her ponytail didn't obey, falling freely around her face. "Not right to end your life like that."

"I agree. I'm working on it."

"I know you are. While you're working on that, I've plenty to do myself—the box on the floor filled with Pita's folders, her paintings up in the loft, closets to clean out." She shrugged. "And I haven't even cleaned up yet from my run," she added as she untied and kicked her running shoes to a spot by the door and then straightened them, a movement she'd learned from Pita. Organization is very important.

"No apologies needed. You look great." His statement hung between them for a few seconds.

Pulling out the red elastic thingamajig that held her hair together and slipping it around her wrist, she said, "My scrunchie. I have a million of them. Don't know what I'd do without them," she snapped it on her wrist and fluffed her blond curly hair, letting it spill over her shoulders. "You know, I thought six months would be enough time for me to face what had to be done here, but it isn't, it really isn't."

He could see that she was becoming emotional. "I'll help with anything I can," was all he could think of saying.

"Thanks. Let's have that coffee. We can both use a good strong cup."

Reaching for a coffee cup in the top cabinet, he stopped. "Sorry, I used to just help myself."

"Please, help yourself."

He poured a cup and filled hers. Having doctored his coffee, he walked to the living room.

"I've always loved this room," he said, standing behind the puffy red and yellow flowered sofa. "Pat was such a collector of old things. She'd scour the flea markets and find things that most people wouldn't even notice. Like that blue bookcase, You should have seen it when I helped her lift it out of the car, but she rebuilt and sanded it and finally painted it," he pointed to the structure that was covered with golden starfish, shiny oyster and quahog shells, and even a few brown hermit crabs peeking over the top.

"You know, she and I painted the scenes on the walls." The east wall reflected sunrise over the water and the west wall mirrored the sunset over the Harbor. "You were here a lot." Jamie interrupted his thoughts.

"I was." This was the first time that Jack had been back inside the cottage since the night that Pat had died.

"Can you tell me how it happened?" She sat down at the table with Jack across from her.

"Are you sure you want to talk about this now? Maybe we could do this after you've adjusted a little bit more to being here?"

"Please, I need to know."

Maybe she was stronger than she looked. Maybe.... "It was Friday about 11 AM. I remember because I was writing up the reports for the week. The phone rang. Pat's voice was barely audible. I grabbed my keys and headed out. I knew that she wouldn't call unless something bad had happened.

"About six months ago, she sat me down for a heart-to-heart chat, as she called it. I always dreaded chats. My Dad's talks ended up as a dressing down about my friends or my driving or girlfriends. When I was older, those discussions were with those girlfriends about my job, my hair, my something.

"Anyway, Pat said she had heart failure. She had been on drugs for years, but they were slowly refusing to help the fluid buildup. She knew eventually the drugs would run their course. We didn't know how long, but she made me promise not to tell you. She said that she didn't want you worrying, running down and fussing over her. I thought about contacting you, but I'm not a good liar and I bet you aren't either. She would know. It was easy for me to keep her promise because our paths never crossed. I assume she kept her secret from you?"

"She never said a word."

"I prayed to God that I'd make it in time, that she wouldn't die alone. I don't know how much you know about our relationship, but she was like a second mother … I couldn't let her die alone." He sipped his coffee.

"It should have been me with her." She looked away.

"I knew if I called you, you would never have made it."

Jamie nodded, blowing her nose.

"Are you sure you want to hear this, Jamie?"

She nodded. "Please…."

"When I came in, she was in front of the sliders. I knelt and cradled her head in my lap. Her eyes fluttered open and she smiled that all-knowing smile, you know the one, like she could read your mind?"

Jamie nodded, swiping at the tears on her cheeks.

"I told her to save her breath. She kept trying to talk. I told her that we were going to make it. She reached up, touched my face, and shook her head. She knew and so did I." He paused and took another sip of coffee. "She crooked her finger for me to come closer, kissed my cheek, her breathing hard and then asked me to promise to take care of you. Her words were that you would be 'broken again' and would need someone strong. When I hesitated, she grabbed on to me tighter. I had to promise. Her hand slipped from my shoulder. She still had a smile on her face as her breathing stopped. I'm so sorry Jamie, I couldn't help her."

"I know that." She grabbed another tissue from the box on the table. "I'm sorry to take you through that again, but I needed to know what her last minutes were like." Her voice caught. "Thank you so much for being with her when she… went. I should have come down months ago. I just couldn't. What am I going to do without her?" She dabbed at her eyes.

Jack knew that he wasn't expected to answer.

"I'm sorry…."

"Never apologize for asking me questions." Jamie had somehow endured so much sadness in her life. "And you already know that I'll only answer what I want to." He tried to lighten the conversation. "And a warning, I'm changing the subject now. Pat said you travelled a lot? What exactly do you do?"

"Hard to explain my job—I catch bad guys like you, but find them in cyberspace. I go after hackers who irritate my clients. I'm like the wizard in Oz… hiding behind the green curtain, waiting and watching."

"Really? You're correct. I haven't any idea what you do."

His comment almost brought a smile to her face. "Well, speaking of needing help, anything new on the woman on the beach?"

"Not that I know of. Phil, the coroner, the man on the beach with me, he's still doing his thing."

"Well, if I can help, I will. I'm pretty good at my job."

"Maybe I can help with Pat's stuff?"

"That would be terrific," she hesitated. "I'm embarrassed to say that I really don't know what she did with a lot of her time down here, so maybe you can fill in the blanks?"

Through the screen door, Jack's car radio cut into their conversation. He had to check in at the office. Maybe it was information on the drowning.

"Sorry. Sounds like they're looking for me." He hesitated for a second before adding, "How about I bring over some dinner tonight and we make a dent in that box?"

"I'd love that."

"How does six o'clock sound?"

"Perfect." She began to shoo him out the door when he turned and said, "Your coffee was great."

"Stop by any time. There's always a pot on."

When he reached his car, he turned and saw her standing at the window watching him. He'd be damned, but she was a dead ringer for the women on the beach. As he slid into his seat, he remembered he had forgotten all about taking her statement.

Chapter Four

Jack sat behind his desk, absentmindedly tapping his pencil on the pad of paper in front of him, thinking about the call he had taken a moment ago. Withdrawing a manila folder from the bottom of the pile on the floor beside his chair, he opened it and jotted notes inside the cover. A thick stack of papers secured to the back cover stared back at him. This case had plagued him for over two years. As good as he was at busting cases wide open, he couldn't find this case's elusive first clue.

A young Boston woman, Justine Colbert, vanished from her South Boston apartment. She didn't figure to be a runaway and she never turned up dead. And, that's what baffled him. Why would she run away? Everything pointed to her being happy—she was engaged and planning a big wedding. Her parents appeared to be pleased with her choice of husband.

But there was no evidence that pointed to someone taking her or killing her. Where was she then? Somewhere, among all the bits and pieces of information in this folder, there was a hint. He rubbed his temples as he reread the reports.

Justine's fiancé, Thomas Cramer, lived and worked in New York City. Jack flipped through the sheets and located his partner's notes from the interview with Cramer. He'd written, "Thomas appears reasonably distraught over Justine's disappearance and has supplied no additional information from what her parents had said. He confirmed that they were engaged, happy, and looking forward to a life together. Did I think he was being truthful? Not sure. Something made me feel there was something he wouldn't or couldn't say."

He flipped through more pages, finding the copies of the old email messages, letters, and phone records that Justine had with Thomas. They showed nothing. Rereading his scribbling in the margins, he remembered how he had thought that it was funny their correspondence showed no romance, no "I love you," no "I miss you." Maybe young people didn't write things like that. How could he judge when he had never written anything like that to Lizz. But then, he didn't really love her. Was that the clue he was missing? Thomas and Justine's love had vanished like his and Lizz's had? And if it had, wouldn't they have just broken the engagement off like he did?

Exasperated, he snapped the pencil in his hand. "Damn it," he said as he threw the pieces into the wastebasket, the noise of chunks hitting the metal echoing through the office.

The clue existed in here somewhere. He thumbed through the notes again. No one knew what Justine was wearing when she disappeared. Her workday seemed normal. After work, she met a girlfriend for dinner. They both left the restaurant around 9 p.m. and had gone their separate ways. A taxi dropped Justine off in front of her apartment building. The driver said that she appeared happy and upbeat, and gave him a very generous tip. The security man had seen her at about 9:15 p.m. She said good night to him, took the elevator to her floor, and evaporated into thin air. Jack picked another pencil out of his top drawer. His stash was running low. He scribbled a note to his secretary.

He had been the lead detective on this case. Justine's mother phoned from Connecticut to report her daughter missing. Three hours later, both parents stood in his office discussing what they knew about her disappearance. Every question he asked, every answer Dr. and Mrs. Colbert provided, had been chronicled in this folder. He flipped to another sheet.

The forensic report stated that there has been no sign of foul play, no blood evidence, and no sign of a struggle. Forensics unearthed nothing. Justine's apartment looked like no one had ever lived there, it was so clean. Jack had solved many missing person's cases, but this one baffled him. Even though the Boston Police department had placed Justine's folder in the cold case file, Jack and others kept it open.

Talking to Justine's parents frustrated him. Her mother had been involved in many of Justine's daily activities, talked to her constantly, and looked forward to her visits home. When she went missing, her mother's life had stopped. Justine, like Jamie, was an only child. Jack felt sorry for her parents, but didn't know how to encourage them to start living again. He knew that there was a good chance that their daughter might never be found. How do you say that to a parent? He leaned back in his chair and stared up at the ceiling. He had been over this information time and time again and... his gaze shifted to outside his office where Jamie stood, watching him. He waved her in.

Sticking her head inside the office, she asked, "Am I disturbing you? You were so engrossed in that file." She hesitated. "I thought I'd stop by and see if you wanted me to pick up anything special for tonight. I'm sorry if I interrupted."

"Absolutely not. Come in." He flipped the folder closed and stood up. "What a great surprise." When he stood in Pat's kitchen this morning, he realized how much he missed having someone to talk to, a person to trust. Being a small town Police Chief made him an outsider. He maintained a professional distance from his deputies and officers. The few locals he met for a beer weren't really friends. With Pat, he could stop by her place any time, day or night, and she would welcome him as family. And today, Jamie appeared, bright, attractive, and easy to talk to, a lot like her aunt.

"Do I sense that you're afraid of the concoctions I might make tonight? I'm actually a pretty good cook on the grill. It's still in the shed, isn't it?" Without a grill, he was dead in the water.

"I haven't looked in the shed yet,"

"When I come over tonight, I'll haul it to the deck so you can use it all summer. I'll pick up some charcoal. You might think about buying a gas grill. I tried to convince Pat last summer to buy one, but you know her."

They both stood there as his last words hung in the air.

"Anyway" he continued, "let me know if you're interested." When he looked at her, she was shaking her head. He was rambling and trying too hard, but she tilted his world.

"I'll pick up something to drink and see you at six?"

"Pick out a good local beer for me." He nodded as he walked her out of the station. "Where's your car?" he asked, scanning the parking lot for her convertible.

"No car today. Took the bike after I had the tires checked. I needed the exercise and fresh air." She kicked the bike stand back, turned the bike around, and pedaled out the parking lot into the street, waving backwards to him.

He waved, visualizing Pat on that very same bike.

He strode back into his office, shutting the door behind him. He dialed the state police. They had no ID on the dead woman and no one had reported her missing. Then he phoned Phil, who had no new information. The autopsy had shown no forced sex, no bruises that proved the woman had been choked or held underwater. The cause of death was drowning. Phil still awaited other tests results, but so far, he found nothing that indicated foul play. Jack knew otherwise. He couldn't prove it, but it was murder.

Chapter Five

Jamie placed two hand-painted glass plates with matching wine glasses onto the lilac cloth that draped the small round table sitting in the corner of the living area. A milky sea green vase overflowing with daffodils from the side garden sat in the center of the table. She dismissed the cut glass candleholders—too intimate. She pushed the carton overflowing with Pita's files close to the couch and checked her watch. Five-thirty, time to get dressed.

Her phone rang as she walked into the bedroom. "Hi Kate. How are you feeling?"

"Great, no morning sickness yet. What's up with you? Feeling better?"

"A bit. Can I call you back later or tomorrow?" Jamie yanked a pair of slightly worn jeans from the closet. Rummaging around in the bureau drawer, she located her favorite blue sweater. "I have someone coming over."

"You have a date? Wow, this guy wastes no time. Is this the Chief?"

"Kate." She hit the speakerphone button so she could continue dressing. "It's not a date. He's coming over to take my statement from this morning," she blurted out before she knew it. "He's helping me go through some of Pita's folders as well." She knew Kate would pick up on what she said.

"Why would he need a statement from you? What happened out there?"

Kate would badger her for the truth, but Jamie had been warned to say nothing. "I can't really say, Kate. I'm not really sure…." She was a terrible liar. When she broke up with Aiden, she told Kate it was mutual, but Eddie suspected something different and confronted Aiden.

Aiden, not knowing what Eddie knew, spilled the entire story, saying it was a lack of judgement. After a few choice words, Eddie ended their friendship.

"What are you not telling me? Did you have an accident this morning? Is that why the police were there?"

"No… no, of course not. Something happened on the beach—not to me—and the Chief's coming tonight to tell me what… it was. That's all I can say."

"Is dinner involved?"

"Kate." Jamie took a quick turn in front of the antique full-length mirror.

"I'm not criticizing. Is he old or young? You didn't say much about him. You know how I feel, I want you to find someone, be happy like me," Kate said.

"I'm not… please Kate, I have enough on my plate these days. I don't have time to contend with a man right now."

"Okay," Kate interrupted. "But it's been a long time since Mike and Aiden. Maybe having a man in your life is exactly what you need. I'll call tomorrow. Keep your eyes and heart open. Love you. Bye."

Kate was exasperating sometimes, but then, she always meant well.

Jamie and Mike had been together throughout college and then, one day after graduation, he said, "I'm going to California." "Why now?" she had asked. He said he needed to travel, take his bike on the road. "This is a perfect time to go," he'd continued. "No strings." That comment had hurt her so deeply and still did. She was not a string.

"Come with me?" he asked, when he saw her face. But she knew that she didn't fit in his plans. With her background, she wanted roots, a home, not the road. "I have to do this," he said. "Wait for me?"

Ten years later, she was still waiting and he hadn't reappeared. She had never told Kate, but she had done a number of computer searches looking for him—he had just dropped off the earth.

Opening the top drawer of her jewelry box, she chose her mother's opal necklace. Pita had given Jamie the small wrapped box on her eighteenth birthday, promising that the opal had magic and would keep her safe. Jamie had stopped believing in magic years ago and didn't need a necklace to keep her safe. She fluffed her hair, deciding to wear it loose for a change.

The sound of the kitchen timer alerted her that the brownies were ready. Baking used to be one of her passions, but being alone, she didn't cook much anymore. Tonight was an opportunity to mix up a batch of her mother's delicious brownies, the ones that had filled the house with a wonderful smell when she returned from school.

Maybe her mother's blond squares would soften that mysterious facade of Jack's.

Chapter Six

Jack hauled the grill from the shed to the deck, cleaned it, and lit the charcoal. Sitting on the couch, he and Jamie chatted about Pita's garden gnomes and his typical day.

"Usually I have twenty calls about howling coyotes and barking dogs to start the day. It only gets worse and more dangerous as summer comes on. Then, we're into loud parties, drinking teens on the wharf, and speeding cars. I mean, this is a tough job," he said, trying to sound serious, but missing the mark.

Jamie laughed.

The sunset seemed to bath the room in softness and quiet. And then Jack's phone pinged.

"Everything okay?" Jamie asked as he checked it.

"Just an update on this morning." Jack rose to check the charcoal.

"Anything you can tell me?" she called out to him.

"Not yet. Maybe later," he replied, sitting back down next to her.

She draped her arms around her knees, her bare feet sticking out. "You know, I'm pretty damn good at finding out information—even hidden stuff?"

"I don't doubt it." He meant what he said; he wasn't going to talk about it. He stared at her bright red toenails.

"Yup, I'm a painted woman."

"That color seems at odds with you. I mean, you aren't the flashy type." He was obviously embarrassed at being caught staring at her bare feet.

She stretched out her foot. "I kind of like them. In Catholic schools, I couldn't wear jewelry, makeup, my hair had to be pulled back or up, but"—she hesitated for a second—"the nuns couldn't see my feet. How horrified they would have been if they saw my bright red toenails. I still laugh when I paint them."

"Catholic school girl, huh?"

"That was years ago. Haven't been to church in a long time." She would leave it at that for now. Could she coax him into sharing something of himself? "Did you grow up around here?"

He swiped his hair back in a nervous movement. "Wyoming. After my Dad died, my Mother took the family east to be near her sisters in upstate New York."

"So that's why your Dad chose Shane."

He nodded, "My Dad was born and raised there."

"When I was a child, we camped in a town called Ten Sleep. We even went to a rodeo." She shook her head. "Funny what sticks in your mind, isn't it? My parents camping, now there's a memory. Your mother didn't like it out there?"

"No, too far away from civilization, she would say to my father. He would just smile. So when he died, she headed east."

"I'm sorry. How old were you when your father died?"

"Twelve." He flicked an imaginary fleck off his brown sweater.

"My father and mother died when I was sixteen." She uncoiled her legs, slipped her feet into flip-flops, and rose off the couch, declaring that they'd better eat or they would never have a chance to sort through Pita's boxes.

"The sunset is one of the fiery ones." she called from the kitchen. "My Dad used to say, 'Red at night, a sailor's delight; red at morn, sailor be warned.' We have a sailor's delight going on." She hustled around the kitchen making and tossing a salad. She had become an expert at hiding her emotions from everyone, or so she thought.

Chapter Seven

"I'm stuffed." Jamie said as she stacked the plates in Jack's hands. "That was delicious; I don't usually eat red meat."

"Why didn't you tell me? I could've grilled fish."

"Not a big deal. I eat it, just careful where. It wasn't hanging in a window, was it?" She added dishes to his pile. "Please put these in the sink for me? I'll wash them later. Thanks. You said you were on call?"

"Always" he answered matter-of-factly, storing the salad dressings on the top shelf of the refrigerator. As he closed the door, he said, "You know Pat loved getting your postcards." Pictures of England, India, Spain, and the South Pacific covered the door. "You travel a lot."

"Not so much now. It wears thin after a while. Oh shoot, speaking of traveling, I forgot to ask Kate to check my mail." Picking up a pink piece of chalk from the chalkboard next to the door, she said, "See, I make lists now, not a good sign." She wrote, "mail – call Kate" to a long list of items, one of which said to call Matt. She wiped her hands on her jeans. "And speaking of weird things, Pita told me you were a Boston policeman and a lawyer?"

"Weird things?"

"The chalk board, not you."

"Phew, I was afraid I'd been made," he laughed. "Anyway, to answer your questions, law wasn't my thing, not a suit or court kind of guy." He shrugged, wondering who Matt was. "My poor mother almost dissolved when I became a Boston patrolman, the night beat. She had lived through years of wondering if my Dad would come home. One day he didn't. She was afraid the same thing would happen to me." He'd been caught in a number of firefights,

Judi Getch Brodman • 38

one that disabled his partner and another had him in the hospital with a flesh wound in his side. At night he chain-smoked; off duty, he drank with the guys. He was sliding down the slippery slope of self-destruction. His workouts kept him sane… barely.

"Did you live in the city?" Jamie asked.

"The West End."

"I live close to there. Pita never told me why you left."

"The violence. It never stopped." His mind went back to the dead women on the beach. "Course I thought I had left that all behind until a couple of weeks ago." He checked his phone again. No new messages or calls. "That's it." Pat didn't know many of the details of his life, especially about Lizz, the woman he had lived with, who had created most of the angst in his life.

"How did you end up in Oyster Point, of all places?"

"Saw the job opening and I have family on the Cape. And it's quiet here, most of the time."

"You have family here in Oyster Point?" she asked as she slid the dish of warm butterscotch brownies on the coffee table in front of the couch. "My Mom's recipe."

"Maybe after we make a dent in these papers? We should get going."

He avoided the question about family. She let it slide. "You're correct, Counselor." Dropping to the floor, sitting cross-legged in front of the box, Jamie grabbed a bunch of documents wrapped in an elastic band.

"Before we start, can I ask you one question?"

"Depends," she answered.

"Since I answered a slew of questions for you…"

Jamie interrupted, "I'm sorry. I didn't mean to pry. I just wanted to know more about you since you were so close to Pita."

"I didn't mean that comment in a bad way. You'll learn that I answer what I want to and ignore the rest."

"Okay. Can I use the same rules… tell if I want to, ignore if I don't?"

"Yes ma'am," he laughed with his hands up in front of him.

She shook her head. "Dangerous, you know that. What did you want to ask me?"

"I'd like to know about your summers here as a kid." Pat was Jamie's guardian after her parents were killed, but he wondered what her childhood had been like.

"Well now, let's see what I can remember." Leaning back on her elbows, stretching her legs out in front of her, she began, "Once upon a time, when I was very young, Pita and Frank brought me here. Since they had no children and I was so adorable, they couldn't resist having me around during the summer. I slept in that hot, stuffy loft." She pointed to the upper level. "When I was about ten years old, the skylight magically appeared in the roof. Each night, I would lie on my cot, feeling the cool night air blow over me, watching the earth turn, and the stars drift in and out of view. They became my friends, appearing regularly in the dark sky. I knew them all by name and would ask them where they had been and what they had seen that day." She appeared transfixed as she looked up. "How I envied them traveling all around the world, together as a group. They always had each other, always."

Jack looked at the photographs of Jamie hanging on the walls and her smile never seemed to reach her eyes.

"And when my parents died, I needed them. Sounds silly now, but they helped me through those black nights. I told them everything. And they listened. I still love looking up and seeing them in the night sky. I wonder if they remember me." She picked up her glasses and wiped the lenses on her jersey. "Enough about me, shall we return to the box? Or we can talk about you again?"

"It doesn't sound silly to me at all." Jack always had a houseful of sisters and friends around when he was young. It was hard to think of Jamie growing up all alone.

"I guess that's a no, so let's get started." Putting on her glasses, she held a group of papers. "These are folders about the town, tours, even about this cottage. I don't need any help with those." She placed them on the floor beside her. "But these, these look they might be yours? Case NY 121? BOS 362?" She passed him one of the manila folders. "They look like old cases maybe. Here's one that I found open on the table with 'Justine Colbert' written on the tab." She adjusted her glasses. "Why did Pita have them?"

He didn't have to look at the folder in his hand. "They're old unsolved cases."

Jamie fingered the items in the stack, counting them, looking up at him as she reached the last one. "Twelve of them?" Her words hung in the air.

"Come, sit here." He tapped the spot next to him. "You know Pat was the very first person to welcome me to this town. When I found out that she lived alone, I'd check on her or have the guys check on her. It wasn't long before she asked me to dinner. Most nights I'd pick up something for us to share. She loved mysteries and enjoyed hearing about my unsolved cases. We'd eat, talk, and share a sunset. My Mom's gone so it felt nice to have someone worry about me. I guess like you, I was an orphan too. Pat worried about you as well. She was afraid that when she died, you would be alone again. That's why she made me swear to look out for you."

"She was always overprotective. You don't have to watch over me. I can take care of myself."

"There are many things I don't have to do, but I promised her. Would you break a vow that you had made to her?"

"No, but then I might not have made a promise I couldn't keep. Now, tell me again why she had these cases."

"They're unsolved. The Boston guys and I still meet once a month in a bar in the city to talk about any new leads. I'd tell her what I heard, and then, she'd question me about the crimes and the people involved. She made notes. Maybe a week later or so, she'd call or stop by the station with a clue that would sometimes break the case. She helped us find a little girl who had been missing for years. Don't ask me how."

"I taught her to use the computer. You think she did computer searches?"

He shook his head. "Doubt it. We spent hours, days, sometimes months checking out leads." Jack removed his phone from his shirt pocket and read the message that flashed on the screen. "I have to check in at the station." He began collecting the folders.

"Don't worry about those. I'll go through them and make sure that none of Pita's papers are mixed in before you take them." She pushed the stack away with her foot. "Don't forget the leftovers I packed for you. And my brownies."

"Thanks." Jack slipped on his jacket and headed to the door as Jamie bagged up the containers of food. "I'll have to return these plastic things. Maybe I'll see you tomorrow?"

"Probably."

"Lock the doors please."

"Talk about being overprotective. No one ever locks their doors down here."

"That was then, this is now. And use the bolt."

Chapter Eight

"Kate, everything okay? You're up early again." The phone call had once again interrupted her early run. She only hoped that the baby was alright.

"Well, look who's talking. I was going to leave you a message, but you're up too. I called for a couple of reasons, but first, what happened last night? Wait, am I interrupting something? You sound like you are out of breath."

"I'm running, Kate. Honestly. We had dinner, we talked, and he left. He's very nice."

"Well, I guess that's a good getting to know you date."

"It wasn't a date." Jamie could envision Kate's smug smile.

"Okay. Okay. Anyway, the reason I'm making this pre-dawn call is because I'm on my way to the airport. A trip to LA came up. I'm thinking while I'm on the West Coast, I'll fly up to Seattle to see my Dad. Check on him. Tell him the good news in person."

"Lucky you. You're okay to fly?"

"Absolutely."

"Give him a hug for me. Are you on your way now?"

"Waiting for the cab, why? You need something?"

"A small favor? I forgot to forward my mail. Can you or Eddie stop by my building and shove whatever's there into my apartment?" Kate and Eddie lived around the block from Jamie and they both had keys to each other's apartments. But now with Kate expecting, they might start looking for a house out of the city. Jamie would miss her.

They had always lived steps away from each other. She would cross that bridge when the time came.

"Done."

"Jamie?" A voice came from the dark to her right.

Turning, she saw Jack, dressed in sweats and a T-shirt, making his way through the sand toward her. She waved. "Kate, happy trails. I have to hang up."

"Hopefully that's him? Too early for you to be out there alone... please be safe. I know something's going on down there. You'll tell me when you can?"

"You know me too well. Thanks for taking care of my mail, safe trip. Call me when you get in. Love you."

"You too, sister. Enjoy the Chief." Kate hung up.

"Is this your place?" Jamie asked as Jack reached her. She always wondered who lived in the beach house that seemed to grow out of the dune.

"Rent it. You're out early, sun's not even up. Can I join you?"

"I couldn't sleep." She didn't need to tell him that every time she closed her eyes, she saw seaweed mixed with blond hair and a shriveled white hand with pink nails.

"Well, you have good excuses for not sleeping, given with what you've been going through lately. Me, couldn't sleep either," he replied, running by her side.

"I finally brought the folder on Justine Colbert to bed with me to see what was so interesting – the one Pita had been looking at?"

He nodded.

"I did some computer research on her, but found nothing unusual—just her age, place of birth, company she worked for. It produced nothing but bloodshot eyes this morning."

He laughed, "I get it. It's a weird case, isn't it?" his breathing heavy from running in the soft sand. "She just disappears without a trace. By the way, you should be careful running alone this early on a deserted beach. You know what we found yesterday. I don't know if she was killed on the beach, somewhere else, or just drowned. So until I do, please be alert."

"I'm not alone, I'm with the Chief of Police. And stop hovering."

After a few minutes, they turned around and headed back. The sky showed the tiniest hint of purple.

"Come on up on the deck, watch the sunrise, and have a cup of coffee?" Jack's house, nestled in the dunes, had a perfect view of Oyster Point Harbor.

Jamie sat taking in the view and the solitude of the morning. She had shared the sunset last night with Jack and here she was sharing the sunrise with him.

"I hope this coffee's okay. I like it strong," Jack stated as he placed the coffee pot and two cups on the table between them. "By the way, I never asked Pat if you had been married."

"Wow, a question like that before coffee, Counselor?" His directness surprised her. "No. How about you?"

"Not really."

"That sounds like an almost to me. What happened?" She figured she could conduct her own interrogation as well.

"The job. She felt ignored and truthfully, probably was." He rested his feet up on the railing.

"And?"

"She kept pushing for what I couldn't give her, more time, more energy, and more of myself." He sipped his coffee. "I'm sure you must have had a close call or two?"

"A few."

"And?"

She shrugged, "Too young. He wasn't ready for something serious, maybe a little immature. He had things to do and they didn't include me. End of story." Mike seemed like a vague memory today. "The last thing I heard was that he had gone to Afghanistan."

"Would you like me to see what I can find out?"

"Wasted energy—it was a long time ago." She couldn't even remember what he looked like anymore without taking out a photo. "Thanks anyway."

"Let me know if you decide you want me to." He poured cream into his coffee. "By the way, who's Matt?"

"Matt? Where did you come up with that?"

"You had a note to call him on your board yesterday?" He poured her more coffee. "Too strong? I know he's not your brother."

"Boy, you don't miss a thing. Are you building a 'Jamie' case folder?" she asked.

"Maybe. Will it be a large folder?"

"Doubtful. Just ask and I'll pretty much tell anything you want to know. Matt's a friend in Boston." She emphasized the word 'friend.' "He's the lawyer who's handling Pita's estate. How about you, anyone you need to call here or back in Boston?"

He stared at her with that raised eyebrow and she started to laugh. "By the way, the coffee's great."

"Building a case file on me? You think me having a girlfriend is funny?"

"No, not at all." She waved her hands at him and equated her outburst of laughter to a lack of sleep. "I'm just tired and …" She started to laugh again.

"No one I need to call. Maybe life's simpler that way?"

"Simpler maybe, but lonelier."

He avoided her comment, asking, "Have you seen the inside of the house? Want a quick tour?"

"Can I trust you?"

"Do you have a choice?"

***

After walking Jamie back to her cottage, Jack followed the shore back to his place. The sound of the waves helped him to think. He stared at the fading stars, remembering Jamie's story.

"Hello, Jamie's friends. Travel far and have a good day." Sitting on the rocks in front of his house, he craved that early morning cigarette so badly. "Watch out for her," he added, looking out on the dark water and remembering blank green eyes.

When he'd visited Phil's office last night, the woman's parents had arrived to sign for the release of her body. They provided a little more information. Trisha, the thirty year old dead woman, had broken up with her boyfriend and wanted to get away. Her mother couldn't speak without sobbing. Her parents didn't understand why she had drowned. She was an excellent swimmer. He had asked them if they thought that she could have been distraught enough about this breakup to take her own life.

"Absolutely not. In fact, she was glad to be rid of him," her father stated.

Could be the ex-boyfriend? Or a predator that might have a type—tall, young, blonde—just like Jamie.

Chapter Nine

A loud noise jolted Jamie out of her daydream. Justine's folder lay at her feet, pages riffling softly in the light wind. She checked her watch. Noon.

Her vision, so real, had taken her into a dark, dank room where she looked down on Justine's case folder lying in a box marked "Unsolved—Cold Cases." When she lifted it, there was another folder underneath marked, "Marya and Ralph Janson," Jamie's parents. The hit and run driver had never been found. The car had been stolen; the driver ran into the cold icy night shadows. Even with all her computer abilities, she hadn't found him.

"I will find you, coward," she said, picking up the remnants of Justine's life and placing them back in the folder.

After she'd showered, Jamie had read through Justine Colbert's folder. Justine emerged sounding just like her—an only child with a high powered position at a research institution, who lived in a renovated section of South Boston with a few close friends and family nearby in Connecticut. But that's where the similarities ended. Justine had been engaged to be married, both her parents were alive, and her family was wealthy. Jamie bit down on her yellow pencil as she wrapped her scrunchie around her wet hair. She scribbled a note to research Justine's job. When she had questions, she dialed the telephone number listed for Jack on Pita's chalk board. They agreed to meet at the village coffee shop for lunch to talk about the case.

Carrying the folder, she hurried inside, slipped into a pair of jeans and a sweater, brushed her damp hair, grabbed a jacket off the hook by the door and rushed down the road, hoping to make it to the village by 12:30.

When she reached the corner, a police car stopped and Jack rolled down the window. "Can I give you a lift or were you planning on being late for our date?"

She dropped her sunglasses to look at him. "Actually, a ride would be great. And it's not a date. Are you sure you're not too busy for lunch?"

"Trust me, they can find me anywhere. And I'm hungry." He leaned across the seat and opened the car door for her. "Hop in."

As Jamie fastened her seat belt, a huge furry head emerged from the back seat, banging against her. "Who's this?" she asked, receiving a big wet kiss.

"Are you okay? Maxine, get back. I'm sorry, did she hurt you?"

"A slight concussion, nothing really. I can shake it off." She scratched Maxine under the chin. "Great name. I didn't see her at the house this morning?"

"I picked her up at the station. She makes the rounds. My guys adopted her so she wouldn't be put down." He pulled up in front of the village coffee shop. "Some nights I take her home and we run on the beach." He held the door for Jamie. "Maybe I won't need her as running partner now that you're around," he whispered in her ear as they entered the restaurant.

"Great, I'm replacing a dog," she murmured.

Jack escorted Jamie to a corner table where he could see everything. A redheaded waitress appeared, wearing a jersey that fit a tad too tight and hung a bit too low. She stood so close to Jack that her hip touched his elbow. Addressing him by name and never taking her eyes off him, she took their orders of blueberry pancakes. Neither of them had eaten any breakfast.

"Specialty of the house," she answered in a low, sexy voice, giving him a wink and turning toward the kitchen.

Returning a moment later, she said, "Here's your coffee with some cream, honey. Just the way you like it." The waitress leaned forward, adjusting his coffee cup, red mane tumbling over her shoulders, and her jersey gaping enough to give him a perfect view of her ample breasts.

"Thanks, Bev." Jack never took his eyes off Jamie as he reached for his coffee cup.

"Okay, so what's going on?" he asked after Bev reluctantly moved on to the next table.

"What's going on there?" Jamie raised her eyebrow, nodding toward Bev.

"Bev? Don't know. Don't care. Not interested." He dismissed the waitress.

"Hmmm, I thought she might be one of your not so serious friends?"

"Not likely. Why, you think she might be a good match for me?"

"Depends on what you're looking for, I guess." Jamie tossed her hair and winked at him.

"Not bad." He tried to keep from laughing. "But for some reason, you look ridiculous doing that."

"Thanks. So much for sexy this morning. Anyway, before I'm sidelined over Bev—" she exaggerated her name— "I told you that Justine's folder lay open on the table when I arrived. Pita must have been scrutinizing the notes, reports, and interviews." Her words became softer as she leaned forward. "It's driving me crazy. I just can't picture Pita solving crimes with clues hidden in those pages. By the way, any more information on the woman who drowned?"

Jack's eyes never stopping moving as he listened to her. "This isn't the best place to talk," he stated matter-of-factly. "Too many eyes and ears around. You'll find that out pretty quickly," he warned as he acknowledged a group of men entering the restaurant.

She nodded. "I guess that's part of figuring out if I belong here now."

"I hope you do. You know more about these people than I do," he added.

"Not anymore, I'm afraid," she answered, noticing that she didn't know a single soul in the entire restaurant. "Is tonight okay? But I'll cook this time."

"Can we eat at my place? I have notes and computer files that might be useful to us. But I'll let you cook. How's that? I'll pick you up on my way home?"

"Sounds great. Would Maxine like some treats?"

"Don't worry about bringing her anything. She has tons of stuff, even her own bed." He looked embarrassed.

"I wondered if the couch was her place."

"When I'm working in the living room, she lays there with one eye closed, the other watching my every move."

"You know what they say, nothing attracts a woman more than a man with a baby or a dog." She put her chin in her hands and batted her eyelashes at him.

"Stop, really, that's so not you." He laughed so loud that the whole place turned to look at them. "Small town gossips will be out today, especially after we're seen here together. I hope you have thick skin."

"Very. I'm tougher than I look." She moved her purse from her lap to the chair next to her, as Bev arrived with their pancakes.

Dropping Jamie's plate in front of her, she asked, "Anything more I can do for you, Jack?" Her meaning was quite clear as she adjusted his silverware.

"Can't think of a thing right now, thanks, Bev."

"More coffee please, Bev?" Jamie answered. Bev shot her a cold icy stare. Jamie smiled, suppressing an urge to stick out her tongue.

"I'm around if you change your mind, Jack." Bev turned on her heel, sashaying away toward the kitchen, hiking up her skirt to a very unladylike level as she reached inside her apron pocket. She cast a last look at Jack over her shoulder as she entered the kitchen.

Jack ignored Bev's maneuvers. Jamie noticed, but decided to join Jack in consuming the blueberry pancakes and the pot of coffee that Bev eventually left on the table. When they finished, Jack paid the bill and placed his hand in the small of Jamie's back as they walked out the door.

**

Bev hid in the shadow of the kitchen door, watching Jack and Jamie laughing and touching each other as they spoke about tonight.

Chapter Ten

Unpacking the food on Jack's kitchen counter, Jamie called over her shoulder, "I'm putting the casserole in the oven to heat. Dinner will be ready in about twenty minutes."

"Great. That'll give me time to jump in the shower, if that's okay? Smells terrific."

"Fine, I'll set the table," she replied, peeling off the old blue checked oilskin stuck to the gouged table. She threw on a flowered tablecloth that she had brought from the cottage.

Jack's organized kitchen had four of everything including an old mismatched service of silverware, dishes, and old jelly jar glasses like Pita's. She had to laugh. A true bachelor pad.

She placed the last piece of silverware on the table as Jack appeared in the doorway, pulling on a sweatshirt over his lean, muscular chest. He wore jeans, no shoes, and his hair was all tousled. Her cheeks colored as she met his eyes.

"Sorry, I didn't mean to startle you." He combed his wet hair with his fingers. "I guess I'm too used to living by myself."

"I just wasn't expecting to see you there," she answered. "You said you have sisters? Any brothers?" She struggled to make conversation. It dawned on her at that moment how socially awkward she had become. Kate was correct, she lived like a nun. Her life consisted of work, her rented apartment, and more work. She had cut herself off from life. After Clementine, her cat, had died two years ago, she hadn't even gotten another animal. Death was too hard to cope with....

"Two sisters. Both married with two children each. No brothers. The kids are adorable, two girls and two boys. Jessica and her family live in Dennis. Debra lives in upstate New York." He waited for a response as she folded the napkins.

"Are you as overprotective with them as you are with me?"

He laughed. "I try, but like you, they fight me all the way." He walked to the kitchen area. "Feel like a glass of wine and a view of the sunset?" He poured her wine, grabbed a cold beer for himself, and led the way to the chairs out on the deck. "I gather you didn't want to eat on my antique tablecloth?" He pointed to the two chairs on the deck.

"I figured a little color might brighten things up. You can keep the cloth if you like. Pita had about thirty of them in the closet." She read his body language, "You think it's too girly, don't you?"

"Well, if I was having a bunch of guys over to play poker, not sure I'd use it," he joked. "But thanks. Not that you could tell, but I scrubbed that blue and white thing. Drab, huh?"

She would never imagine how at that moment she filled his kitchen with color by just being in it. His life was gray as well.

"Problems?"

"No, just thinking how upside down everything is." She swished her wine around in the glass.

"How so?"

"Well, my only living relative dies. I thought I knew her, but find out I didn't. I have inherited my childhood sanctuary, which I'm cleaning out and selling. My best friend's pregnant and in California. I can't find the ghost who's clobbering my client's website. And I end my run at a dead body. Other than that…." She stared at the reflections of the setting sun. "And, on top of all that, for

some reason, I feel I need to be here. I don't know why."
She felt so silly saying these words out loud. "Does any of
this make any sense?"

"You've been through a lot."

She wanted to dispute what he said, but couldn't.
Pat's death, Kate's pregnancy, women who washed up on
her beach dead and all the memories that confronted her
constantly —she had trouble coping with it all.

"And there's still much for you to sort through. And
I don't mean just the physical stuff. You can keep the
cottage, use it, rent it, or sell it. Take a breath and think
about what's important to you. The cottage contains a lot of
your life."

"My work's the only constant I have right now. I
live alone and work fills my life—like you. Down here, I
feel… freer, more able to be myself. Everything has shifted
quickly for me. This is like a parallel universe. Why are
you smiling like that?"

"Just agreeing with you. It's not quite real down
here. Maybe that's why I stay. And maybe that's why you
shouldn't sell too quickly. This is home to you."

She nodded. "But, alas, I have to return to the other
universe to see my client in a day or two. Is there anything I
can do for you while I'm up in Boston, anything on the
cases that I can research?" She started to stand.

"Can't think of anything off hand," he said, getting
up and heading inside after her. "Look," he said grabbing
her hand, "one of your friends is flashing up there." They
stopped and watched a shooting star blaze across the sky.

"Funny, you made me remember my night buddies.
Now there are two up there… I haven't thought of them in
a long time."

"Maybe it's time to show them how bright and
strong you've become…."

"Maybe…. Anyway, let's eat."
***

All during dinner, Jamie and Jack studied Justine's folder. She asked question after question—how many interviews were conducted, was everyone in Justine's apartment building questioned, were accounts searched for activity, what was her boyfriend like, and so on.

Jack answered them as fast as she fired them—fifty interviews were conducted, everyone in the building was spoken to, all her bank accounts were searched for activity over the last year.

"Two of my detectives spoke to Thomas, her fiancé. He's wealthy, earned some on his own, and inherited family money. I didn't talk to him until later. He checked out okay." He slouched in the chair with his feet stretched out in front of him, his hands folded across his chest.

"What are we missing?" Jamie tapped her pencil on her notes. What would she have done if she were Justine? She hated to admit it even now, but she had thought about running away after her parents died. Pita was great, but sometimes she felt like she was drowning in memories... "Where would you go if you wanted to disappear?"

"Wyoming," he stated. "Why, think I should?"

"But I could find you there..."

"But only you could. And you would keep my secret."

"I would. So who would keep Justine's secrets? Her girlfriend? Thomas? Her parents?" She hesitated, "What was the weather the night she disappeared?"

"Why would the weather have anything to do with her disappearance? Should be notes in the crime scene report."

"That's usually captured?" She scanned the pages, stretching her legs out in front of her in a similar pose to Jack. "Nothing, there's absolutely nothing about the weather."

"Well, if it's rainy, the investigators note that fact in their crime scene report because evidence could be compromised. It rained the next day when Justine's parents and I drove to the apartment. We got soaked in a downpour, I remember that."

Writing the weather question on her folder cover, she added, "Maybe I can locate a weather report."

"Why do you think it's important?"

"I don't know...I'm trying to see if maybe thinking outside the box might help. Was it foggy, rainy, or clear? And her research, I'll look up her company. I know a couple of people who might be able to help with that."

"Be careful, that's all. We don't know what happened to her. If you become visible to the wrong people... " He didn't have to finish the sentence.

"Yes, my protector." Jamie rose from the chair, stretching. "Boy, am I stiff." She checked her watch. "We've been sitting here for over two hours and all we have are sore butts." She touched her toes, slowly unrolling, shaking her hands and arms. As she reached her full height, she held her hands behind her back to stretch them and twisted her head from side to side.

Jack's eyes never left her.

"What?"

"Nothing, absolutely nothing. I'm thinking I should have been a Yoga teacher, not a cop." He raised an eyebrow appreciatively.

"Oh, for heaven's sake, you have been living alone too long. Time for me to leave." She collected the files and dropped them into her box. "My mind's swimming in useless information. How do you do it?"

"I'm used to it." He stood. "Hell, I can hardly move myself. These chairs are terrible. We should've worked on the couch by the fire."

"That would have been productive. I would have been asleep in five minutes," she added, picking up her box. "Maybe buy some cushions for these chairs?"

"Okay, a deal if you go shopping with me." He took the box from her. "You grab the dishes."

When they were driving back to her cottage, Jamie decided to share the dream that she had had earlier in the day.

"I didn't realize the guy who hit your parents was never apprehended."

"No, but I'll find him some day. As you say, that first clue's all you need."

Jamie unlocked the cottage door, turned on the lights and Jack did a quick walk through of the rooms.

"You were expecting that I was hiding someone?"

"Nope, force of habit." He stood at the front door, his hands in his pockets.

"Thanks for checking the house. I shouldn't make fun of you."

"I don't mind." Hesitating for a second, he touched her cheek. "Call me tomorrow before you leave and tell me what your plans are, okay?"

"I will. Goodnight." She stood silhouetted in the doorway, wondering if he had been about to kiss her. She wasn't sure how she felt about that. It was hard to trust anyone these days, even Jack.

"Lock your doors, please," he called over his shoulder.

She watched him turn on the car's spotlight, swipe the light over the surrounding trees, and drive away. Then she closed, locked, and bolted her door.

***

As he drove away, Jack thought about the heartache that Jamie carried at never having a resolution in her parent's deaths. He would do that for her, he vowed.

Chapter Eleven

Jamie paused in front of the bay window of her Boston apartment waiting for Jack to answer his phone. Her view across the Charles River to the boat houses didn't seem as exciting as it once had. The living room, decorated in soft colors and fluffy chairs, had been a refuge from the pressures of her job, loud city noises, and the lifeless world outside. Now, it was just another flat in the city, a temporary place for her to stay, not home.

Feeling a chill, she flipped on the gas fireplace. Jack's distracted voice startled her.

"Hi. You're busy." She sat down in front of the computer, her eyes fastened on the large painting that hung above the mantle. There, on the right side nestled in the dune, Pita had painted Jack's house. She hadn't noticed it before.

"Not at all. Believe it or not, you shamed me into unpacking some boxes and guess what, no chair pads or whatever it was that you called them. How was your drive up?"

"Well, after I crossed into my parallel universe, I found that nothing had changed." The emotion she felt as she left the Cape drifted through her words. "We can shop for cushions when I come back. It's good to hear a friendly voice."

"Kind of lonely here, too. When do you think you'll be home?"

Home—she felt like someone other than Kate cared about her again. Jamie's phone clicked. "Jack, hold on, Kate's calling."

"Hi hon. Everything okay?"

"Now that's a greeting," answered Jack.

"Oh God, I pressed conference. Hang on."

"No, wait. Hi Jack," Kate squeezed in before Jamie could cut him off.

"Hi Kate. Jamie and I were discussing chair cushions. Any ideas?"

"Hey, you guys, should I just hang up?" Jamie butted in.

"Bye, Kate. See you soon. Let me know about the cushions," Jack added

"You bet. JJ, I'm at my Dad's. He's doing great but anxious to finish up this job and come home." Kate's Dad was a structural engineer who worked for a Boston architectural firm.

"How excited was he when you told him the news?"

"We conferenced in my mother and he cried when we told him."

"Tell him I send my love. I have to get back to Jack, if I didn't disconnect him, thanks to you."

"He's one sexy sounding guy. Send me photos please and don't forget to call me back. Cushions? In front of the fireplace? Hugs sweetie." Jamie heard the click and switched lines.

"Sorry about that. Kate's visiting her Dad in Seattle and was checking up on me."

"So, I'm not the only protector. How's it going?"

"For me? Good. I'm hoping to be done Thursday afternoon. I'll catch the apartment manager and alert him that I'll be away for most of the summer and then go to the post office to have my mail forwarded." Leaning back in her chair, she added, "By the way, it was foggy."

"Weird. It's clear here." She heard the door to the deck slide open. "Your friends are very bright tonight. They're missing you."

"Really? Tell them hello and I'll see them soon." She felt a pang of homesickness, something not experienced since her college days. "And it was foggy the night Justine disappeared. Not heavy fog, but I guess a light patchy fog?"

He said nothing for a few seconds. "Funny, I don't remember fog."

"Foggy nights are high crime nights, right? No moon, shadowy figures moving in the dark, disappearing people, hard to see faces." She laughed. "Reading too many old London crime novels, huh?"

"Definitely."

"Well, at least it's new information." They were both quiet. "You should go back to your cushion search and I to my presentation. I don't want to be up all night and look like a tired old hag in the morning."

"Impossible. You look gorgeous all the time. Want me to call tomorrow night?"

"You have the knack of saying the right thing at the right time. Thank you. I'll call you when I get settled in for the night?" She heard the dog in the background. "I'm glad you have some company tonight. Give Maxine a hug for me. Good night, Jack."

"Will do. Give 'em hell tomorrow. 'Night."

***

Jack walked inside, wondering if a little fog could have obscured faces the night Justine disappeared. He had to think about it; maybe Jamie hadn't been reading too many Sherlock Holmes stories. Maybe that's why they had trouble recognizing people on the street?

"You know Max, you used to be company enough for me, but you have stiff competition now." He patted Maxine. "She's changed my life in a few weeks. Why aren't my music, case folders, and you enough anymore? What happened?"

Opening another box, he answered his own question.

"She happened."

Chapter Twelve

Jamie's client meeting concluded at two o'clock. The discussions had gone well and Jamie and her security co-worker thought they had found a set of tracks that might lead to the person who was messing up the website.

When she reached her car, she stood thinking about her options—drive right back to the cottage or make a slight detour by Justine's apartment building, a few blocks away. Photos were just that, pictures, one dimensional. If she stood there, wouldn't she feel more?

Jamie squeezed her Mustang into a parking spot in front of a plain yellow shingled building in one of the revitalized section of South Boston. The structure was an older triple-decker built around the turn of the 20th century for newly-arrived immigrant workers like Jamie's grandparent's had been. In fact, Jamie's family had lived a few streets away from Justine's condo. What surprised Jamie was that Justine hadn't chosen to live in one of the tonier sections of Boston like Beacon Hill.

When she reached the door, she almost turned around. What did she expect to find that Jack and his detectives hadn't found almost three years ago? She had no experience in physical crime solving.

She removed the hairpins holding her hair up, fluffed it loose around her face, and opened her top button. She would use anything she could to obtain information. She tried the front door and of course it was locked. Peeking through the sidelights, she spotted a man dressed in a dark blue shirt a size too small with sweat stains under the arms, slumped over a tiny table reading a magazine. She knocked and knocked again louder on a glass pane.

Glassy black eyes peered over half lenses as the man closed the magazine and dropped it beside his chair. He rose, pocketing the glasses, smoothing his sparse hair and wiping the sweat from his brow in a continuous motion.

She waved to him.

He strolled over, adjusting his pants as he opened the door.

"Hello. I'm sorry to bother you, but my rental agent told me that there might be an apartment for lease here?" She flashed her brightest smile. "I was wondering if you could help."

He nodded.

"I'd like to know more about the people in the building before I actually commit to taking the flat. You know, a woman can never be too careful." She tossed her hair back with a sexy little move. "Are you the security guard?"

Straightening himself up to appear taller, he glanced at her left hand. "Yea, pretty lady, I head security here."

Trying not to laugh, she added sweetly "Oh, that's wonderful, I mean that the building has a security force." She wrote that down in her notebook. "And you would be?"

"Officer Ocalivitch, but Andy to you." He smiled as he moved outside the door closer to her.

"Well Andy, nice to meet you. How long have you been head of security?" She didn't extend her hand.

"Five years."

"So you know everyone who lives here?" Looking down at her notebook, pretending to read some comments, she pushed him for more information. "Someone told me there had been an incident here a few years ago? Something about a tenant disappearing?"

He looked down the street, fumbled with his belt, and finally answered, "I remember now. Nothin' big. A guy packed up and scooted."

"Hmmmm.... A man? My information must be wrong, it says a woman disappeared. That can't be the same one?" She frowned, hoping he would think that whatever had happened would keep her from renting in this building.

"No...well...." He rubbed his hands together and shifted his feet as though nervous all of a sudden. "The renter left... two or three years ago I think."

"She left?" Her frown became even deeper. "You did say a woman, correct? Do you happen to know where she went?"

"Yea, a female." He shrugged, "No one knows why."

"She packed up her things and moved out? Were you on duty the day she left?" Now she tried to look horrified.

"Not ... not exactly. I wasn't on, Angell was."

"Angell?" She scribbled the name, not looking down.

"Yea, Angell Barcardi. He's our night guy." He pointed to the table and chair where he had been sitting.

"And Angell worked here how long?"

"Five years." She pushed a little more. "And there are cameras here?"

"Front and back door."

"That's great. I assume all the tenants have keys to the back door? And you and Angell watch the cameras?"

He nodded.

"And no one saw this woman leave or anyone come in?"

He nodded again.

"Did the police talk to everyone after she disappeared?"

"Yup, me and Angell first." His watery eyes narrowed. "Why do you want to know all this stuff... happened years ago? Are you a reporter or somethin'?"

She had to be careful... too many questions. "Well, as I said, a woman can never be too careful these days. Were all the apartments occupied when the police came?" Again, she pretended to write something down. "I mean rented?"

"I know what occupied means."

"I'm sorry, I didn't mean that. I just wanted to know if the apartments were all rented, not if the people were home when the police came."

"Yup, full." He glanced away and said, "Wait, the guy in 3B left right before this woman did, a Terry something. Terry Connors?" He shrugged his shoulders indicating the name meant nothing to him. "Big guy. Saw him with that gal some mornings. Think they were getting it on." He moved his tongue across his lips.

"Really."

"Anyway, he left. Cops went through his apartment, but said it looked like he never lived there."

"Are all the apartments rented?"

"Sure are, even that woman's apartment. I mean she's not there, but the rent is paid. Which place did the realtor say was for rent? Maybe her place? No one else told me they were leaving." Now he wanted information.

"My agent didn't give me an apartment number, but I'll look at the flat when it's available." She flashed her smile again. "Thank you so much, Andy. You've been a big help."

"My pleasure, Miss. It's 'Miss', right? Leave your name and number and I'll call when something comes up." He moved closer. His breath smelled of onions, his body of sweat.

"My realtor might be upset if I did that. But I'll stop back if I have more questions." She avoided his offered hand by fumbling in her purse looking for her car keys.

"Thank you, Andy." Stuffing the notebook into her purse, she turned, wanting to leap down the steps two at a time, run to her car, and lock the doors behind her. Instead, she marched down the stairs, surveyed the area as though it could be a prospective home, and hummed loudly.

Andy leaned against the doorjamb, watching Jamie until she got into her car. He took out a small scrap of paper and wrote something down as she drove away.

Chapter Thirteen

Jamie's little red car sped across the Sagamore Bridge onto Cape Cod with a gorgeous sunset as a backdrop. The time spent in Boston had been very productive—her recommendations for improving her client's website security had been approved. The persistent hacker still knew how to hide from them, but they were getting closer.

Her charade with Andy, Justine's security guard, might present something new to Jack, especially the nervousness that he had shown when talking about the empty apartment and Angell. If it didn't, Jack would be madder than hell with her mucking around in his case. She probably should have let him know what she had planned although at the time she really didn't have a plan.

After her exchange with Andy, Jamie had contacted Andrew, her security guru whose specialty was accessing background information.

"Both these guys are sketchy to say the least, but that doesn't make them murderers," she told him, giving him all the information she had on Andy and Angell. "And could you send any information you find on Justine's genetic company and her involvement in any projects that might have been active when she worked there?"

Terry Connors, the renter who lived next to Justine, was a dead end. Andrew's research uncovered nothing, no driver's license, marriage license, or birth record for a male in his thirties or forties. He said that he had found an eighty-six year old man, Terrance O'Connor, who had lived in that neighborhood, but had died ten years earlier. A stolen identity, she wondered. Maybe another clue?

"Thanks for the update, Andrew." She clicked off.

Fog began a slow crawl across the highway. Jamie clicked on her high beams. It was as though a cement wall had been created in front of her, reaching right down on the road. The moisture reached inside the car. Her hands tightened on the steering wheel. *Fog veiled crime, shadowy figures, and abduction.* The words repeated in her mind.

"Stop it," she said aloud. "It's fog…you are on the Cape, not the London streets." She slowed and clicked on her hazard lights in case there was anyone else stupid enough to be driving in this mess.

She blamed Andy—he had creeped her out. He was the type who would enter an apartment and steal underwear. She had to smile, visualizing him lurking over an open underwear drawer, fingering the silk material, drooling.

The phone rang and Kate could be heard on the speaker, "Well?"

"I know, I know. I didn't call back. I'm sorry, but time's moving quickly."

Concentrating on the solid yellow lines in the middle of the road, Jamie finally caught a glimpse of the "Entering Oyster Point" sign. Only a couple of miles and she would be home. She flexed her hands, stiff from gripping the wheel. The drive had already taken her over three hours.

"No, you didn't. Where are you?"

"I'm driving home from Boston."

"Home, is it now? So, tell me more about our Chief."

Jamie slammed on the brakes as she passed the small rowboat that signaled her street. "Damn it," she stated, angry with herself for making such a stupid mistake.

"Are you okay?" Kate asked.

The fog had lightened a bit in the village, but thickened as Jamie crawled over the hill heading toward the Marina. Holbrook Street, one of her favorite streets, showcased some of the town's most beautiful old rambling Cape Cod homes, covered with wild roses in June, and gifted with high views of Cape Cod Bay. Tonight though, her view was barely the macadam in front of her.

"I'm fine. Just missed my street in this murky stuff."

"Fog? Okay, drive carefully and call me when you get in?"

Jamie checked the time—barely 9 p.m. "I think I'll stop at Jack's. I'm sorry, but life has been upside down lately. How are you feeling? Our little one causing morning sickness?"

"I'm fine, hon. No sickness. You sound great too. All's good here so we will connect when I return in a week or so. Love you."

"Love you too."

The fog thickened again by the water. Jamie slammed on her brakes imagining someone or something to her left. Nothing. Eerie rolling shapes melted away. Pulling into Jack's driveway, every muscle in her neck ached from being hunched over the wheel for the last couple of hours.

The garage door clanged up and Jack appeared, framed by the old light in the ceiling. Jamie pushed the driver's door open and was immediately clobbered by paws and a huge black head.

"Maxine. I missed you too." Maxine jumped up and licked her face.

"Maxine, sit." Jack commanded as he rounded the front of Jamie's car. Maxine backed down and sat with her tail wagging wildly as she looked from Jamie to Jack and back again.

"Thought you were staying in Boston tonight?" He grabbed hold of her trembling hand, helping her out of the seat. "You okay? The fog? It rolled in quickly. One minute I had a beautiful view of the bay and the next minute, I couldn't even see the deck railing. Maybe you should have waited till morning?"

"Well, I'm glad to see you too." She rubbed her hands together. "The city's too noisy, too busy, and too lonely." Jamie moved her head side to side, loosening the muscles in her neck and shoulders. "I was fine until I crossed the bridge, then, from there on, I battled the fog. By the time I entered Eastham I could barely see the road."

Jack put his arm around her shoulders and shut the car door. "Looks like you could use a massage?" He raised an eyebrow.

"I could, to tell you the truth. Are you offering?" He looked different tonight. "I've never seen you with glasses."

He rubbed her shoulders.

"I need the glasses for reading. Usually I can't find them."

She shook her head, smiling, "They look great on you." She leaned back, enjoying his hands on her neck. "They make you look studious."

"Great. Just the look I was going for." He tightened his arm around her. "Well, the 'Prof' says let's get you inside, out of this dampness, and make you something hot to drink."

Maxine trailed behind them and then stopped abruptly at the door, sniffing the air, ears up, her hackles slowly rising.

"You comin' in, Max?" Jack asked, holding the door open.

Max looked back at him and then sat on the bottom step, still sniffing the air.

"Something out here? Make sure it's a not a coyote, girl. Stay close." He closed the screen door, but left the cottage door open a foot in case Max needed him.

Once inside, Jack made two cups of steaming tea.

Jamie wrapped her hands around the cup.

"So how did everything go?" Jack asked.

She explained some of what that they had done for her client. When she finished, Jack had a great question, "Could you secure our database at the station?"

"I can certainly take a look at it. Sometimes just a few simple changes can make it more secure."

"Great. Let's do it. We've been hacked a few times and now I'm afraid to put real data out there." He jotted himself a note on a yellow sticky and pasted it to a folder on the table. "I'm pretty sure I can even dredge up some funds."

"Perfect. By the way, I drove by Justine's apartment on my way back," she blurted out.

Jack scowled. "Tell me you didn't go near the building." His tone became flat.

She ignored his comment. "I spoke to the security man, a guy named Andy." Fumbling in her purse for the notebook, she flipped to the last page, "A strange little man, heavy set, sweaty." Her words flew out of her mouth in a flurry.

"You talked to him? Why would you do that? You were alone." He stood up and paced. "You realize that he could be a murderer?" Not waiting for her answer, he took off his glasses, placing them on the pile of folders and leaned on the table looking straight into her eyes. He spoke so softly that she could barely hear him. "Don't you ever, and I mean ever, place yourself in that kind of danger again without me, do you understand? This isn't child's play, Jamie. Justine could have been murdered by one of these men." He continued on, his voice rising. "If he made Justine disappear, he could make you disappear," he stated. "How would I have found you?" His tone softened. "You would have been gone, just like her."

She had acted impulsively and placed herself in danger. "I'm sorry. It all happened so fast. I found a parking spot, so I took it. Her apartment is a few streets over from where my grandparents had lived. I know that neighborhood and was surprised that Justine would choose to live there." She rubbed her eyes; she was tired. "I peered into the lobby. I wanted to see what she saw every day. And there the security guard sat, so I knocked."

Jack sat down across from her, folding his hands on the table, his steely eyes fastened on her.

"I said I had heard there might be an apartment available soon and I'd like to know what it was like living there and what the tenants were like." She stopped, debating what else to tell him.

"Go on."

"I told him that I had heard a woman had disappeared."

"Damn, it just gets worse."

"I was careful." Jamie removed the band from her wrist and pulled her hair back into a ponytail. "First, he told me about a guy who skipped out five years ago. He spoke of Justine packing up and leaving no forwarding address. After I pushed a little more, he told me that she was listed as missing and that her parents still paid the rent for the apartment. He seemed to get really nervous when I talked about Justine." She watched as Jack put his head in his hands, and then, raised it enough to look at her.

"Is there more?" he asked.

She had been angry with him a few minutes ago, but now, as she retold the story, she realized how careless she had been. She didn't use her smarts today—unlike her to be irresponsible.

"I didn't think. I was feeling so good about my meeting that I thought maybe I could pick up some new information for you. You're right—I should have checked with you or at least told you what I was planning."

"Please, don't do anything like that again? I would have gone crazy looking for you." He paused and then asked, "Do you think he got your license plate number?"

She stared at him. "I don't know. I guess he could have. I never thought about that."

"No, you didn't."

Chapter Fourteen

Jack followed Jamie back to her cottage. Once inside, he locked the windows, checked the closets, and even peeked up in the loft. He volunteered to sleep on the couch if Jamie would feel safer.

"Don't be ridiculous. Even if he had taken down my license plate number, he would have my Boston address, not this address." What she didn't tell him was that she had returned to her apartment after her encounter with Andy and then driven here; someone could have followed her.

Jack paused at the door, touching her face. "If you feel at all uncomfortable, please call me, use my cell phone. I keep it right next to my bed. And lock and bolt this door after I leave." He started down the walk. "By the way, Kate sounds like fun," he called back.

"She is. Thank you... I'm sorry."

"I know you are. Get inside, please," he called over his shoulder.

"'Night, Jack."

Once inside the car, he flashed the spotlight around the yard; the dense fog hid everything.

Leaning her head against the bolted door, Jamie realized how foolish she had been. Why didn't it occur to her that the creepy guy could be the murderer, that he could get her license plate number? Maybe because she wasn't trained to think that way...like Jack was. She shut off the outside light and then switched it back on, just for tonight. She flipped the deck light on as she headed to the bedroom. She was exhausted.

***

"Damn fog." Jack switched off the car spotlight. The heavy mist shrouded Jamie's cottage. The outside light on the cottage dimmed and then brightened.

He had spooked Jamie, he knew it, but he had to make her realize that she could be dead, murdered by that pervert. His alibi had checked out, but he could still be involved in Justine's disappearance, could have locked her away in some dark, dank cellar for his own deviant pleasure.

As he turned around in Jamie's driveway, he watched the light on the back deck flash on. Dialing the office number, he asked, "Scott, do me a favor please? Pick me up an egg salad sandwich and a cup of black coffee and deliver it to my house?"

"Sure Chief, what's up?"

"Just an impromptu stakeout. Heard there might be some trouble around the Marina tonight, so I thought I'd sit and see what materializes."

"I can send one of the guys to cover it so you don't have to spend the night out there?"

"Nope, I have nothing else to do. Just send someone with the coffee."

"Okay, Chief, give me a few minutes."

"Thanks Scott."

Pulling into his driveway, Jack waited to see if he had been followed. Nothing. But then again, with this fog, someone could be lurking ten feet away and he wouldn't see him.

When he finished loading Maxine into the back seat of the car, his coffee and sandwich arrived. He thanked Scott and drove up Holbrook. Turning the car around, he shut off his lights and rolled down the hill, pulling into an empty driveway where he could sit without interruption. Settling back into his seat, he watched billows of fog rolling by. Jamie's cottage lights were barely visible. He cracked the window so he could hear noises, a car engine, or footsteps. The best thing about fog was that sound traveled well in it.

"If it's him, Max, he'll be here tonight. He'll be too impatient to wait," he said aloud. Max laid on the back seat, her eyes open and ears up, listening as well.

Chapter Fifteen

Worn-out by the happenings of the day, Jamie stumbled into the bedroom, kicked off her shoes, and flopped down on the bedspread. She propped up the pillows, turned on her side, and fell deeper and deeper into a haze of dreams.

Loud creaking sounds filled her head. Heavy fog pushed on the sides of the cottage and the walls pushed back, buckling and undulating like the sea. The waves rocked her, the smell of the ocean engulfed her, and the mist smothered her.

Thunder rolled above as the fog pressed her down. Hands around her neck pushed her under the water, holding her there. Gasping for air, she lashed out at the form above her, scratching and kicking. On top of her, he moved with the waves. Then he was gone. She thrust herself through the water, gasping for breath. She tried to stand, but fell, her ankle tied to something.

Jamie screamed for help, her cries echoing off the walls, waking her up. She shivered. Swinging her legs over the edge of the bed, she pushed her hair back off her face gasping for air. She peeked through the bedroom curtains. The fog had lifted and the sky reflected the possibility of dawn. Switching on the bathroom light, she splashed her face with cold water. From the mirror, a ghostly face stared back at her.

"A nightmare, it was just a nightmare," she repeated, her hands shaking as she grabbed the sink to steady herself.

After a few minutes, she walked into the kitchen, turned on the light and the coffee maker. A knock at the door caused her jump. She pushed back the curtain and saw Jack standing there.

***

"What are you doing here?" she asked, opening the door.

"Was someone here? Are you okay?" One look at her pale face, he knew something had happened. How had he missed someone coming to the cottage? He pulled her close. "What happened?"

"It was a dream, but felt so real, the water, noises, splashes, and fog. A man clamped his hand over my mouth. I couldn't move, couldn't scream." Her words came between sobs. "He held me under the water and moved with the waves above me, trying to rape me, I think. He tied me to something."

"Shhhhh, remember, it wasn't real." He stroked her hair, thinking of green eyes and wet blond hair on the beach. "Just a nightmare. Shhhhh. It's okay. I'm here." She quieted. "Your clothes, you never changed." The woman on the beach had the rope around her ankle, the bruises on her neck. "Did you sleep at all?"

"I... I... After you left, I fell down on the bed for a minute. I must have fallen asleep." She shuddered, touching her black slacks. "They're my good slacks." She sounded amazed, "And probably ruined. What the hell happened to me?" She looked up at him with a hint of fear in her eyes. "It felt so real."

"Please, jump in the shower. You're shaking. Stand in the hot water and warm up. I'll get you a cup of coffee. I promise you'll feel better. I'm right here—no one's in the house, but me."

Janie headed to the bathroom, steaming coffee in hand. Jack stood at the kitchen sink, splashing cold water on his face. He hadn't slept all night. When the bathroom light flashed on, his gut told him that something was wrong. He had been out of the car and up the hill in seconds, Max running ahead of him.

Sipping his coffee, he walked out onto the deck where Max sat, watching him. He could hear the shower running.

Jack groaned as he sat down on the swing. He was really too old for this stuff, or more likely out of shape. The fog thinned over the wharf for a minute and then rolled back over it. He thought back to Jamie's nightmare and the blonde they found on the beach. He was sure that there was no mention of a rope, so how did Jamie know about it? She looked so pale and fragile when she opened the door. How could he protect her if he didn't know what he was protecting her from? He heard the shower shut off.

Jamie appeared wearing a blue terrycloth bathrobe tied loosely around her waist, a towel wrapped around her hair, her feet bare. He smiled at the woman standing in front of him as she removed the towel from her hair. Bending from the waist, she fluffed her hair with the towel. Her position provided him with a clear view of everything under the robe. He fought the urge to take advantage of a view he didn't have the right to, at least not yet. She moved next to him.

"Now who's embarrassed? Have I been living alone too long?" she joked.

"Maybe we have both been alone too long," he said, looking up at her.

"You look so tired." She pushed his hair off his forehead and sat on the arm of the swing. "You never answered me before. Why were you at my door so early this morning?"

By the look on her face, she had the answer before she finished the question.

"You sat outside all night, didn't you?" She petted Maxine's head. "Why didn't you stay on the couch? At least you could have slept a bit."

"If you remember, I volunteered to do that, but you threw me out."

"Well, if memory serves me correctly, I said you didn't have to stay because I was afraid. But, that didn't mean you couldn't stay if you were afraid." She smiled as she shook water drops out of her hair onto him. "You could have taken a swim with me."

She joked, but the nightmare had upset her. "I'm sorry I came down so hard on you last night."

"No, I deserved it. I was careless." Her tone became flat. "I've had nightmares before, but not for a long time and not like this."

"Are the dreams always the same, a drowning?" He pushed a bit.

"No, this one with me in the water is a first."

He decided not to ask anything more for now. "Are you okay? Would you like some breakfast?" he asked, wondering if the other nightmares were as real to her.

"Absolutely. I skipped dinner last night. Give me five minutes to throw on some clothes and we can be off."

"Okay, a deal." He relaxed on the swing, thinking there wasn't a woman alive who could dress in five minutes.

***

Laying the afghan gently over him, Jamie ran her hand over the stubble of his beard. She nudged his hair back from his forehead causing him to exhale and shift slightly. He hadn't slept in more than twenty-four hours. Was he so protective because of the promise he made to Pita or because he was the Chief? He had many faces, detective, friend, brother, dog lover—and wore them all well. She doubted that she knew everything about him. He was complex, as he had joked.

She stepped over Max and plopped herself on the arm of the chair next to the swing. How calm the bay looked with traces of fog still hanging over it. She slid down into the chair, wrapped her legs under her, and leaned back to watch the gauzy haze slowly evaporate. She closed her eyes, listening to the gulls, her hand resting on Maxine.

Chapter Sixteen

Jack grabbed for his gun. He could hear waves splashing as he cracked one eye open. Why the hell did he have a pink afghan over him? His disorientation faded as he recognized the deck. How long had he been asleep? He placed his gun back in its holster, rubbed his eyes, and stretched his stiff body. He could still taste the onion from the egg salad sandwich he ate last night. He pushed himself to a standing position, his body telling him that it had missed this week at the gym. He spotted Jamie on the other chair, her hand on Max, her eyes closed. He placed the pink afghan over her legs.

He thought of Lizz who had been a lot like Jamie when he met her—well educated and very independent. But then she changed, became clingy and needy. Or, maybe he had changed. Eventually, nothing about him pleased her— not his job, his friends, not even his looks. First, she asked him to take a desk job at the police station. Then, she attempted to convince him to don a suit and join her Dad's legal team. Jack had spent a few weekends with her family at their lodge on Lake Winnipesauke in New Hampshire. He and her Dad would go out fishing and talk for hours. But, as much as he liked her father, he wasn't about to give up his job. Lizz refused to accept that he loved being a cop, wanted to be a cop, and chose to be a cop. She felt that he could be more. That's who he was; he didn't want to be more.

At the end, they fought constantly. "Why won't you do this one little thing for me, for us?" she had pleaded. "Why don't you love me enough to change your job?"

Eventually, he had packed up and moved out. Lizz married within months of their breakup, and her husband,

Phillip, had taken a marketing position in her father's company. Jack heard all the dirt from his sister Jessica who seemed to know everything about Lizz, even though she never liked her. In the end, Lizz had gotten what she wanted and he was happy for her.

Physically, she was maybe five foot two and resembled a young, sexy Liz Taylor. She was beautiful and knew it. She used her looks to get anything she wanted, including him. They met at a Boston Policeman's Fundraiser and she came on to him immediately. She dressed to show off her best physical attributes. Coming from a wealthy family and being the only daughter, she was used to being pampered.

Jamie, on the other hand, was tall, willowy, and athletic with curly blond hair that flew everywhere. She had a smile that lit up a room, her laugh was throaty and real, and her large blue-green eyes showed everything she felt. He doubted that she even knew how to flirt. Genuine, vulnerable, but tough, she had overcome challenges that would have crushed another woman.

"Penny for your thoughts. With that tortured look on your face, you must be thinking about a woman," Jamie quizzed him as she stretched.

"You're too damn good for me. How are you feeling?"

"Hungry," she stated as he grabbed her by the hands and pulled her to her feet, the afghan dropping to the floor.

"Let's go. I'm starving, too," he said, watching her fold the pink square and place it on the back of the chair. It was special to her; perhaps Pat had made it.

"Well, was I right, a woman?" she asked, locking the cottage door behind them.

"Close, two women." He tossed a piece of gum in his mouth and they headed for the car with Maxine following behind.

Chapter Seventeen

Jamie's fingers flew across the keyboard. Buried among her words could be a tiny detail that might break Justine's case, something about the building or even Andy. As she wrote the details of her nightmare, she felt the fear resurface. Finishing her daily journal, she wiped her sweaty hands on her jeans.

Now on to her to-do list for the cottage—the first and largest task being the loft.

Climbing the wooden ladder, she remembered all the nights that she had taken this journey to her bed. She loved this cottage and all the memories that filled it. Selling it would be the last chapter of her life in Oyster Point. Was she ready to let this cottage go?

"Only brick and mortar," Kate said. "What are you going to do, stay down there all by yourself? Sell it." Kate was a black and white person; Jamie was not, especially when it came to matters of the heart. If Mike had done to Kate what he did to Jamie, she would have blackballed him and moved on. But Jamie had loved him and believed that he would come back.

"Maybe I'm just a poor judge of men," she said, reaching the top of the ladder. She pushed the clutter at the front of the loft aside and picked up Pita's easel and a few unfinished paintings. Juggling them, she made her way down the ladder, almost falling twice.

Going back up, she dangled her bare feet over the edge with Pita's shoe boxes stacked beside her. Secrets, the word used in her will, hummed through Jamie's mind. What secrets did Pita have here that no one knew about?

She untied the white ribbon on the top box and lifted the lid. There sat a white envelope with her name on it. She sniffed it, inhaling the smell of Pita that still lingered. She removed a single sheet of paper that read,

My dearest Jamie,

As I write this letter, my heart breaks because I know that you are alone at Lemon Pie. I wish I could put my arms around you and kiss away your tears. We both knew that the day would come when I would have to leave you. You have been my joy, my sole reason for living all these many years.

When your mother and father died, your grandmother and I thought it best if you came to Oyster Point for the summer. How nervous I was. I remember picking you up at the bus stop. You looked so sad and lost as you stepped off the bus. Your life had been shattered. One minute you were a normal, happy teenager; the next, you were all alone in the world. Our loss cemented us together that summer forever.

Tears slid down Jamie's cheeks as she recalled how empty she had felt that summer. Pita had breathed life back into her by giving her a place where she belonged, here at Lemon Pie. She taught her that although nothing would ever be the same, she could go on and live her life.

She read on…

When it came time for you to return to school, I wanted to keep you with me, but I knew that it was best if you returned to finish your education with your friends. It was then that I knew how much I really loved you, how you belonged to me, my beautiful Jamison. You had given me a reason to live. Funny, isn't it, how life works. When I look back I can't imagine my life without you, it would have been drab and colorless.

Your college graduation, a bittersweet day shrouded by your parent's ghosts, showed how tough you had become. You knew how proud they would have been. Job offers came in from all over the country, but you

choose to stay close to home. Secretly, I was ecstatic. I knew you were staying for Mike, but I was thrilled anyway.

Later that year you arrived unexpectedly. I knew when I saw your face and the look in your eyes that he was gone. I had seen that look in my own mirror years ago. Your heart would mend, but the scar would be there forever. You needed a mother to turn to, to comfort you; instead, you turned to me. I hugged you, cried with you. Your hurt reopened an old wound of mine, one you never knew I carried. The pain I felt, although the same, came from different circumstances, but in the end, both men left our lives forever.

Placing the letter down beside her, Jamie sobbed for her Pita and for the wound that had been reopened in her own heart.

The telephone ringing rescued her. Rummaging around, she finally found it under a pile of unread letters.

"Ahh…hello…." She blew her nose and wiped her face.

"Well, that's quite a greeting. You okay?" Jack asked.

"Just a bit distracted." Her voice cracked. "I'm up in the loft going through Pita's old photos and letters and I found a note for me."

"That's nice, right?" he asked.

"It's beautiful." She needed to hear his voice. "Are you busy? I could read the last paragraph?"

"Sure, go ahead."

Jamie read, "I know that we talked about what would happen to the cottage when I died, but who else could I leave it to? Who could love and care for it more than you? No one. You are like me in many more ways than you know my sweet one. And in time, you will learn all the secrets of the Lemon Pie Cottage."

"What's all the secret stuff?"

"I don't know. The same words were in her will, that everything in the cottage was intentionally left to me, including the secrets." She paused, looking at the sheet of paper in her hand. "You can read the whole thing when I see you. I also found a letter written by someone named Billy. Looks like it might have been their first year of college? Strange that she left it for me to read, don't you think?"

"Did you think that there was never anyone else in her life but Frank? She was in her thirties when she married him. That's pretty old in her day."

"I only remember Uncle Frank. Did she ever say anything about Billy to you?"

"Not exactly. But I'm not surprised that she was in love with someone before Frank. She was like you; she would light up a room even when I knew her. So I'm sure she had many, many admirers."

"What do you mean, not exactly?"

"Well, one night when she was grilling me about my ex-girlfriend, she hinted about an early relationship. She never went into the specifics, but from what she said, it ended sadly. She went quiet, like she was remembering him. She must have wanted you to know."

"She must have, but it seems odd to leave old love letters around. By the way, she did mention you in her letter."

He was silent, waiting for more. "That's it, aren't you going to tell me what she said?"

Jamie laughed, "Nope. You'll have to read it yourself. So, what's up?"

"How would you like to go to the Club for dinner tonight, my treat? They have live music on Friday nights. I thought we could both use a break from cooking. And some loud music might be just what the doctor ordered for both of us."

"Make it Dutch treat and I'm in."

"Sold. I'll pick you up around 6:30?"

"Perfect. By the way, I found her journals as well."

"Excellent." He paused and then said, "Don't be too hard on her, huh? See you at 6:30."

"*Ciao.*" She headed down the ladder to the deck with the letters from Billy still in her hand and a shoe box under her arm.

Chapter Eighteen

Jamie thumbed through Pita's old photographs. The one that caught her eye showed a group of men and women standing in the sunshine in front of a seawall with arms around each other, laughing. The women, dressed in sleek dark dresses, high heel platform shoes, boas thrown casually around their necks, with short cropped hair, resembled movie stars from the 1930's. Using her magnifying glass, Jamie read the names on the back of the photo. She flipped the photo. There was Pita, her light colored hair combed to the side, fluffy and curly around her face, made her look like Jean Harlow. Jamie touched Pita's face, imagining the happiness she must have felt at that instant, with all of her life ahead.

The soldier behind her wore his hat tipped, with light hair falling across his forehead, his chin resting on the top of Pita's head. Jamie, focusing the magnifying glass on him, tried to see his face, but the shadows hid it. She was sure that Pita had met Frank after the war. So this must be her Billy.

Delving further into the box, Jamie found tattered brown envelopes postmarked in the late 1930's and early 1940's. The name above the address was Billy Lawrence. The earliest postmark was October 6, 1939. Jamie unfolded the sheet:

My Dearest Patsy,

It's only a week since I left and it seems like forever. I miss you so much. When we talked about going to different schools, I didn't think I'd be so lonely without you. Our parents said we did the right thing, but I still miss seeing you every day. How's your art coming? I'm studying hard, nothing else for me to do here. See, I'm being good.

All kidding aside, how lucky I feel to be in college with so many people struggling these days. I have to admit, I feel guilty sometimes, I really do. I know you, you will try to make me feel better by saying I can do more to help people with my schooling behind me, and you are right, I suppose.

The guys here are talking about the war in Europe and the invasion of Poland. Roosevelt hasn't said much about it, yet. But my buddies say we should go over there and punch them back. You know how guys are, tough, huh? Especially when they are sitting in a place like this with no worries and that includes me as well. As they say, war clouds on the horizon. Oh well, I won't take up any more of the little time I have to write to you about war. I'm sure you know what's going on.

But right now, I wish I could see you, talk to you, and give you a kiss. You sounded pretty lonely in your last letter too. Just keep thinking of our dream. That's all I've been doing lately. Less than four years.

Let's hope this week passes quickly. I can't wait for this weekend. Every time the clock jumps a minute, I miss you more.

'Till then... I love you. Billy

The words stunned her. Had she actually married him? Was this one of the secrets that Pita had alluded to?

Chapter Nineteen

When Jamie came to the door, Jack looked like a schoolboy on a first date. All he needed was a bouquet of flowers.

"Hi, you look great," he commented, helping her on with a suede jacket. She fluffed her hair from under the collar and the smell of flowers and springtime filled the air.

"Thanks, you clean up pretty well yourself," she countered, locking the cottage door.

Silhouetted in purples and grays, they walked down the dirt road past the Marina.

"Tell me a little more about Kate. She sounds like a character."

"A character? Really?" Jamie shook her head. "You might say that. It was college orientation. There she stood, blue spiked hair and long blue strands that ran down around a slim porcelain face. Her hair color matched her gorgeous huge blue eyes. She was my assigned roommate."

Jack gave a belly laugh. "Definitely my kind of gal. I gather she doesn't look like that now?"

"Oh please, she's the epitome of the business woman, short black hair, business suits, stiletto heels, and her attaché. And so conservative—if she had a daughter who did that today, she would go crazy," Jamie laughed.

Jack held the door open for Jamie, his laughter entering the Club before them. "So she did that just to get everyone's attention?"

"Absolutely. And it worked."

Jack introduced Jamie as Pat's grandniece to the people he knew at the bar. His eyes swept the area. His gut told him that there was a murderer lurking in the local area so he wanted to see who was eyeing Jamie. She fit the profile. One man alone at the bar stood out.

"Jack, your table's ready," Lily, the hostess, broke into his thoughts. Jack, his hand resting on small of Jamie's back, followed Lily to a table near the window. Jack held the chair out for Jamie. His seat had a view of the entire Club, including the bar where the stranger drank alone. He stared into his glass seemingly oblivious of everything around till a woman bumped him accidently. He turned so abruptly that he almost knocked her over. He smiled and offered to buy her a drink. She shook her head and walked on.

After Lily left menus on the table, Jack continued the conversation about Kate. "So when am I going to meet this quirky friend of yours?"

"Quirky? Great description of her. Why, interested?"

"Always interested in someone who's protective of you. Is that what you mean?"

"Just thought that the dark haired, blue-eyed beauty might be your type."

"Nah, been there, done that," he replied, looking away.

"Ah, must be the ex you mentioned?"

"Could be. So what treasures of Pat's did you uncover today?" He shut the door on the Lizz conversation. Not someone he wanted to discuss tonight.

"I know what you just did. I'll circle back, trust me."

"Is that so? Well, let's go back to Kate then. I need her telephone number by the way."

"Really? Do I get Jessica's number?" She passed him a napkin, opened up her purse, and pulled out a plastic baggie and a pen. "I'm sure your sister would love to share stories ...." She offered him a pen.

He just stared at her with a silly grin on his face. She had gotten him.

"Okay, moving on. Remember I told you Billy wrote love notes to Pita? His letters stopped after 1944." She poured the contents of the bag onto the table. "He wanted to enlist. I thought I'd try to find some information on him. Maybe my security buddy Andrew and I might be able to access his military records?" She hesitated. "Now this is where I would call Kate to get her opinion. But, what do you think?" She handed him the pen.

"I don't know what Kate would say, but I know you. It doesn't matter what I say, you're going to look him up anyway." He scribbled Jessica's number on the napkin.

"Now, those would have been Kate's exact words," she said.

He handed her the napkin and gave her his. "Kate's number, please?"

"Are you really going to call her?" She scribbled Kate's number, then handed him some photos.

"Only in an emergency, how's that?"

"Well, not knowing what constitutes an emergency, I would say if I was dying... okay? Would you look at these photos, please?" She tucked Jessica's number into her pocket. "That's Pita on the left. See the young man behind her? Billy, maybe?" She leaned forward, pointing to the young man wrapping her grandaunt in his arms.

What Jack saw a young man, happy to be with the woman he loved. And Pat was beautiful, full of life, and content to be with this mystery man.

"Could be. She was a looker, wasn't she?" He laid the photo on the table. "What information do you want on Billy? Maybe he came home, maybe they broke up, or maybe he never came home. Are there any other photos of them together?"

She pulled out more photos from her purse. "I think this is her college picture. And she's with Billy, I think."

"Look at them, so full of life and hope. Now they're probably all gone."

"Wow. Where's that coming from? Are you talking about her or yourself?"

"Maybe a little bit of both. Life goes by too fast. If you don't grab that brass ring when you can, you may never get another chance." Their fingers touched as she offered him more of the contents of the bag. "If you want, I'll see if my contacts can find out anything about him. No promises. What else did you find?"

"Any info will help. Thanks." She squeezed his hand, opened it, and dropped two men's rings into his palm. "I found these in the box too, a high school ring and a Colby College class ring dated 1941, both with the initials WJL. They must have been together all that time." Her face softened as she looked at the striking young woman with her handsome soldier. "I have to admit, I never thought of her being so young and in love with someone other than my uncle. Something must have happened, because they seemed so much in love." She passed him more photos. "Although, I guess even that's not enough sometimes."

"Now who's talking about themselves? Want to share his name and then we'll be even?" He saw the beginnings of a smile. So, someone had hurt her in the past.

"Not really, but thanks. I told you I found the journals? My next task is to read them and find out as much as I can about Pita's life."

He barely heard the rest of Jamie's words as he stared at the young woman in the photographs. If he didn't know any better, he would have thought that it was Jamie.

"You look just like her." He glanced up at her. "I saw the family resemblance when she was older, but look at these."

Jamie waved him off. "Not really. She was beautiful, wasn't she? Like a 1930's movie star. I thought of Jean Harlow. And that special smile of hers and the throaty laugh, only she had." Embarrassed, she tried to change the subject. "I'm stumbling through this and you're not helping with that smug smile. So thank you for the compliment. Now, as to the other photos?"

He had to laugh. "I don't care how much you protest, you are a young Pat, the smile, the laugh, even the hair. And you're just as pretty." He hesitated, "Actually you're more beautiful."

"Stop it. You are making me blush. People are watching."

"It's a pretty shade of pink." He was enjoying the banter. "Okay, I'll be good. But it's true—you're prettier. And yes, I'll look through the other photos."

A drum roll filled the room and the band members beckoned to Jack.

He apologized. "I should run over and talk to the guys for a minute. If that's okay, I'll be right back."

She nodded, adding, "Absolutely fine with me. I'll just sit here by myself, all alone, not knowing anyone in this entire room." He started to sit back down. "Oh, for God's sake, I'm kidding. Go." She gave him that killer smile.

The musicians kidded Jack as he stood with his both hands in the pockets of his crisp tan slacks, his brown crewneck sweater hanging loosely around his waist. When he turned toward Jamie, he shook his head. His conversation continued for a few more minutes, arms waving and sheet music being exchanged.

"Who's turning pink now?" she added as Jack returned to the table. "I gather you know the band playing tonight?"

"Yes Ma'am. Local group letting off a little steam. Good therapy."

"Sounds like you know what you are talking about."

He felt his tough guy façade crack a bit as he tried to focus on the menu and not his dinner companion.

Chapter Twenty

As Jamie and Jack discussed dessert, the band launched into Beatles and Rolling Stones pieces. When the final set came to a deafening halt, the leader signaled for Jack to join them. After pointing to their melting ice cream sundae, Jack excused himself, walked up to the stage, and said a few words, resulting in laughter from the band members. Picking up the guitar, Jack settled on the stool and spoke to the crowd.

"I'm only in for this one song. Tonight, I'd like to sit back and enjoy the music." Almost on cue, everyone turned toward Jamie, embarrassing her even more. "Please give these guys all the support you have. Ready, one, two, three."

Jack's transformation from Police Chief to lead singer in a rock band amazed Jamie as he began to play and sing Kenny Chesney's song, *Boston*.

"Everyone." Jack encouraged the crowd to sing along.

This was definitely a different side of him—more relaxed and at ease. When they met on the beach, he came off as a bit overbearing, standoffish, and all business, but now it was like he had performed in front of a crowd all of his life. Maybe that was the key; he knew and trusted these people. The room filled with the words of the chorus.

When the song ended, Jack leaned the guitar against the stool and walked back to Jamie as the audience continued to clap. He waved a thank you, and sat down wearing a boyish grin.

"I'm sorry. I thought we would have a nice quiet dinner. I didn't plan on any of this tonight."

"Sorry for what? That was fantastic. Never in a million years would I have thought of you as a rock star. Never." All the women in town must be dreaming about him, especially Bev who sat across the room shooting daggers at her. "You never mentioned that you played in a band?"

"Complex, I told you. And thanks, I guess I'm more of the professor type?"

"Phew, not after that performance. That was hot." She fanned herself with her napkin.

"Okay, okay, I get it. Like to dance?" he asked as the band broke into a slow piece.

"Absolutely. How can a girl turn down an invitation from the most popular guy in town?" she teased while holding his hand behind her as she headed out onto the dance floor.

He wrapped his arm around her, holding her hand close to his chest. She felt his heartbeat—strong and steady. She couldn't remember the last time she had been this close to a man. Maybe at her cousin Alicia's wedding, when she had been forced to dance with Aiden. They had argued even then, under their breath, so it couldn't be overheard by the rest of the wedding party. His words still rang in her ears. "Why are you so mad? I don't love her, I love you." Aiden had almost made her forget about Mike, almost.

Jack rested his chin against her forehead and she wrapped her hand around his neck.

Aiden had cheated on her, had slept with one of Kate's friends. And because it happened only once, he thought that he should be forgiven. Jamie found out about it when she had accidently overheard a young pretty redhead ask Kate if Aiden could be her usher. Kate explained that Aiden and Jamie were almost engaged. The woman's mocking response was, "Really? Then why was he in my bed last night?" Jamie snuck out of the room without either of them knowing that she had overheard the conversation.

"Awfully quiet. Want to tell me his name?" Jack whispered in her ear. "It's only fair."

She pulled away from him, sure that her thoughts were written across her face. *Damn Aiden, damn Mike, even after all this time.*

She hesitated, never having shared these hurts with anyone. She never even told Kate what happened. "Aiden, his name was Aiden."

He pulled her closer. "Thank you," he whispered.

***

Jamie had said nothing more than his name, but Jack saw the hurt in her eyes. As they walked back to her cottage, his arm casually draped around her shoulder, she hummed the Chesney song. He would find out about this ex. Kate would know.

"Now you're quiet. What's up?" she asked, turning to face him.

"Nothing really, just thinking about tonight."

"I had a great time."

"Me too." He stopped walking. "You know..."

She pressed her fingers to his lips. "No, no talk of Lizz or Aiden tonight, promise?"

"Okay, but..."

"No buts."

He had a feeling that she could make him agree to anything. He nibbled at her fingers.

"I didn't realize you were so talented." She changed the subject and withdrew her hand. "What other secrets are you concealing?"

"I'm not terribly good at hiding anything. What you see is what you get." He looked her straight in the eyes as he said it because he wanted her to know that he wasn't Aiden.

"We'll see." She started to walk again. "By the way, did you ever figure out who that guy at the bar was?"

He laughed and shook his head. "Was I that obvious? Here I thought I was being circumspect, but everybody, including him, probably knew I was watching. I never saw him before. Also never saw the tall, long haired blonde who came in later and joined him." He shrugged his shoulders. "Might just be visitors."

"Might be."

Chapter Twenty-One

A few weeks earlier, Jamie had stopped at the Blue Wave Art Gallery to ask the owner, Marge Kramer, if she'd be interested in some of Pita's paintings.

"Interested? Are you kidding me? Her watercolors will sell within a week once the collectors arrive. Patrice is one of our most sought after artists." Marge went on to explain how, this year, Patrice's paintings would be prized even more. They both knew what she was saying; the death of an artist raises the value of their work because there will be no more.

Jamie and Jack had spent a few hours over the weekend packing up Pita's paintings from the attic. She offered Jack any paintings he wanted and she held out the ones she would keep. The rest would be given away as gifts, donated to the town of Oyster Point, or sold with the money going to the Oyster Point Historical Society. Jamie didn't need the money and the Society could buy something in Pita's name.

Jamie lugged the paintings inside the Gallery, standing them by the front desk as she searched for Marge. When the two of them returned, a group of people hovered around the desk.

"Are you the artist?" a woman inquired, holding up one of Pita's pieces.

"I am an artist, but these paintings were done by Patrice Dalton."

"I would love to buy this one," the woman now spoke to her friend.

Marge, overhearing the conversation, asked Jamie if she would like to bring in some of her own works and, if her paintings were popular, the Gallery would represent her in a show of her own next summer.

"I'd love that. When I finish the pieces I'm currently working on, I'll be back." The sounds of a bidding war going on for Pita's paintings followed her to the car. Next year, who knows where she'll be. Life had changed so much in the past year, Pita had left her life and Jack had entered it; she owned a home, but it would be gone by fall.

Max planted a big wet kiss on her cheek as she opened the front car door of Jack's SUV. "Where will we be in twelve months, Max?" She rubbed the dog behind her big floppy ears. Max had been staying with her since the fiasco with Andy. Jack believed she would feel more secure with the dog in the cottage. Whether or not she felt safer, Jack did. She wouldn't put it past him to have a patrol car check the cottage every night. She didn't ask and he didn't say.

Today was too beautiful to work indoors, so Jamie drove to the Cove to paint. She had a choice of subjects, roses cascading over the rickety wooden fence, high dunes, or Oyster Point Harbor with a few boats that had already claimed their moorings.

Max pushed by her as she unloaded her paints and easel. The shadows crept along the sand as the sun lowered. Max returned from the water, dug a hole in the sand, and curled up at her feet.

Jamie covered her paper with colors and washes. As ships' bells rang in the distance, Jamie realized that she had been painting for over two hours. Her creation with the dunes flowing down on the left, an old worn and chipped red boat pulled up on the sand, and the blue-green water sneaking through the sea grass on the right had caught a bit of haze over Indian Head in the distance. The juicy purple shadows ran across the paper in stark contrast to the light sand. She'd take a few photos and finish up at the cottage.

She leaned down, removing her camera from the bag when Max's bark caused her to look around.

A dark colored car sat at the end of the road, facing the water. The low sun glared off the windshield, blinding her for a second. Even though the driver's window appeared open, it was too dark to see inside. Something flashed. A wrist watch? Ring? A camera? Damn it, she had left her sunglasses back in the car. Her heart began to pound. The car just sat there.

This didn't feel right. Max kept her eyes on the intruder, the hair on her back rising.

Jamie hated to do this, but she pulled out the cell phone from her short's pocket and pressed Jack's number. It rang and rang.

"Answer Jack, damn it, answer the phone, please."

Chapter Twenty-Two

As Jack sat checking the police reports filed last night, his cell phone rang.

"Chief Hereford," he answered, flipping to another report.

"Hi, it's me."

"Hi. I called the cottage before and you weren't there." He could hear Jamie's breathlessness, like she had been running. "Having a good afternoon? Did you have any trouble dropping the paintings off at the gallery?"

"No, none. Jack, I...I...I think I would like you to send someone down to the Cove please."

"What's the matter?" He grabbed his car keys and was halfway out his office door before she said another word. There was fear in her voice.

"I'm just feeling..." Her deep breath cut off her words. "It's probably nothing, but a car drove up and parked. It's just sitting there. I can't see who's in it because of the glare from the sun." Her words ran together. "Now, when I'm telling you, it sounds foolish. It's probably nothing, just someone enjoying a few minutes by the water."

"I'm on my way. Your intuition's always spot on, never doubt it." He tore out of the station parking lot onto Main Street, lights flashing. All he could see were cold green eyes and wet blond stringy hair twisted in seaweed. This might be how the murderer stalked his prey. Phil wouldn't like his use of the word "murderer," but he knew that they weren't accidental drownings.

"I'll be there in a minute. Keep talking. What color is the car, what's the model?"

"It's a dark blue or black. I can't tell the make, damn it. I'm too far away. A sedan. Looks new. Probably American, not foreign."

"Don't move. Anything else you can tell me? Is the engine still on?" He had to keep her answering his questions.

"I think so. I hear a hum and there aren't any boats around."

Damn, she was alone on the beach. "There's no one else there?"

"I don't see anyone. Wait, the car is backing away. I can't see it anymore. I'll go to the road's edge and read the license plate number for you."

"No," he shouted. "You stay where you are. Hopefully I'll meet him at the corner." When Jack approached Old Wharf Road, he still hadn't passed any cars. "How's Max? Did she stay with you?"

"She's the one who alerted me. I lose myself when I paint."

"Great. Just what I need to hear. From now on, please let me know where you're heading?" He shut off the flashing lights and drove up the lane hoping he could spot the car.

"I don't see anything. Damn it. Where did he go?" He headed back to the beach. "I'm pulling up now."

His phone went dead. He watched her push through the loose sand toward him, Maxine right behind her. As he stepped out of the car, she landed in his arms, almost knocking him over, her straw hat flying off in the breeze.

Maxine barked, jumping on them both. "Good girl, Max, good girl." She licked his hand.

"Am I glad to see you," Jamie whispered in his ear, arms wrapped tightly around his neck.

"Better be careful, a guy could get used to this," he nuzzled her ear, trying to relax her. He could smell the sun tan lotion on her skin, feel the heat from her naked back.

"Where did the car go?" She pulled back.

He could never tell if she heard his comments and just chose to ignore them. "Must have turned onto Old Shelter Road heading toward the Neck." He enjoyed holding her just a little too much, he realized, moving his hands along her back. "You okay?" he pushed a loose strand of her hair back behind her ear. She leaned her forehead against his chest.

Lifting her head, she pushed her hair back behind her ear before he had a chance to touch it a second time. The afternoon sunlight had tinged her face with a healthy sun kissed look; her eyes held a spark of fear and anger. All of a sudden, like lightening, it dawned on him that he had to protect her, not just for Pat but for himself.

"This is ridiculous. I can't live like this. I've never been afraid of anything and now, when someone parks at the beach, I panic?" She tried to pull away from him.

"Not yet." It was like he had known her forever: the tone of her voice when she joked; the way she tossed her hair when her temper flared; or the use of her hands when she spoke; the smell of her hair and her perfume. He pulled her close. "I'm sorry I involved you in my cases." He rested his head on hers. "Should have stopped it right off, but I never dreamed you'd go off by yourself. Now we're both…" he hesitated, trying to find the correct words "…on edge."

"It's not your fault. I had to play detective and stick my nose right into the middle of your investigation." Turning from him, she said, "Well, he's gone. I need to pack up my gear and you need to get back to work."

"First, this is my work. Second, I'll help you pack up and, third," he declared, "I'll follow you home. And, by the way, thanks for hanging up on me before." He needed to see her smile.

She gave him that wonderful quizzical look, and then, that lopsided smile he loved. "I guess once I saw you," she shrugged, her opal necklace reflecting a glimmer of the lowering sun between her tanned breasts. She placed her straw hat back on her head, and sauntered through the deep sand to gather her easel and paints with Max following close behind. When Jamie picked up her bags, Maxine headed straight for the water.

"Don't Max. You'll ride in the back deck," Jack warned.

The dog gave him a look, growled a bark as if to say, "We'll see," and splashed into the water.

Jack swore he saw her wink at him before she submerged.

Chapter Twenty-Three

The stranger eased his car up to the rise where he had a perfect view of the beach below. He took a bite of his donut, the jelly sliding out the bottom, down his chin. He wiped his face with an old shirt from under the seat, and sipped his coffee.

Jamie made quite the picture, standing by the water's edge close to where the tall sea grasses grew, intently painting with a dog at her feet. Her straw hat drooped over her head, her hair blew in the slight breeze off the water, and her skimpy pink halter top tied around her long slim neck completely exposed her back except for the tiny pink bow that held the halter in place. She eased back a few feet to look at her painting, tilting her head to the side, her long tanned legs emerging from her white shorts, bracing her in the soft sand.

He raised his camera, scanning the length of that soft skin leading to her tiny waist. The sand caused her hips to sway as she stepped back to the easel. Facing him, she bent over looking for something in her bag.

Click.

"Now that's quite a view," he mumbled, adjusting his long range lens. The fullness of her breasts between the strands of blond hair cascading over her shoulders increased his breathing. A slight tug on the bow behind her neck and everything would be his. He could feel the heat of her breasts in his hands. He took another photo, shifting his legs further apart, uncomfortable from his daydreams.

His coffee cup tilted. "Damn." He wiped at the spill, spreading jelly on the crotch of his pants. When he refocused his camera, Jamie stood looking up at the car. Her beautiful body straightened, her breasts straining against the thin fabric as she pulled her hair to the back of her neck.

Click.

He threw his empty coffee cup on the rug floor. "Now's the time to come to Daddy, my beauty," he said, grabbing for the door handle, placing the camera on the seat next to him.

"Shit," he yelped as a red flash caught him in the eyes, blinding him. He shielded his eyes with his hands. When his vision cleared, he heard the low murmur of Jamie's voice as she spoke on her phone. He couldn't be found here watching her. He had squandered his opportunity.

"Damn it all to hell." He hit the steering wheel with his hands. "I could have had her. No one would have ever known what happened to her except me." He started to back up the car. "You will be mine, I promise you, Jamie."

Making a U-turn, he floored the engine so that the rear wheels skidded in the sand as he headed to the intersection. Turning right, he pulled into a hidden driveway, pleased as he watched the flashing red and blue lights turn toward the water in his rearview mirror.

"Good luck, Chief," he smiled. "Happy hunting." He sped away.

Chapter Twenty-Four

Jamie sat on the deck reading Pita's journal. Her words painted a picture of a teenage girl falling in love with a young man on their first date.

Billy walked toward me tonight at the dance and my heart jumped right out of my chest. I wanted him to ask me to dance so badly. And he did. Can you believe it? He asked ME! He's the captain of the football team and very popular. I'm well-liked, but not "cheerleader" popular, if you know what I mean. We stayed together the rest of the night and then he asked me for a date. I couldn't say yes fast enough.

The slamming of a car door interrupted her reading. Maxine headed around to the front of the cottage. It seemed early for Jack, but then, tonight was Friday night at the Club. Maxine's bark eroded into a growl. Jamie put the journal down and stepped inside. Through the screen door, she caught sight of a dark colored sedan. She hid behind the wooden door. He had followed her. Her cell phone, where was it? On the night table, damn it. Could she reach the one on the wall? She grabbed the door handle and pushed with all her might, but a wing tip shoe kept the door from closing. Her bare feet slipped on the tile floor and he flew through the opening, tumbling onto the floor.

"Matt? What the hell are you doing? You scared me half to death." She offered him a hand. He reciprocated by grabbing her so she fell on top of him.

She screamed, "Stop." He held her tightly to his chest.

A shadow fell over both of them as Jack jerked open the screen door and stood with gun drawn. Max bared her teeth, ready to pounce if given his order.

"No, Jack, please. It's okay," Jamie said, pushing herself up against Matt's chest. She extended her hand for Jack's help.

He pulled her up, watching as Matt's hands traveled all the way down her bare back as she pushed away.

Matt gave a low whistle. "Impressive. You have your own bodyguard?" He stood close to her, fooling with the tie at her neck.

Jack eyed Matt as he continued to fool with Jamie's halter straps. He turned to her, eyebrow raised, awaiting an explanation.

"Jack, this is Matt. I told you about him?" She felt a pain in her chest seeing how he looked at her. "Stop it." She pushed Matt's hand away from her neck.

"You did?"

"Remember, Matt's my friend from Boston who's handling Pita's estate. He's the one parked at the beach today. Matt, this is Jack Hereford, the Oyster Point Chief of Police. Jack, this is Matt Hollings." She shifted her gaze to Matt, looking for confirmation. "That was you, wasn't it? At the beach? I recognize the car."

"Christ almighty, I left because I thought the entire police force would be on me, just for trying to surprise my girl." He slipped his arm back around Jamie's shoulder.

"You're just lucky I didn't catch you when I drove down the road." Jack stared at Jamie. He slipped his gun back into his shoulder holster, never taking his eyes off her.

"I just didn't think, Chief. Figured I'd surprise her at the cottage instead of at the beach. More private." Matt's words conveyed his intention. "Or so I thought."

"When Max barked, I thought it was you. When I opened the door, Matt jammed his foot in and I..." she blabbered, pushing Matt's hand away from her again. Jack had to realize that this guy meant nothing to her, but his frown said it all.

"I'll just take off since everything seems more than okay here." Jack extended his hand to Matt, giving him an intimidating look. "Matt."

"You'll be back? We're going to the Club later?"

"I'm playing tonight." He looked into her eyes. "Maybe I'll see you there." He turned to leave.

"Wait." She touched his arm. "Matt, I'm going to walk Jack out. I'll be right back."

"No, don't bother. I can find my way to the car. You have company." Jack closed the screen door behind him.

Running down the walk after him, Jamie heard the screen door slam behind her. When she turned, Matt stood watching them.

"Jack, will you stop for a minute and listen?"

"There's nothing to listen to. This is the guy from Boston." He kept walking.

"I told you about him the first night we ran together. He's just a friend. There's nothing between us."

"You did tell me," he stated. "I guess he slipped my mind over the last few months. It's fine. I'm heading over to the Club to help the guys set up. I'll talk to you later." He hesitated a second, "By the way, good friends don't usually use the term 'my girl'." He slammed the car door shut.

"Jack, please don't go this way," she whispered.

He turned around in her driveway and gunned the car down the hill.

"Please." She stood watching him drive away, feeling nauseous all of a sudden.

***

Matt met Jamie as she stood at the end of the walk, "I have to check for my wallet," he smiled. Jamie nodded and headed back to the cottage. Maybe this was his time; she was upset with the Chief. He gazed down the road where he saw a police cruiser hidden in the trees. He kicked the tire.

Chapter Twenty-Five

A hush fell over the Club's dining room when Jamie entered with Matt. As much as she tried to convince him that they could find a quieter place to catch up, he insisted on grabbing dinner at the Club, the place that Jack had mentioned. He was intrigued, he said.

She turned to Matt, "Let's leave." But it was too late as Lily, the hostess, approached them.

"Two?" she asked looking at Jamie. "Is this your brother?"

"No," Jamie added and followed Lily to a corner table in the back, away from the stage. The table that she usually shared with Jack remained unoccupied.

"Thank you, Lily. He's a friend from Boston."

"A good friend," Matt added, pulling out her chair.

Jamie stared at him, a coldness coming over her. "Thank you, Lily." She felt Jack's eyes on her as she sat down. When she looked over, he stared at her for what seemed like forever and then, turned back to hooking up his guitar.

Jamie excused herself, telling Matt that she needed to say hello to the band. The guys greeted her as usual, but Jack's cool response surprised her.

"Are you playing all night or only a few songs?"

Not looking up, but continuing to work on his guitar, he responded, "I'm not really sure. I haven't checked out tonight's songs."

That wasn't true; the band always planned a week ahead. She forced him to look at her when she asked, "Will you come over to the table on your break?"

"I don't think so. I'd be intruding." His dark brown eyes softened a bit as they held hers.

"You wouldn't be intruding at all." She tried to keep the pleading out of her voice, knowing that everyone in the Club, including Matt, was watching them.

When he didn't respond, she asked, "Come by the cottage after you finish here?"

Jack stared over at Matt and then back at her. "I'm tired tonight. I've had a long day. I think I'll just go home and you have company." He didn't say it in a mean way, but with disappointment and sadness that cut right through her.

"I'll be there. Please, we need to talk," she whispered. When he didn't reply, she smiled at the band, wished them luck, and made her way back to her table.

***

Jack slammed the sheet music on his stand. Jamie looked back; Jack looked away. What a fool he had been for getting involved with her. Hadn't Lizz taught him anything? When he held Jamie today, he knew that he had to protect her. What a fool he was to think someone like her would be unattached. This guy didn't seem her type...or maybe he didn't know her type.

Matt had given her a long rope, not seeing her since April. How attached could he be? If the tables were turned, he would have been on her doorstep every day. But she was taken. He wasn't sure what was going on between them, but he didn't need to be a third wheel.

Matt jumped up and pulled Jamie's chair out as she returned to the table. His look to Jack said, "Stay away from her."

Chapter Twenty-Six

A gentle breeze blew the white gauze curtains, filling the bedroom with the smell of evening primrose. The moonlight cast silhouettes across Jamie's bed like lovers moving to the rhythm of a slow dance. Jamie lay on her side replaying the events of the day. How had the situation with Jack and Matt gotten so far out of hand? Jack hadn't believed her. Why?

When the clock showed three o'clock, she threw off the bed sheets. She was too agitated to stay in bed. Maybe reading one of Pita's journals would be a better use of her time, although in her present mood, reading Pita and Billy's love story might not be the cure for her insomnia.

A rare blue moon lit Jamie's way through the living room to where Max, sprawled upside down in front of the sliding door, blocked her way to the deck. She shifted Maxine's hind legs over. The dog turned over and started to snore.

"Max, you're such a great watchdog," she clucked in the dog's ear, patting her on the head. "Glad someone's asleep in this house."

Jamie stepped out onto the deck in a camisole, cotton shorts, and bare feet. The balmy July night air felt good. White tipped waves slapped against the posts at the marina in a predictable rhythm. The moored boats bobbing on glistening waves cast long undulating shapes across the water. She looked up and saw her childhood friends twinkling above her.

"Where have you been today, dear ones? You don't know how glad I am to see you. I made a mess of tonight and don't know how to fix it. Everything has fallen apart. Matt appeared acting weird, Jack's angry with me...

somehow I thought destiny had led me here, but maybe I was wrong?" Somehow, she believed that fate had played a part in bringing her back to this town and this cottage. She didn't quite understand it, but maybe she would someday. "As much as I love it here, I should never have come back."

"So? You wish you had never come back?" Jack questioned.

Jamie's eyes flashed open. "Oh my God, you scared me half to death. What are you doing out here?"

Jack patted the spot next to him on the swing. "Couldn't sleep. Come sit."

The swing creaked as she sat down next to him. "Me either." Jamie noticed a light go on in one of the moored boats. "Thought I'd come out and have a chat with my friends. I've been ignoring them lately and tonight I really needed them." With her eyes still focused on the light in the boat's window, she asked, "I didn't hear your car?"

"When I can't sleep, I walk. I ended up here on your swing. I guess in spite of everything that happened today, I still feel comfortable here at the cottage."

She said nothing.

"I'm really sorry about tonight. I acted like a jerk, rude and insensitive. You deserve better than that from me."

Twisting to see his face, she found she didn't have an answer for him. "I don't understand why you were so angry with me—why you didn't believe me." She wanted him to say how he felt.

"Where's Matt?"

"I sent him back to Boston. He attempted to wheedle an invitation to stay, but in a small town like this, his car would be noticed outside my cottage overnight, and," she added, "no one would know he stayed on the couch." *Especially you*, she thought as she looked away.

"Really."

"Yes, really." she snapped. She couldn't see his face. "Do you think I'm lying? You know me better than that…at least I thought you did. Check inside. You'll find nothing. Matt's probably back in Boston by now."

"No, I believe you." He hesitated. "But he didn't go back to Boston."

"Yes, he did, I saw him leave…" her voice trailed off. "He turned right onto Commercial Street." Yet she had no idea where he had gone after that.

"He saw Bob sitting at the end of the road, I'm sure. When I drove by, his car was parked in front of the cottage, so I headed to Dunkin's for a cup of coffee hoping that when I drove back, he'd be gone. He passed me as I pulled out of the parking lot, so I followed him until he pulled into a little dirt road just over the Eastham line."

"You followed him? Tonight?" She didn't understand. Then it registered with her. "You mean you and your guys are spying on me?" Her voice rose. "You thought he was going to stay here overnight, didn't you?" She lowered her voice, knowing how sound carried across the water at night. She leaned in so close to him that her heated whisper touched his cheek. "How dare you? Is that what you think of me, that I invite anyone into my bed?" Her voice was low and her words slow. "What gives you the right to watch me?" Why was she so angry? Then it dawned on her. "You really don't trust me."

"Matt didn't go back to Boston. And it's not you I don't trust, it's him." He was calm. "And besides, it's my job to keep you and everyone else in this town safe, especially with what's happening on our beaches." He shifted a stray piece of hair behind her ear. "You know me, I'm a bloodhound. I don't like Matt, obvious reasons aside. Something about him doesn't click, too smooth, too preppy, too possessive after not seeing you since April. After the Club, I drank a beer out on my deck and thought about this afternoon. Why would he frighten you like that? If you were my girl and I found you painting on the beach, dressed like you were, and I hadn't seen you since April, which by the way never would have happened." He adjusted the back of her camisole. "Anyway, I would have jumped out of the car, run down the beach in my wing tipped shoes, and grabbed you up into my arms." His feelings for her were written across his face, but she couldn't see them.

"You would have been mad as hell for me interrupting your painting concentration, but I would have done it anyway. But he didn't. Why? He sat watching you, waiting for what?" He didn't expect an answer. "And then, when he knew he had frightened you to the point of calling someone, he took off. Why didn't he just identify himself? You could have cancelled the call." He kissed her shoulder. "Don't be mad at me, but I called Kate."

"Oh good Lord, no."

"I had to ask about Matt. Something just didn't add up. We only spoke for a few minutes."

"And?"

"The Matt she described was nothing like the Matt I met today... yesterday." He stretched and placed his arm behind her.

"He acted so weird. You know something else? He rented that car, said work was being done on his Jaguar," Jamie added. "But I know that the dealership provides him with a loaner Jaguar."

"I know," Jack responded. "I checked the plate. It's rented to his father's law firm."

"I should have known you would be a step ahead of me. What are you thinking?"

"I don't know. Maybe he wasn't looking for you? Could he have driven to the Cove for another reason? He couldn't have known that you would be there. Did he stop by the cottage first? Has he been to the Cove before?" he asked. This was the Chief probing, not Jack.

"Never," she stated without hesitation. "In fact, he has only been down here once, last summer when we visited Pita for the day to go over her will. And we never drove to the Cove. Not sure I ever mentioned it to him. We didn't share a lot of personal information."

"So, does he know anyone else down here?"

"Not that I know of." She knew very little about his personal life. They were both busy and when they met for dinner, they discussed work and little else. She knew more about Jack and his family and she had only known him a few months. She felt chilled all of a sudden, like when Matt had looked at her at the Club.

"Cold?" Jack asked.

"A little."

He took off his sweatshirt and put it on her.

"His arm around my shoulder and the 'my girl' comment felt creepy. We talked about our relationship ages ago and agreed there was nothing between us. He's never touched me that way." Jamie knew that Matt placing his hands on her in such an intimate way had angered Jack.

Playing with her hair, he responded, "I'm glad."

"About Matt being a creep? It was so unlike him. He's usually so professional."

"That's just what Kate said. Enough about Matt," he said, slipping his hand behind her neck, gently pulling her close to him. He closed his eyes and kissed her, a gentle, innocent kiss. Pulling back, he outlined her lips with his thumbs and leaned his forehead against hers. He caught her green opal in his hand.

"I'm sorry. I don't know why I did that."

Pushing his hair back, she ran her hand over the bristle of a day's growth of his beard. "Don't be sorry. I'm not." She laid her head against his chest.

He wrapped his arms around her, rested his chin on her head, and closed his eyes.

Chapter Twenty-Seven

Jack left Jamie at dawn with a promise to take her on a surprise trip. After he showered, he called the office. His secretary said his day was clear, go and enjoy and she would call if he was needed.

Last night had changed a lot of things for him. Until now, he had protected Jamie because she had belonged to Pat, but now, he wouldn't let anyone hurt her because she belonged to him. He would find out more about this Matt guy. For some reason, the man that he met yesterday was a threat to Jamie. This could be the way that the murderer stalked his prey, seeing the women alone, unprotected?

Now that he sat outside Jamie's cottage rubbing his beard, he thought maybe he looked too grubby. He hadn't shaved. Too late. He lifted the bouquet of flowers off the front seat. His mother always said flowers were best served as a surprise. He hoped that she liked boats. He hadn't asked. He jogged up the walk in his shorts, a T-shirt, and a Boston Red Sox baseball cap, with his dark reflective sunglasses adding a touch of mystery to his looks.

When Jamie opened the door, Jack greeted her with a large bunch of flowers. Hugging him, she whispered, "They're beautiful. Thank you so much."

"A little peace offering to say I'm sorry again. Somehow they reminded me of you when I saw them," as did everything these days.

She walked to the kitchen sink, the flowers held to her face.

"Whenever you're ready, we can get started."

"Let me put these in water. A pure white bouquet, how beautiful. I love flowers."

"I know," he said as he came up behind her, kissing her on the top of her head. "My mother, bless her soul, had special meanings for all the flowers she grew, the daisy, purity and loyal love; and lily of the valley, sweetness, beauty, humility; the rose… a rose I guess." Moving to pick up her bags by the door, he said, "I'll throw these in the car. Is this what you're taking?"

"Wait." She grabbed him by the arm, stood on bare tiptoes, and gave him a quick kiss. Slowly wiping her lipstick off his lips with the tips of her fingers, she answered, "Yes, that's what I'm taking. Thanks again, for everything."

"I haven't done much," he said, carrying her bag out the door.

He leaned on the deck of his SUV, with arms crossed, waiting for Jamie to lock up the cottage. Her response to the flowers was so… not Lizz. Lizz had been blasé whenever he brought her flowers, as though they were expected. She'd throw them on the counter, letting them wilt. Jamie, on the other hand, acted delighted, stopping everything to put them in water, fussing over them—and him. Another big difference between the two women.

Chapter Twenty-Eight

Taking Jamie's hand, Jack helped her down into a boat moored at the marina. "Hope you like boats. I never asked."

"I love boats. Did you rent this one?"

"She's pretty, isn't she?" He called back as he stashed their gear into the lockers at the rear of the boat. "Nope, not rented."

"Borrowed?"

He responded, almost embarrassed, "Nope, mine."

"Yours? You're kidding, right?" She scanned the 36' Sea Ray.

Jack gave a little shrug. "What's a single guy to do with his money? You live in a place like this, you need a boat." He placed his sunglasses on his cap visor.

"Do you ever take her out?" Her questions kept tumbling out.

"Not often. Sometimes, if I need to get away, I'll go out, do a little fishing."

"Boy, what else don't I know about you?" She walked to the front and called back, "Good golly, this thing is huge. What's her name?"

"Jackie's Oh," he came up behind her, "a stupid play on words."

"I get it. Very cute, very cute indeed."

"Ready? Let's take off. I want to be there at low tide. Today's perfect, a full moon with good tide pulls."

"Ready when you are, Captain." Jamie hopped back up on the wharf and slid the mooring ropes off the pier. Throwing them back to Jack, she grasped his hand and jumped down into his outstretched arms.

"Not bad. You make a pretty good first mate."

"That I do. Had a little practice with my Dad." Jamie twisted her hair up and through the back of her Boston Red Sox cap. She faced the sun, the wind blowing against her, watching as Jack piloted the boat out of its mooring, past the channel markers into the outer harbor, past Great Island on the right and the Neck on the left. His two day old beard lent him a salty, seasoned look. His eyes were hidden behind his sunglasses. His set mouth indicated that his mind was elsewhere.

"A penny for your thoughts?"

A sly smile spread across his face. "They're worth a lot more than that."

"You never told me what Kate said?"

"About what?"

"About whatever you talked about."

"She profiled the Matt she knew and like I said, it didn't fit the guy I met yesterday." He wasn't about to tell her that he had asked about Aiden. Or that Kate talked about Mike. If Jamie asked him directly, he wouldn't lie and he told Kate that. Otherwise, it was their secret. "She said the same thing that you did, he never rented a car. Just doesn't add up."

Jack picked up the radio transmitter. "Dan, Jack here. Looks like we might have a poacher taking on someone's lobster traps just past the jetty. He thinks he's hidden. Normally I'd stop, but I'm on my way out. Thanks Dan. Out." He clicked the hand held microphone back on the dash and continued to guide the boat past the hidden shoals as the boat entered Cape Cod Bay.

"You have eyes in the back of your head," Jamie commented.

"Yes I do, so beware."

Blue skies, light wind, little chop, and big, puffy white clouds hanging over the mainland made the day perfect. The coast of Plymouth to the west and the

Provincetown monument to the north were both perfectly outlined.

"Isn't this the life, cruising out here on a day like this?" Jack pulled her near, saying, "Will you take the controls for a minute?"

Taking the wheel, Jamie warned him, "Don't leave me alone with this thing too long unless you want to own a pile of rubble. It's the only thing you own, you know; you should protect it."

His laugh was infectious. "We're far enough out that there isn't much you can hit. If you see another boat, swerve." He rummaged through a pile of maps. "I thought we would cruise for a while and enjoy being out on the water, and then, head over to Billings Island for a picnic. Have you ever been there?"

"It's usually underwater, isn't it? I think Uncle Frank took me out there clamming when I was a kid."

"Normally, but with an extra low tide like today, the island should be about eight to ten feet out of the water. A perfect day for a picnic."

"Should I turn at any point?"

"Stay in sight of land for now," he yelled from the back of the boat where he reshuffled the gear they had brought on board and then disappeared below.

"Hello," she shouted. "Don't leave me up here by myself. You'll be sorry."

"You're doing great, JJ," he called back to her, appearing on the stairs carrying a large cooler and some blankets. "By the way, there's a head down there, a galley, bunk, whatever you need."

"Ah, JJ? I can tell you've been talking to Kate."

"Bad to call you that?"

She shook her head. "My Dad called me that and now Kate does."

He moved behind her, putting his arms around her as he took the wheel. "I'll take over now, if you want. If it's too personal, I'm okay with that." He kissed her on the nose as she turned to face him. He wasn't sure how it happened, but she had become part of his everyday life. She hugged him back, kissed him on the neck, and ducked under his arm. He put all thoughts of the green-eyed women away for today. He actually felt happy for the first time in a long time. He felt her grab his arm as he made a wide turn and headed back toward the island. He placed his hand over hers as he slowed the boat and maneuvered his way around the sandbars and shoals, coming in close to Billings Island.

"You can call me JJ. I love the nickname, but I don't let most people call me that. You are joining a small group of three."

Chapter Twenty-Nine

Jack dropped anchor and jumped into the water. He had pulled the boat in as close to the island as he dared, but the water still reached his chest. With the cooler and the blankets held over his head, he waded onto shore. When he returned and made it to the top of the ladder, he froze. She appeared from below, slipping on an oversized T-shirt over a flowered bikini.

He gave a low whistle.

"Well, if I have to wade in, I better have my suit on. Let's go, Captain."

"Yes, ma'am. Dressed like that, I'd follow you anywhere." He fell backwards into the water. When he surfaced, he stood at the bottom of the ladder appreciating the view as Jamie backed down the ladder. When she reached the bottom step, he scooped her up into his arms.

"Put me down. What are you doing?" she cried.

"You're barefoot. Too many broken shells on the bottom."

"I brought flip-flops. Why didn't you tell me?"

"Because this is too much fun." He faked dropping her in the water.

"Don't you dare," she shrieked, grabbing him around the neck as he splashed up on shore.

"See, wasn't this better." He slid her to the ground, gently kissing her.

"Okay, I have to agree, not half bad." She adjusted her T-shirt.

"Looks absolutely perfect from here."

"Where's the blanket? Here, help me with this please."

Jack had brought it all—dishes, napkins, forks, knives, and food and drink, including his favorite chocolate chip cookies, enough to feed an army. They ate and laughed, enjoying each other's company.

"How often do you do this, pack lunches for ladies and abscond with them to a deserted island?"

"I'd say, by the way I feel right now, not half as often as I should. I can't remember the last time I took a day off and went to the beach. It's like cutting class."

Jamie sat facing to the sun. "It feels great, doesn't it? Cutting class?"

"I bet you never cut class." Jack started to stand, "Hell, I left the pillows on the boat." Jamie grabbed his arm.

"Forget them, too much work. Rest here on my lap," she said, patting her legs. "If I want to relax, I can lay back on my bag." She moved her beach bag behind her. "I just want to sit and take it all in." She rubbed her suntan lotion on her face and arms.

"Need any help with that?" He positioned his head on her lap, taking off his baseball cap and placing it on his chest. When he looked up, the sight of Jamie's curly hair spilling down her shoulders reflecting the sunlight like a halo was burned into his memory. No matter what happened, he would have today.

She looked at him and pushed his hair off his forehead. "Not yet."

He closed his eyes and relaxed. "Tell me about your parents." He felt her body tense. "Forget I asked that."

She sat quietly for a few minutes. "No, no. You should know. My Dad was a bank robber, my mother, his moll." Her laugh caused his head to bounce on her stomach. "I had to say that, you sounded so serious. What would you like to know?"

"Do you look like your mother? What were your parents like? Did you have a good relationship with them? Tell me anything that helps me figure out who you are."

"You're travelling down an impossible road, trying to understand me. I don't even know what makes me tick."

He waited.

"My mother was beautiful, much smaller than me with short light brown hair that always fell in her eyes and beautiful green eyes. She always sang with the radio," she continued. "One of my most vivid memories of her is when my grandfather died, her sobs frightened me. I was eight and had never lost anyone. She held me, explaining that's what happens when you love someone. When they leave, it breaks your heart. I couldn't understand how love could hurt so much. I learned." A tear escaped from under her sunglasses. "She smelled like lilacs. There are days I know she's near because I can smell the lilacs." She swiped at her cheek.

"I'm sorry. We can talk about something else, my mother, if you'd like." He tried to make her smile.

"It keeps them alive, doesn't it? When you talk about them? My Dad, what can I say about him? He had a great laugh and a terrific sense of humor—everyone loved him. I could always count on him to be there when I needed him, strong yet gentle. I've missed him every day since he died."

"What did he look like?" Jack pushed, wanting to know more.

"Tall, but shorter than you, with curly dark blond hair. That's where all this comes from," she added, tousling her hair.

"I'd like to thank him for that." He tugged on a curl. "What else?"

"He loved to dance and played all kinds of instruments, guitar, accordion, and mandolin. You two would have gotten along so well. He would have put you to shame on that stage."

"I wish I had met him." Jack questioned that her father would be happy about his only daughter being involved with a cop. "How'd they meet?"

"A dance. He had broken up with a longtime girlfriend, saw my mother, asked her to dance and the rest was history. The way they told it, lightning struck both of them. I guess it happens that way sometimes."

He thought back to how his heart hammered in his chest when he looked up and saw her for the first time chewing out his deputy on the beach. "Yup, sometimes."

She acknowledged his words with a shake of her head, but said nothing.

"You're a combination of everything good from your parents." He kissed her palm. "Bright, beautiful, a killer smile, a warm and gentle person, and that hair."

She smiled, stroking his beard. "I'd like to think so, at least in some ways, but in others, I'm not sure." She twirled his hair in her fingers, her smile disappearing.

Chapter Thirty

Jamie realized that she had about an hour or so to do some investigating before this island disappeared. Jack stayed behind to return the blankets and cooler to the boat.

Strolling along the damp sand, she stepped over half buried rocks that could have been part of a town that had existed on this mile long island over a hundred years ago. While Jack had snoozed, Jamie refreshed her knowledge of Billings on her iPhone. Around 1644, mackerel and whale fisherman built fishing huts and lived on the island from April to November. As years went by, a thriving little town arose with a school house, a whale processing plant and a lighthouse. All the makings of what seemed a blissful place until a great storm surge in 1855 split the island in two, killing many of the inhabitants, sucking their houses out to sea.

Jamie stepped inside a large circle of seaweed covered granite stones, the foundation of the old lighthouse. She wondered if the keeper had lived through the storm?

Any remaining structures had been destroyed by a winter storm in 1915. And so, the town of Billings, a navigating hazard, disappeared except for a few hours at low tide.

Turning to check the tide, she caught sight of Jack splashing ashore returning from the boat. He waved. As she waved back, she felt her world tilt a little. She closed her eyes. A dizzy spell? She knew better.

"Don't let it happen here, not in front of him," she prayed out loud. The visions didn't stop once they started. As she opened her eyes, Jack disappear into a dark murkiness crawling in from the water, low at first and then creeping higher. It encircled her, leaving a taste of salt on her lips, the feel of mist on her hair.

"Jack, help," she yelled. A thick black mass swirled around her ankles, like a snake slowly encasing her legs and anchoring her to the sand. The water rose, covering her knees. She spun around trying to locate Jack, calling again, her voice muffled by the fog. The force of the waves finally knocked her to her knees. Suddenly, she felt a hand on her shoulder, the water reaching almost to her chest.

"You frightened me. Thank God you came." She tried to stand.

The strong hand closed around her neck, choking the air out of her, pushing her down under the water. She dug her fingernails into his hands. He released his hold for a second. She pushed up through the water, gasping for air. Too dark to see him. He straddled her, pressing her down under again.

The water, so cold. Air, I need air. She slipped down slowly, her strength ebbing. *Oh God, Jack, help me.* Her last thoughts as she drifted silently under the water.

Chapter Thirty-One

Jack watched Jamie wander around the old lighthouse base, her curls blowing every which way in the wind, her tee-shirt obscuring her bikini, and her tanned legs extending a long way as she bent to pick up shells. Splashing ashore after placing the cooler and blanket on the boat, he waved to her as he made his way through the shells, carrying the last towel that he had rescued from the beach.

She dropped to her knees.

"Are you okay?" he yelled. "JJ?" When she didn't answer, his heart rate accelerated. He slung the towel over his shoulder and ran as fast as he could in the deep sand. When he reached her, she lay, face up, barely breathing.

Grabbing her, he shook her, calling her name, pushing her hair back from a deathly pale face. "JJ? Jamie?" His own words were lost in the thumping in his ears. "Cough, damn it, cough." He banged her on the back as he sat her up.

Pale and frightened, she coughed, clutching his shirt. "Thank God. The fog rolled in so fast. I called again and again. It was cold and dark and wet." Her breathing came fast and her speech so rapid that Jack could barely understand her.

"Slow down. Take a deep breath. Tell me what happened." He rubbed her back trying to relax her. "It's over. I'm here."

"I was walking and all of a sudden a dark, heavy fog rolled in. Something anchored me to the sand. I couldn't move. The water rose swiftly. I called to you. Then he appeared, choking me, pushing me under. I couldn't breathe, gulped in water. As he held me under, he climbed on top, moving with the waves, like he was raping me." She coughed.

"Who was he? Did you see him?" Jack could feel the fury building inside for this guy who didn't even exist, or did he? Green eyes flashed in front of him.

"Vaguely, but I was under water. I scratched his hands." Shivering, she looked around at the bright sunshine and touched the dry sand. "Where's the fog? And the water?"

"There's no fog. I saw you all the time – I saw you fall." He looked away for a second, "It's like the nightmare you had the other night." He held her close.

"I can't explain what triggers these things, or if it's happening to me or someone else."

"Anything you can remember about her?"

Jamie tied her hair back. "I saw blonde hair like mine floating in front of my face." She looked up at Jack. "He was large and strong. I think he drowned her and raped her at the same time." She grasped his hand and he pulled her to her feet. "Who is she? Do you think it was the woman on the beach?"

"I don't know. Do you remember anything at all that might tell why she was here on this island?"

"Not really. It was so normal at first, then the fog rolled in, the mist covered me, a hand grabbed me. At first I thought it was you, but then he grabbed my throat, pushed me under."

"Do you remember a name, who she called to?" Jack asked as he took her arm, heading back to her beach bag for a towel.

"I was calling to you." Still shivering, she picked up the towel and wrapped it around her shoulders.

"I'm sorry if bringing you here caused this," he said, wrapping the towel snugly around her.

"You didn't cause this."

"Maybe I did, by frightening you…"

"Please don't do this. None of this is your fault."

Jack picked her up and carried her through the rising water to the boat. This time, she wrapped her arms around his neck, laid her head on his shoulder, and didn't fight him.

Chapter Thirty-Two

A huge explosion of multi-colored bursts cascaded down in the moonless sky illuminating the entire harbor. Jamie and Jack curled up on the deck, his arm around her with his hand resting possessively on her hip, as they watched the fireworks in the harbor.

Leaning his head on hers, Jack debated if he should ask the question that he had been trying to answer for weeks. Every time he had brought up the episodes, Jamie had joked about them and changed the subject. She wasn't telling him everything.

"You know you don't have to answer if you don't want to, but I'm concerned about what happened on the Island." The fireworks burst and hissed in mid-air. "Have you had those episodes, nightmares or whatever you call them, before?"

Watching the explosion above them, she answered, "Not this bad until I came down here. The nightmare I had when you refused to stay on the couch was similar to this last one." She patted his hand. "I'm joking because I can't answer you. I've experienced these dreams off and on my entire life, but nothing like the one on the Island, never during the day, never that realistic. The first time I had a premonition was a few nights before my parents were killed." She hesitated, and when he said nothing, she asked, "Why?"

"I was wondering if maybe Pat had these or maybe your mother." Did Jamie's visions portray future or past events?

"You think that somehow this, whatever it is, has been passed down to me?" The fireworks continued to brighten the sky and spill down with a hiss to the water.

"I don't know. Could be something inherited, right?" He patted her hip reassuringly. "The dreams take a huge toll on you." He didn't want to scare her, but he worried about these visions happening when he wasn't around. The latest episode, resembling a seizure, had panicked him. "Do you think," he paused, "maybe you should see a doctor?" He had heard of health problems that could cause a disconnection with reality for a few seconds. "I'm okay with this, you know. I'm just trying to understand it. Not sure if they are about you or someone else." He thought for a minute and then added, "Maybe they're tied to Justine's disappearance? You said they started down here."

"I've had dreams." She shifted a bit, sitting up straighter. "I saw the crash that killed my parents before it happened through my mother's eyes."

Pulling her closer, Jack knew that he wasn't expected to do anything but listen. He hated to admit it, but the connection between the dead women on the beach and Jamie was becoming stronger. Did these dreams mean other women would die? Or was it about her?

"And, to answer your earlier question, I've seen doctors and psychiatrists. There's no physical condition that causes this. It's a gift," she shook her head. "That's what the doctors called it, can you imagine that? A gift, they said. What kind of gift is it when you don't even understand it until it's too late?" She swiped angrily at the tears spilling onto her cheeks. "Do you think there's going to be another drowning? You're thinking it's murder?"

"I wish I knew, on both counts." He wanted her to know that this gift, as she referred to it, didn't change his feelings for her. If anything, he felt even closer to her because she had shared what she knew with him. "It's okay. We'll figure it out. I promise you." He hugged her, while the fireworks lit up the sky around them.

"You asked about Pita. She knew things that others didn't. It spooked me when she sensed what I needed. When I asked her about it, she said that I always come to Oyster Point when I'm hurting. She asked me once if I ever had a feeling that something was going to happen before it happened. I told her about seeing my parent's crash in a dream. She nodded and we never talked about it again."

"You think that she had the same gift?"

"I don't know." She thought for a minute, "Maybe. I know there was more to her 'knowing' than she told me. Maybe there's something in her journals? I'll start through them again tomorrow." She leaned her head against his chest as they watched the rest of the fireworks. "Maybe that's how she came up with the clues for you? Wouldn't that be a hoot."

"Maybe," he said as he held her close.

Chapter Thirty-Three

"If I never heard from him again, could I blame him?" Jamie said aloud, adding a touch of cream to her cup of coffee. "Damn it. He had to be the one to see it happened both times. Crazy, that's what he'll say, she's crazy." She picked up Pita's box. "And you know what, Maxine, he'd be right. I must be crazy," she commented as she spread the photographs from the folder labeled "Lemon Pie Cottage" out in front of her on the floor. Maxine, with ears up, listened intently to Jamie's rant.

"Let's learn about the cottage, especially if we plan to sell it."

There was the deed. Pita and Uncle Frank had purchased the house in the mid-1950s and Pita lived here after Uncle Frank died.

"Now I'll probably be driven out of town because I'll be labeled the 'mad woman of Lemon Pie Cottage'." She picked up another photo. "Serves me right for getting mixed up with a cop." As she began reading Pita's notes, Maxine growled and headed for the door.

"Just what I need, another interruption." Jamie pulled herself up from the floor and looked out the kitchen window. "It's okay, Maxine, probably just someone stopping by to get a look at the mad woman. My fame has undoubtedly spread though the town. They'll all be driving by to get a glimpse." She had barely finished the sentence when she noticed a dark colored car in front of the fence. She jumped at the sound of a knock on the door.

"Matt, what a surprise." Jamie stepped outside the house. "The dog's a little uneasy with strangers. What in the world are you doing here?"

"A dog now? How domestic." He smiled his adorable little boy smile. "I was thinking about you, wondering if after you sell this place, if you'd be returning to Boston. Can you have a dog in your apartment?"

"She's not my dog, only on loan." She scrutinized him. "This isn't exactly around the corner for you?"

Matt must have recognized that Jack tailed him to the town line the other night and seen him take the left onto the small dirt road in Eastham instead of heading back to Boston. What he didn't know was what she knew.

"Well, I'm not sure if I ever told you this, but I have a friend who owns a place in Eastham."

She turned away from him.

"It's only a little house, similar to this," he said.

"Really," she answered facing him, "Funny, you never mentioned it before."

"I guess it never really came up. When I left here, after you kicked me out the other night," he chided her, "I was so exhausted, I thought I'd crash at his place for the night and head back to Boston the next day. Are you sorry I didn't stay?" He touched her cheek and leaned in to kiss her.

She stepped to the side, careful not to fall off the stone step. "What are you doing? We decided ages ago that there was nothing between us?"

"A guy can change his mind, can't he?" He seized her arm and attempted to pull her close.

She pushed against his chest. "Ouch. Stop it. What's the matter with you?"

A car door slammed.

"Crap, it's your Chief, once more to the rescue." He freed Jamie, causing her to lose her balance and fall backward off the step.

An arm snatched her just before she hit the shells on the walk. "Are you okay?" Jack asked, standing her up on her feet.

"Yup... I..."

"What the hell's the matter with you?" Jack said, heading for Matt.

Jamie grabbed his arm. "It's okay. Don't."

He halted a few steps from Matt. "It didn't look okay to me. Matt, you want to explain how Jamie ended up almost cutting herself to bits on the shells?"

"Jack, please, I lost my balance."

Jack gave Jamie the "I'm the Chief of Police, let me do my job" look.

Stepping back, Matt bumped into the closed door. The top of the Dutch door flew open exposing him to Maxine's bared teeth as she jumped at the door.

"Christ, now I have everyone after me, even the goddamn dog." Matt was cornered with no place to go. Maxine tried to devour him from behind; Jack glowered in front of him. "Jamie lost her footing, like she said."

"And you had her by the arm because...?" Jack scowled. "It looked as though she tried to push you away and fell backwards."

"Look, Chief, we were fooling around, weren't we, JJ?" Matt misspoke her name. Jack's raised eyebrow said he knew no one ever called her JJ. Matt sent Jamie a pleading look, putting up his hands. Without any reason, Jack could manufacture something out of this incident and he would end up in jail overnight, or more.

"Jack, please, it's not a big deal. Matt had been teasing me and I didn't feel like joking so I tried to push away. When he heard you drive up, he let go. I lost my footing and fell off the step. That's all there was to it, really." Jamie gave Jack a look that said, "Trust me about this; I know what I'm doing."

"Okay, but be careful, you could get hurt," Jack replied, his meaning clear. "It's been a tough day, so I'm sorry if I jumped to conclusions."

"What happened? Anything you can share?" she asked.

"Another body washed up on the beach," he stated matter-of-factly watching Matt's face.

Jamie grabbed Jack's arm. "A woman?" she probed.

"Yes. Be doubly careful, please. We'll talk later." Jack turned and left.

Chapter Thirty-Four

Jamie felt a chill sitting in the July sun. After Jack left, Matt suggested that they go inside and sit down because she looked so pale. Not trusting him in the house after Jack's warning, she suggested that they walk to the wharf for coffee and some fresh air.

"Another woman washed up," Jack's words echoed through her head. What if today's body was the woman in her vision? Could it be a simple drowning, like the coroner said the previous ones had been? Not three of them, all looking the same, all looking like her.

The harbor looked so calm. "Please don't let this woman's death have anything to do with my nightmares," she whispered.

Matt placed the hot coffee down. "I'm sorry, what did you say?" He reached for her hand. "Are you okay?"

She wrapped both hands around her cup, willing the warmth to melt the iciness that crept through her body. "It's the news of a woman drowning. How does that happen here, in the harbor?"

Matt's face showed no emotion. "Did Jack say any more?"

"No." Matt was fishing. "As far as I know, there's nothing more to tell. I'm sure at some point he'll tell me what he can." She swirled the swizzle stick in her coffee. She forced herself to breathe. Because of her nightmares, Jamie dreaded hearing the details.

"I'm sure it's just a drowning. She might have fallen off a boat? Accidents happen." He coughed, wheezed, and pulled an inhaler from his pocket. He tried to hide it.

"You have asthma?" Strange, she never remembered Matt using a nebulizer.

"I'm fine, just a left over from a winter cold. Are you sure you're okay? You're shivering." He took a breath and pocketed the inhaler.

"I'm fine." She didn't remember Matt being sick this winter. "It's frightening, that's all."

"A drowning happens." He watched her. "I heard there were other drownings?"

"You heard about them?"

"In the newspaper. Jack has an easy job down here, usually. Just summer and winter beer parties?" His words held ridicule.

Jamie focused on a fishing boat coming back into the harbor. "I'm sure there are days like today that aren't easy."

"What's going on between you two?"

Jamie's head jerked around. "Going on?" She stared at him.

"Just what I said. Are you two involved? He's around Pat's cottage every time I am." He didn't flinch as he locked eyes with hers. "How well do you know him?"

"First, the cottage is mine now." Her words flared. "And the reason he's around is none of your business."

"Look, hold on, I'm not prying. I just want to make sure that you know him, really know him, especially if you two have a thing." He coughed again.

"What are you insinuating?"

"When he worked in Boston there were issues— before he came to Oyster Point."

"So?" Her words came fast and furious. "Issues? What kind of issues?"

Holding up his hand in front of him, he said, "Don't get angry with the messenger. You should know what you're getting yourself into, that's all. I looked into his background. Your Chief was connected with guys who were brought up on charges. One of them was his partner."

"I say again, so?" She didn't need to deal with this today.

"Three detectives were accused of improper classification of crimes, solving crimes by assigning them to someone who may or may not have committed them. They were suspected of accepting bribes. One of them was Hereford's partner." This last sentence carried a judgmental tone. "I bet he never told you that."

He acted so smug, so unlike Matt. "Were they convicted? Was Jack ever accused of anything?" she snapped.

"Not sure any of them went to trial. They resigned or retired before they could be brought up on the charges. From what I could uncover, Jack wasn't accused, but resigned as well. So who knows what he did?" He left his words hanging out there for her to grab.

His self-righteousness turned her stomach. He had never been interested in anyone but himself. Why this sudden change? "Your point is?" she responded again.

"The talk on the street is that Hereford has a lot of money stashed in bank accounts, houses, but they could never tie any of those possessions back to illegal activities."

"The boat?" she whispered.

"Excuse me? I couldn't hear what you said. A boat?"

"Oh, no. I thought I knew that boat pulling in." Her stomach churned. Had she ignored Jack's faults? Not done her homework? Matt, for some reason, relished uncovering Jack's flaws. Why did he care about Jack or, for that matter, what was going on between them? Whatever it was that she and Matt had shared in Boston, it certainly wasn't romance. And, today, he was killing off the intangible that they had. His information must have come through his father's corporate connections. But why?

The wind blew her hair across her face. She nudged it behind her ear when she heard him say, "I always liked your hair up." She thought back to the night that they had first met. Her client, winning an important lawsuit against one of their competitors, threw a huge party at a posh Boston hotel. When she arrived, dressed in a black sleeveless sheath with black heels, hair pulled up, the president of the company joined her. Beside him stood the lawyer who had represented the company in this lawsuit— a tall drop dead gorgeous man with dark blond hair that fell over the collar of his very expensive suit. He flashed a killer smile.

Jamie held his stare as he clasped her hand, repeating her name. Her client mumbled, stepped away, and left the two of them alone.

Matt knew her immediately as "the security consultant who had helped the company protect the money-making patented products."

Her cheeks colored slightly. "Matthew Hollings III, you won them the patents." Her recognition of him made him smile even more.

"Matt. Please, call me Matt. Luckily I wasn't an athlete. My name would never fit across the back of a jersey," he joked.

It was a well-practiced statement, but was still funny. After a while, they headed out to the patio for some cool air. He asked her out to dinner and she accepted. And, so began their very amicable relationship. Being together gave them time to vent about their work and to feel like someone cared, even if they didn't. She smiled, remembering those first few minutes. He had changed.

"What are you smiling about?"

His question brought her back to reality. "I was thinking back to when we met, at that cocktail party?"

"Whatever made you think of that?"

"Your comment about my hair. You seemed so different then." He stared at her. "And I guess when you asked me what I knew about Jack, I wondered what I knew about you."

"Well, you have known me a lot longer than Jack."

"Maybe longer, but what do I know about the two of you?" She was disappointed and frustrated with both the men in her life.

Chapter Thirty-Five

Jack stood looking down at a young woman lying on the beach close to where the other women had been found. He watched Phil do his thing.

"Look at this, Jack." Phil pointed to the woman's leg where a piece of rope encircled it. "Again."

"Too weird to be a coincidence." Jack took off his sunglasses, hung them off his shirt neck, and rubbed his eyes. It was twilight. Again, she had been dropped off in high tide. "We have a serial killer on our hands."

"I hate to say it, but you're probably right." Phil turned the dead woman's head and moved the blond hair behind her ear. "Look, bruises on her neck."

"She's a carbon copy of the other women." Jack turned her head back toward him. He focused Phil's light on her face. "Eye color more blue than green, but her age is around thirties maybe? He has a type."

"I agree. Your gut feeling was right on. He's good though, makes them look like an accident."

"Who found her?"

"A family who had just finished their day and were walking back to their car. One of the little ones tripped over her. They're up there waiting." Phil pointed to the dark shadows on the dune and signaled to his helper to bring the black bag.

"Anything else I should know? Time of death?"

"She was killed a few hours ago. I'll determine the exact time of death back at the office, but she's a recent one."

"Clothes?"

"Like the other women, a top around her neck, no shoes, no underwear, and no ID."

"Could be a collector? Takes the underwear as a souvenir?" Jack watched the bag being zipped.

"That's your area of expertise, Jack. Find the underwear, find the killer."

Chapter Thirty-Six

Jamie's paintbrushes flew across the paper creating dashes of yellow and green color here and there. She thought of Jack standing over yet another dead woman on a dark beach.

"Please be an accident," she said, tossing her brushes into the water bucket. She had to talk to Kate.

"Hello," a sleepy voice answered.

"Hi, it's me. I woke you, didn't I?"

"God, what time is it? No, no, I guess I dozed off." She yawned. "It's your godbaby. He or she is sapping my energy. What's the matter?"

"They found another woman on the beach today."

"What? That sure as hell woke me up." She was quiet and then said, "Are you okay? What did Jack say?"

"He's at the beach." Now that she had Kate on the phone, Jamie couldn't imagine why she had called her. The news would just upset her. But Kate had a way of processing information faster than any one Jamie knew. So she started, "Matt was here today."

"That's why you're calling." Kate responded. "Again? Why?"

"I don't know. He acted weird, possessive. He creeped me out asking personal questions about Jack and me." She decided not to mention Matt's questioning of Jack's background.

Kate's outrage spewed forth. "I hope you kicked his damn ass back to Boston… excuse my Irish." Kate listened as Jamie told her about the beach, the cottage visit, and his comments about Jack.

"What nerve, really. Do you think he lied?" Kate questioned. "It doesn't really sound like Matt, does it? Or Jack either. He called me, you know."

"I know. So, what did you two talk about?"

"He asked for my assessment of Matt and if he was your boyfriend. Some questions sounded like the Chief talking, others sounded like a guy who's interested in you."

"Kate... stop it. What else did he ask?"

"That's about it. I could tell he suspects Matt of something, but didn't say what. I'm sure all these dead women have him on edge. He's thinking serial killer. Did he tell you who they look like?"

"No, who?"

"Ask him. By the way, he sounds very nice and totally sexy on the phone. Take a photo please? And how do you feel about him, if I may ask?"

"Well, that's my cue to go back to my painting," Jamie said.

"Jamie, be careful and do exactly what Jack tells you. I'm worried about some weirdo lurking in the shadows."

"Don't worry, I'm fine. Jack's near. Rest up and keep our baby safe. Love you." Jamie placed her cell phone down on her painting table.

Her paintbrushes sailed across the paper, dabbing colors and swishing water. How could she explain to Kate that she didn't even know what her relationship was with Jack? She dunked her brush into a pool of ultramarine blue paint. And Matt, how dare he talk about someone else. She had no idea about his personal life. His father owned one of the most prestigious law firms in Boston, Hollings and Son, and Matt was a partner there. He loved first-class restaurants, expensive food, and excellent wines.

Grabbing a dash of cadmium red, her ultramarine blue darkened like storm clouds as she added the blood red color. The darkness bled and dribbled toward the Antwerp water.

When she had met his father at a restaurant, he presented himself as a tough, no-nonsense man. The attractive younger woman on his arm was not Matt's mother. Matt had spoken of his mother at a Dana Farber Fund Raiser. Jamie's heart ached for him as he described a beautiful young mother who suffered and died from breast cancer. He shared memories of hospital visits, treatments, and finally her end in hospice. Not a sound could be heard in the room.

As for other family members, she remembered a sibling, a brother or a sister. When she asked more, Matt waved his hand, said "Not important," and changed the subject.

That summarized what she knew about Matthew Hollings III, and, of course, the fact that he had graduated from Harvard Law School—with high honors.

Her brushes continued with browns and pinks. What hidden secrets did Matt have? What did she not know about Jack?

Chapter Thirty-Seven

Jack kissed Jamie's forehead as he entered the room. "Do me a couple of favors? First, ask who it is before you say 'come in', and, second, keep the doors locked?"

"I knew you'd be along." She plopped her brushes in the water, recognizing the look in his eyes. "You think this woman was murdered, don't you?"

"I won't know until Phil finishes up. Until then, be extra careful – please?"

"Was it like my nightmare?"

"Don't know. So what are you working on so intently at this ungodly hour?" He shut down the talk of dead women.

"I decided to paint a little." She moved to the easel.

He grabbed her shoulder from behind.

"What?" she looked from his shocked face to her painting.

"The body today." Jack pointed to her painting where a woman sat in a boat with someone behind her, "Looked just like her, even the pink top." Muted and foggy, only the blond figure could be seen in the painting. "She had long hair, similar to yours and a pink top, just like that." He stared. "How did you know? I didn't say anything, did I?"

"I didn't know," Jamie responded. "She looked like me? Is that what all this lock the doors stuff is about? Kate asked me if you had said anything about the women… you're thinking he might come after me?"

"How could I not think that? Why did you paint her?" Jack's voice dripped with annoyance and tiredness. He ran his hands through his hair in frustration, ending up with his fingers interlaced, resting on the top of his head. "I'm sorry."

"I don't know," she stared at the painting. "I stood here painting, but I don't remember capturing any of those details, her top, or hair. It could be any woman, couldn't it? It doesn't have to be her?" She stepped back from the painting, knocking her brushes and the bucket of water off the table. "Jack." Ignoring the water on the floor, she picked up her brushes, laying them gently on the table. "Talk to me."

He pulled her against his chest, wrapping his arms around her. "I have to find this guy before it happens again." He stroked her hair.

"I know."

"You don't. That could have been you out there today." He cleared his throat. "That's all I could think of when I saw her, touched her cold hands; you, lying there. You have to finish this painting. I need to see who's behind her."

She pulled back. "It doesn't work that way."

"Then tell me why you painted this. Come, sit." He walked her to the couch. They sat with her cold hands in his warm ones.

"I thought about these dead women being dumped like pieces of trash on the beach. Who would do such a thing? I painted. That's all I can tell you."

"But why this one? Look at those ominous clouds...."

She shrugged her shoulders. "I have no idea. Maybe I liked the colors, the feel of it. I remember thinking that I would love to finish a painting Pita had started and sign both our names. I had placed it on the easel so I just added to it." That's all she could tell him, all she really knew.

Letting go of Jack's hand, Jamie stood and adjusted the painting. "I thought painting would relax me while I waited for you," she said. "And pink? I never use pink unless I have flowers to paint and even then…." Turning to Jack, she knew that she had to share what Matt said earlier.

"Matt didn't hurt you, did he?" It was like he was reading her mind.

"No, not physically." She avoided looking at him as she dried her paintbrushes. "After you left, Matt and I walked to the wharf for coffee. He questioned me about us, asked how well I really knew you." She felt her words coming faster as she wiped up the water on the floor with paper towels. She looked over and watched Jack's emotions play across his face, surprise, anger, and then nothing.

"What did he mean, how well do you know me. He asked if you had slept with me? That SOB," he said. "I hope you told him that our relationship was none of his damn business." Jack's temper rose whenever Matt's name came into play. "It's none of his damn business, right?"

"Right." Was that jealousy speaking? "But I don't think that's what he wanted to know." Given the grueling day Jack had, if he thought too much on Matt's comments, he would explode or withdraw. They had to talk this out.

"What was he asking then?" His voice went flat.

Would he feel betrayed if she questioned him about Boston and his partner? Jamie moved to the arm of the couch where she could touch him. How did this summer become so complex? All she had planned to do this spring was clean out the cottage and sell it by fall. Yet, here she sat, involved in multiple deaths, a missing person case, and the life of the Chief of Police. Jamie faced him. She had fallen in love with him, this man with tired, dark circled eyes that shone with a spark of anger and jealousy, his drawn face covered by a day's growth of beard.

How much should she tell him?

Chapter Thirty-Eight

Jack walked to the kitchen and poured himself a cup of cold coffee.

"Sit, I'll make new. That's been sitting there all day," Jamie said.

He waved his hand, "This is fine. Too late for coffee although I doubt anything will keep me awake tonight." But when he saw her face, he wasn't sure that was true. "Just tell me please what the great Matt said that has you so upset?" He searched his pocket for his gum. "Do you have a cigarette around here?"

"Please don't do this to yourself. No, no cigarettes, but I do have some gum, maybe not your flavor, but gum," she said rummaging through her purse. She handed him the pack. "He asked me about your background, your family, and your friends. He brought up your job in Boston. He wanted to make sure that I knew you well enough to trust you, that I wasn't being foolish."

Laying his head back on the couch and popping the gum in his mouth, Jack let out a mocking laugh. "He wanted to make sure you knew me well enough, that you weren't being foolish?" he repeated, emphasizing the "me," rolling his head back and forth not believing what he had just heard. "You? You who don't have a foolish bone in your body, which by the way, he should know." He rolled up the wrapper and tossed it in the wastebasket by Jamie's painting table.

"He's the one who shows up, scares you half to death on the beach, drives away, hides, and then shows up here later? He doesn't think he's acting a bit crazy?" His voice rose along with his anger. "He has a goddamn nerve to question me and my motives with you, or my background." He took a breath, trying to push his anger down. "What else did he say?" He softened his tone. He thought that she trusted him, but now, after what he had seen today, he wasn't sure of anything.

Jamie sat motionless.

God, how bad could it be? She had to be on his side, to trust him, to be in his life. He scanned her face. He read her nuances so well, her frown when she was thinking or her pursed lips when she was so involved in something so deeply that she wouldn't hear him talk, or her large eyes filled to the brim with tears when she hurt. Somehow, in these last few months, she had warmed his heart with her sensitivity, her softness, her ability to connect with people, her gentleness. She made him laugh.

Tonight, sitting here, he couldn't imagine tomorrow without her. He waited for his chance to defend himself. As he watched her, he knew, without a doubt, that he had fallen in love with her. Now what? Would the doubts that Matt had planted cause her to pull away? He knew her history with men. He waited for her to say something.

He would always wait for her.

Chapter Thirty-Nine

"Matt's a lawyer, actually a partner in his father's Boston law firm," Jamie began.

"You said that before."

"Because of that, he has a lot of contacts." She would skip the background check that Matt had performed on him. Her eyes fastened on the painting.

"Do you want me to help you?"

"No, please, let me." She breathed in.

Jack went ahead anyway. "Matt pulled some strings to find out about my job in Boston. He wanted to uncover some dirt, not the good things I've done. He discovered that my partner had been suspended, accused of bribery, falsification of records, am I correct?"

"Yes." She avoided his eyes, embarrassed by the way this conversation was going.

"And me, what did he insinuate about me?" His eyes flashed.

"I think we should have this talk tomorrow. You're tired, I'm tired." Why had she opened this can of worms when she knew Jack wouldn't let it go until they left no stone unturned?

"Just tell me what he said, please. Let's put it on the table, here and now." His voice carried the tiredness that showed on his face. "No use waiting till tomorrow. Actually it's already tomorrow."

She hesitated, but started in before he could add anything more. "He said that they, the inquest, investigated you, but found nothing." Watching him, she continued, "He found out that you had a lot of money, houses and things in your name, but none of them could be tied back to anything criminal."

Jack dropped his head into his hands and finally, looked up at her. "And?"

"He said you resigned soon after your partner was brought up on charges."

"Is that it?" His tone cut through her like a knife.

"Yes."

"And what do you want me to do now, defend myself? Make excuses? Is that what you want?" He started to rise from the couch. "If that's what these last few months have meant... have shown you about me... then...."

"Please, don't go. Just tell me the truth, that's all I want, the truth." Her hand rested on his shoulder so he would sit again. "Pita trusted you, I know that."

"And you? What about you, do you trust me?" Now their eyes met only inches away.

He was not like the others. "I do. Just tell me what happened up there. I need something to fight Matt with."

"I need you to trust me, to believe me. I don't give a damn about Matt. I only care about you and what you think."

She touched his face, ran her hand slowly down his rough cheek. He closed his eyes as she caressed his face.

"Please. If you want to end this... whatever we have, just say it... tonight, right now. I'll go."

"I do trust you," she whispered, leaning her forehead against his. "Oh God, I do. Don't leave."

He slowly pulled her onto his lap.

She held his face in her hands and kissed him gently on the lips. Pulling back, she looked at him, "I do trust you. You don't have to explain anything."

He drew her close, kissing her with a fierceness that took them both by surprise. He kissed her eyes, her cheeks, and took her lips softly.

"I'll do better than explain, I'll show you." He picked her up and carried her to the bedroom where he laid her gently down on the moonlight covered bed.

Chapter Forty

Jack leaned his hands against the white tiled shower wall, the hot liquid cascading over the back of his head. His thoughts splashed all over the place like the water. He had wanted to keep his relationship with Jamie at arm's length, at least for a while longer. But he couldn't last night. It felt so right. She showed him that she trusted him, something he never expected. Her eyes said she wanted him as much as he wanted her. That's all it took and he lost himself. Before he knew it, he had her on the bed. He had no regrets, but would she?

He turned his face up into the water. He hadn't told her about his past, Boston or Wyoming. Wyoming had to be taken care of. He had waited far too long.

Tying a towel around his waist, he tiptoed back into the bedroom. She lay on her side, covers pulled up under her chin, hair falling over her face. Jack slid the strands of hair back from her cheek and kissed her. He lingered, watching her sleep as though saving that vision away for a day when he no longer had her near. He would protect her, no matter what.

She shifted slightly as though sensing him close by.

Falling in love with her had been easy. But a woman like Jamie brought complications that he didn't need right now. His own stuff had to be sorted out before he could honestly commit to a relationship with any woman. And Jamie had her own problems, that damn wall she had built around her feelings. She never said she loved him, but she had trusted him enough to have given herself to him last night. That act spoke volumes.

For some reason, Matt appeared safe to her. Jack slipped on his T-shirt. Safe emotionally, but physically? His gut told him that Matt was a threat to her.

Grabbing his strewn clothes from the floor, he carried them into the living room. It was still dark as he stumbled around pulling on his chinos.

"Not one damn clock in this whole place." He shook his head in disbelief. "How does she live like this?"

Hearing Jack's voice, Max opened one eye, then turned over and fell sound asleep before Jack switched on the lamp beside the easel. His watch said 4:30 AM, early even for him, especially after a day like yesterday followed by a night like last night. He smiled as he checked his phone for messages. Nothing. Phil must have more details on this new woman by now.

Buttoning his shirt over his Tee, his eyes locked on the painting on the easel. He slowly tucked his shirt into his khaki slacks. Was he being stupid thinking that if Jamie finished the painting it would help him solve these homicides? He could see her as the woman, but it also could be one of the dead women. And who was the man who hovered behind her? Maybe Phil had a reasonable explanation for all this.

Jack picked up a pen from the end table and scribbled a note to Jamie.

Morning Sleepyhead,

I couldn't sleep and didn't want to wake you too early. I know you didn't get much sleep. I've gone to see Phil about the latest woman on the beach. Hope I left the bathroom clean... I took a shower. I left a kiss on your cheek. It will have to do until later. Please be careful. J

He underlined the word "please." Placing the note by the coffee maker, he closed the door softly as Jamie reached out for him in the dark.

Chapter Forty-One

Jamie read Jack's note while she waited for her coffee to finish brewing. Wandering into the bathroom, she showered and then, gazing into the mirror, she touched her cheek. The wall that she had built to keep from getting hurt had crumbled last night.

"You just had to reassure yourself about the kind of man he was, had to prove you believed him, trusted him and most of all, you needed him," she spoke to her reflection. "Let's be truthful here, you wanted him." She leaned over and towel dried her hair. She had denied what she felt until last night, when she looked in his eyes.

"You're in deep trouble, girl. Turning back won't be easy." Her reflection said nothing. "You know, you're not helping. You could nod in agreement instead of just looking at me like I'm crazy." She started out of the bathroom, and then turned and said, "You're right, I am crazy."

Jack's focus today would be on the dead women. Were they part of her dreams? She pulled on her shorts and slipped on her Tee. Could there be serial killer on the loose? Fluffing her wet hair, she refocused on the blurred image on the easel. She fingered her paintbrushes... if she could finish the painting. Dabbing a brush in the water and then into the ultramarine paint, she slanted her head left, then right, and squinted. Last night, the brushes flew across the paper. Today, they stayed still. She thrust them back into the bucket, splashing water and blue paint everywhere.

What else could she concentrate on—Pita's boxes? She grabbed the top box and headed out to the deck. Laying back on the swing, the journal opened to a page dated Tuesday, June 4th, 1944:

I'm worried sick about Billy. It's been two weeks since I've had a letter from him. I know letters take forever, and I know that they are censored, and I know that there are battles going on, but I have to know that he's okay. All during the day, no matter where I am, what I'm doing, he's on my mind. I keep trying to put the dream out of my head. I just can't think about it anymore, it's all too frightening.

Jamie sat up straight. She reread the last two lines again. A dream? She flipped back to an entry dated Saturday, May 13th 1944:

I received a letter from Billy today that upset me. He completed his 25th mission and I was so excited. I thought he would be coming home, but instead, he has to fly five more missions. His 26th mission was the toughest so far, he said. He couldn't name where they were bombing, but I can tell from his descriptions and the places that weren't blacked out in his letter.

A group of German fighter planes chased him and hit the tail of his plane. He said it was a real "dog fight." Two of his gunners were shot, one badly. The electrical system shorted out and the oxygen tank was almost empty. But Billy, you know Billy, brought the plane back even though he had to fly low over fields without oxygen. I worry how long he can go without something bad happening. I can't think of it. Please God, make his luck hold out.

The last line struck her heart... God couldn't be relied on. Billy had to get himself home safely. Smudges blurred some of the words as though tears had hit the page as Pita wrote. Now she knew that Billy flew in Europe during World War II.

Jamie flipped ahead to Monday, May 22nd 1944:

I've heard nothing from Billy in over a week. He usually writes like clockwork, a letter arrives every 5-7 days, but so far this week, nothing. I run home every day after work to pick up the mail, hoping to find a letter, but none so far.

I had a terrible dream last night. I woke up screaming, my nightgown soaking wet. My whole body shook, my eyes burned, and I couldn't catch my breath. Helene heard my scream and came running into my room. She looked as pale as a ghost sitting on the bed. I had frightened her. She stayed with me until I convinced her I was alright, that it was a bad dream that I couldn't even remember. I couldn't tell her the truth and put what I saw into words. It didn't feel like a dream, it was so vivid.

I stood in the middle of a sweet smelling meadow, bright red poppies surrounding me. The remains of a bombed out stone cathedral with tall spires cast long shadows over the field. I walked through tall grasses and flowers, enjoying the warm sunshine on my face. It felt so peaceful.

All of a sudden, the ground rumbled and shook, and a roaring noise pierced the quiet. A bird screeched and flew out of the grass, away from me. I covered my ears; the noise made my head ache. I couldn't breathe. Smoke stung my eyes and my throat felt like it was closing. I fell to the ground, covering my head as everything around me turned dark.

Looking up, I saw nothing, but then, from behind me there appeared a plane flying just a few feet above the ground. Black smoke poured from the engines. Fire erupted as it lumbered along, lower and lower, heading right toward me. I stood and ran. The heat and the smoke ate all of the air as I struggled to catch my breath. The roar was so loud that I thought it would split the earth open under my feet. I stopped running with the lumbering plane right next to me. I ducked down, the wing so close I thought it might hit me. I covered my head with my arms.

Glancing over, I could see into the cockpit. The pilot's face was blackened with smoke and covered with blood. His eyes, blue as the sea, stared right at me. It was Billy. Oh my God, it was Billy. Pulling myself up, I ran next to the plane, screaming his name, my lungs burning, my eyes blurred from tears. I tripped and fell, the earth rumbled, a scream... ripped out from my throat.

The journal slipped from Jamie's hands onto the floorboards with a bang. She didn't have to read the rest. The ending was clear. Why had Pita never shared anything about her dreams? Clenching her arms to her chest, Jamie felt nauseous. Did the letters stop after the 13th? She dug through the box. In her rush, she dropped it, causing the photographs and letters to fly all over the floor. Down on her knees, she picked through the papers, trying to read each postmark. The tattered envelopes had been opened many times. She thumbed through them all to make sure she hadn't missed one, February, April, January, nothing later than May 13th.

Placing the box next to her on the swing, she placed the letters inside and returned to the journal. She tried to find her place, but her fingers wouldn't move. She found a page dated Tuesday, July 4th.

Today I went to Billy's house to watch the parade. I took my vacation time to be with his family and mine as well. His mother is doing okay, although I think she's still in shock, as I am. It's hard to do things that you used to do knowing that they'll never be the same. I'm not sure if I'll ever feel anything again. The numbness is there all the time.

Mrs. Lawrence cried when she saw me coming up the walk. When I reached her on the porch, she hugged me so hard I could hardly breathe. We sobbed together. She patted my hair as she always did, trying to console me, but we both know that there's nothing that will ever take away this endless hurt.

The American flag hung from the porch as always. She and I had spent last 4th of July together, sitting on the porch stairs watching the parade go by, clapping and waving. Billy wasn't there, but we knew that he would be *coming home soon. This year, we knew that he was gone forever. The waves and words from others were gentle, soft and subdued. "How are you getting on? Can we do anything for you?" people whispered to us.*

Sometimes I feel I'm walking through a fog, living in a dream, a nightmare, and that Billy will knock on the door one day and surprise me, hold me, kiss me, and...

How can he be gone forever? I can't even comprehend forever. What does forever mean? The word sounded so wonderful when he and I talked about being together forever, but now, being without him forever? I feel like I'm suspended in time, not alive and not dead. I can't explain it, dear diary. There aren't any words to describe the hollowness, the sadness, the aloneness that I feel.

I find myself wondering sometimes, was he ever here, was he real? I have to look at his photos to be sure that he lived, that he was mine. I can't remember what his voice sounded like. How can that happen? How can I go on with my life? What life? I can't picture a life without him. We were going to be married when he came home. I still wear his ring. If I take it off, it means that I accept the fact that he's gone, and I haven't, I won't, I can't. I won't believe it. He can't be gone. He can't be dead. I don't want him to be. I won't let him be. I won't.

Jamie's tears blurred the rest of the page. She reached for a tissue. The words broke her heart as Pita described her intense loss.

Maybe he isn't dead. It's a mistake. But they don't make mistakes, do they.

We didn't even get him back. I don't have a grave where I can go to talk to him, a place where he is. How do you mourn a person when there's no body, no grave? He lies in France, thousands of miles away.

Oh my God, it can't be true. He is, was, so young, we're so young. We had our whole lives in front of us. Now, I have nothing but sadness and emptiness. I don't want to live without him. What I wouldn't give to look into those blue eyes and see them sparkle as he jokes with me; to touch his hair and push it out of his eyes as he works; to see that smile that makes me forgive him no matter what he's done. I want to hear him whistle as he fixes his car, to have him hold me, kiss me, touch my face, my hair. He needs to tell me he'll always love me, no matter what. Please, just one last time. Can't I touch his cheek and hold his hand once more? Why, why can't I? It's not fair. I want, no, I need to say goodbye. It can't end this way, it just can't. Not this way, not for us.

Jamie's sobs came from deep inside, not just for Pita, but for the heartbreak that she had endured years before when Mike had walked away. Pita's words echoed in her head, "I have seen that look before, in my own mirror, years ago. You are so like me."

Gently placing the journal back in the box, Jamie fingered a tiny diamond ring, Pita's engagement ring from Billy. Finally, wiping her cheeks, she walked inside the cottage and picked up her paintbrushes.

Chapter Forty-Two

Jack listened to Phil state the facts about the latest drowning.

"I don't have a positive ID yet. Maybe in a day or so." Phil, being about a foot shorter than Jack, had to look up at him when he spoke. His glasses rested on the end of his nose. Jack guessed his age to be somewhere in the early 50's, but maybe the thinning hair made him appear older than he was.

Jack flipped open a small notebook taken from his back pants pocket and scanned the questions written on the page. "Anything on her blood work? Had she been drinking?"

"So far, nothing's back. I did a quick blood test and it showed alcohol and possibly some drugs. The final tox screen is still pending." Phil pulled out a few pages from the dead woman's folder on his desk. "She drowned, I know that. I didn't find any sign of blunt force trauma. The scratches on her face, knees, and knuckles are similar to the other drowning victims, but still consistent with hitting rocks, dragging on the bottom as the waves pushed her up on the shore. The DNA on her body and under her fingernails was most likely compromised by the salt water, so I don't hold out much hope on that. We're trying to match the rope wrapped around her ankle with the one we found with the other victims. That's all I can tell you Jack, sorry." Phil always referred to bodies as victims; he kept it impersonal.

"You think she was held underwater? Are the marks the same on both women?" Jack slipped his notebook back into his pocket, thinking of Jamie's dream. To him, these deaths were personal.

Phil closed the Jane Doe folder. "The marks are similar, but not exact. With what I have right now, I'd have to say it was another accidental drowning. There's no proof of foul play yet. There's bruising on her neck and shoulders, but they could be from anything, rocks, or a fall. We're looking at everything, Jack, but there's nothing suspicious. Just like the last one."

The blue-green eyes in the colorless face stared up at him. He turned away. "God damn it, Phil, we know these weren't accidents. Give me something to work with."

"I know you want this guy, Jack, but he's smart. There's nothing, really. There are marks under her chin, but they don't mean that she was strangled. No finger patterns. It's just like the last one. She could have fallen, hit her chin, or he could have held her underwater and drowned her. That's all I can tell you right now." Phil patted Jack on the arm. "I know you were hoping for more, but that's all I have. If we're lucky, and it would take a lot of luck, some DNA might still be on her."

"If this guy's a serial killer, he'll kill again and soon. And we know his type, tall, young, and blonde. I'll keep in touch to see if anything pops up in the tests."

"I'm trying, Jack."

Walking to his car, Jack ticked off the things that pointed to a serial killer—the type, the place, and the manner. Could he prove it? Not yet. But, goddamn it, he would.

Driving back to Oyster Point, Jack walked through Jamie's episode on the island. First, anchored to the sand by the fog, could it have been a rope tangled around her leg? Second, pushed under the water and held by a man, yet, had she been choked or just held? Third, his raping movement above her, had salt water destroyed all the evidence of semen?

Jamie's vision must be connected to this guy. If only she had seen him. And who did she call to? Did the woman in her dreams know the man attacking her? And why was he killing now, down here? What had set him off?

Yet, accidents happen. The fog moves in quickly, a woman could lose her footing and fall out of a boat. Maybe a wave hit the boat causing it to capsize and sink, tangling her in the ropes as she fell over? She could have hit her chin and knocked herself out. So, if that were the case, why hasn't the boat drifted in like the body? All of the above could be true, but his money was still on homicides.

How many women can fall off a boat, drown tangled in ropes, and wash ashore on the same beach?

Chapter Forty-Three

"Are you okay?" Jack asked as he muted the TV. "You're awfully quiet."

Jamie had convinced Jack to drive up to Justine's apartment so she could "nose around," as she put it. After a brief encounter with the very strange guard, Angell, Jamie found Justine's apartment to be pretty much what she had expected—well appointed with high ceilings, crown moldings, polished wood and tiled floors. What she hadn't expected to find was a set of keys that fit no one's apartment that they knew of and an old faded photo hidden behind a photograph of Justine and Thomas.

"Sunset's beautiful, isn't it?" She curled her feet under her as she sipped her wine. The cottage felt so comfortable tonight.

"Want to tell me what's going on?"

"Well," she wasn't sure how to say what she was feeling. "Justine's apartment—something didn't feel right."

"Like what?"

"I'm not sure." She closed her eyes and visualized Justine's bedroom. The varying shades of yellow on three walls warmed the room. The fourth wall, painted forest green, set off the yellow and green fabric covered headboard. A large matching buttery and green stuffed chair sat by a bow window with a view of the city. Jamie imagined Justine curling up on the chair with the hand knitted yellow afghan pulled up around her, reading a good thriller on a wintry night with a fire roaring in the fireplace.

"We're not going back, you know that, right?" Jack added, interrupting Jamie's thoughts.

"Don't worry, I'm back there now. Justine lived as I did, in a protected place that she made for herself in the city. Was the apartment cleaned after she left?" Jamie asked keeping her eyes closed. "Did her parents take anything from the apartment?"

"No cleaning and her parents touched nothing, hoping she would be back. After we exhausted all the leads, they closed and locked the door. The photos taken of the apartment are at the office."

Keeping her eyes closed, she replied, "When I look around, there's nothing out of place, nothing at all."

"She was neat—like you. Look at your shoes by the door."

"When I come home from work, I kick off my heels … and yes, I straighten them." She smiled. "I read my mail. If I'm going out, I leave my work clothes folded neatly on my bed and put them away when I return." In her mind, Jamie walked to Justine's closet and opened the painted louvered doors. "By the way, did you happen to find her apartment keys?"

"They were in the dish on the table. I think her parents took them. Why?"

"Well, either someone took her or she never planned on returning. I'm sure you thought through both cases."

"What's your guess?"

"Give me another minute. Her closet's filled with gorgeous expensive work clothes, suits, dresses, blouses, and nice shoes, many pairs of very nice shoes." She thought of her own work shoes, three pairs of heels and three pairs of flats in navy, brown, and black. Justine's closet wall had a floor to ceiling shoe rack filled with Christian Louboutin, Miu Miu, and Jimmy Choo shoes. Jamie was too frugal to spend money on shoes like these even though she loved them. "Where did she keep her casual clothes, shorts, T-shirts, slacks, sweats, walking shoes?" Her mind wandered to a white wicker bureau and opened the drawers. "There are a few casual things, but she must have owned tons. Her closet says she loved clothes. And what hung on all those empty hangers and sat on those empty shelves? Did you see a suitcase anywhere? She traveled a lot, so where are her suitcases? Did she have a storage bin downstairs in the basement of the building?"

"How can you do that, remember everything you saw?"

"I don't know, but when I walk through it again in my mind, it always seems clearer to me."

"No storage areas in the building. Washers and dryers are in the basement for residents who don't have their own. Justine owned all her own appliances. Also, in the basement, there's a walled off area that serves as a semi-apartment for the nighttime security guard. It has a bed, TV, additional monitors…" He stopped.

"What? Do you remember something?" she opened her eyes.

"I'm wondering if we checked those monitors to see if they were working. I think that they might have been off that night. One was reported broken, maybe the back alley one?"

"I'll check the file." She attempted to jump up, but Jack wrapped his arms tighter around her.

"Nope, finish your thoughts. I can look through the file later. So?"

"So where are her missing items like the suitcases, casual clothes, and walking shoes? If they aren't stored and her parents didn't take them, where did they go?"

"I'm not sure I'm following. Are you saying you think she packed up and left? And went where?"

"It's a possibility, isn't it?" She sat up straight. "She's engaged to be married, her parents are thrilled, her wedding date is close, and her parents are planning a huge wedding. Could be cold feet? Or maybe, just maybe, Thomas wasn't her choice." She emphasized the word "her." "Her parents were happy, but maybe she wasn't. She didn't express any love in those emails."

Jack nodded.

"If you lived here and I was in Boston, don't you think our messages would be different from Justine and Thomas's? At least I would say that I missed you."

"Gee, thanks. Those three little words would keep me warm on a cold, stormy winter night, for sure," he pulled her hair.

"You know what I mean." She gave him a quick kiss. "Maybe she met someone who made her heart beat faster than Thomas did?" Like Jack had for her, she thought. "Maybe she had cold feet and ran away? Sometimes stress can make a bride do crazy things."

"Are we talking from experience now?"

"I'll take the fifth. But you've read stories about runaway brides. I wonder if there's more to her story than what you and the police uncovered, that's all."

She closed her eyes and returned to Justine's kitchen. "The sink and counter are bare, no sponge, no dishtowel, no dishwashing liquid, nothing. The dishwasher is empty. It's all too clean, too organized. Who doesn't leave stuff around when they leave for work or go out to dinner, dishes drying that they rinsed out in the morning, dirty clothes." She walked to the bathroom and opened the hamper. It was empty. "She ran, Justine ran."

"I thought that too, but tell me how you know."

"I don't know for sure, but let me look at that old faded paper that she had hidden behind the photo." Removing the sheet from her purse, she held it up to the light. It looked like a negative but there were definitely two shadows like ghosts on the page.

"While you make a copy of that, I'll check for information on the monitors." He pulled Justine's folder from the file box. He had lugged the container to the cottage from his house when they returned from Boston.

"Look at this, two people." She pointed to the figure on the left. "The woman has long hair. Hard to see the features, but the other is definitely a male. Is there a picture of Justine and her fiancé in the file?"

Jack handed her a photo album. "Justine's mother said these were taken at their engagement party."

"Wow, look at this one." Jamie held up a picture of two people standing in front of a large oak tree cast in the glow of the setting sun. Justine, arrayed in a long billowing dress that shone like gold, stood in front of Thomas with her dress cascading around them both like an island of tulle. The gown tumbled off Justine's shoulders into puffy little sleeves. The front dipped into a heart shaped neckline revealing a single large facetted ruby red droplet that nestled between her full breasts. A thick antique gold looped necklace held the ruby in place. Her hands disappeared into the voluminous skirt with only a peek of a fan showing through. Tiny red roses were intertwined with dark curls that cascaded over her bare shoulders. The photo could have been taken on the rolling lawns of Tara in 1860.

Behind her, a foot taller than her stood Thomas, looking like Rhett Butler, dressed in a long beige calfskin jacket, a wide tie, holding a soft gentlemen's hat in his left hand. Thomas' right hand was wrapped around Justine's right shoulder. They looked very serious.

"Well, what do you think?" Jack asked after Jamie had scrutinized the photo.

"The pose, the time of day, the place, everything's perfect. One of them is from Southern heritage?"

"Justine's family on her mother's side. When I asked about her accent, she said her family had pre-Civil War roots in Georgia."

"Justine obviously embraces the Southern heritage. Notice how tall Thomas is and now look at the image in the other photo. He's shorter. Maybe it's her father?"

"No, her father is tall like me."

"Well, another mystery." She flipped to the next photo in the album. The difference in the demeanor of the couple in a close-up amazed her. Thomas smiled, his eyes bright and laughing; he looked directly into the camera with his arms around Justine. His chin rested on the top of her hair. Justine, on the other hand, looked distracted, disinterested. A very large diamond sparkled on her left hand.

"Jack, look at this photo. Do these two look like they're in love? Did Justine's parents ever give you a feeling that she had been pressured into this engagement?"

"Not really. Her mother did most of the talking during the interviews, but we didn't think that unusual." He smiled, holding up his hands in a gesture of surrender. "Since I never spoke to Justine, not sure what she was thinking."

"Didn't she go out to dinner with a girlfriend that night? She must have some idea of what was on Justine's mind. Girlfriends know everything."

"Do they? Kate?"

She placed the open album on the table and curled up again in Jack's arms.

"Yes." Kate knew everything about her. Well, almost everything.

Chapter Forty-Four

"I'd like to introduce my assistant, Jamison Janson. Jamie, Dr. and Mrs. Colbert." Jack had agreed with Jamie that they should investigate the relationship between Justine and her parents a bit more. So here they stood, a week later, on the wide veranda that encircled the front of a large Connecticut Victorian home belonging to Justine's parents. Jack had called and asked if they both could be available for the interview. They had agreed.

"I'm very pleased to meet you both." Jamie shook each of their hands.

Mrs. Colbert waved her perfectly manicured hand to usher them inside the house. Tall and elegantly dressed, she was a woman of about sixty years of age. But her face, like a porcelain doll, with high cheekbones accented by a hint of peach and skin that appeared to have never seen the sun, belied that fact. Her sky blue designer suit hung on her like a model. Her shoulder-length chestnut brown hair, highlighted with light gold streaks, swung perfectly as she glided across the two-story white tiled foyer.

"Is that a Chihuly piece?" Jamie asked looking up at the glass chandelier that hung half way down the serpent-like wood staircase that wound up to a second floor balcony. Made of hand-blown snake-like pieces of different colors, the glass reflected every color of the rainbow magnificently across the stark white lobby.

"Yes, it is." Justine's mother turned to Jamie with amazement written across her face. "How remarkable that you recognize his work. I mean, not that you shouldn't," she corrected herself, "but most people from the East Coast aren't familiar with his pieces."

She had recovered well, Jamie thought, relaxing a bit now that she realized that she had risen in Mrs. Colbert's eyes.

"I know his work very well. I've visited his factory in Tacoma and, when I was in Vianne, France, I purchased one of his pieces for my Boston home."

"You and Justine would have gotten along so well." Mrs. Colbert's clear blue eyes, encircled by long heavily coated lashes, softened. "She loved his work and chose this piece for us."

"It's perfect for this room. I'm sorry that I've touched on a painful memory for you."

"Oh, no, please, it's so nice to have a young woman in the house again." She led them through a library with honey colored wood bookcases surrounding a wood mantled fireplace.

"What a beautiful portrait." Jamie stood in front of the fireplace admiring an oil painting of three women.

"That's my mother and my grandmother with me."

"How much you resembled Justine when you were younger."

"There is no doubt we are—were mother and daughter." Her voice trailed off as she turned, straightened her back, and walked toward the French doors that opened onto a bluestone terrace. In a shady corner, a small black wrought iron glass topped table held four glasses and a frosted pitcher of lemonade. It afforded a view of the magnificent flower gardens and paths that ended at the river's edge.

"What a perfect spot," Jamie managed between sips of the iced lemonade that Mrs. Colbert had poured for each of them. "I think I could sit here and watch the water flow by for hours." She hesitated just a second before asking, "Isn't that the tree in Justine's engagement photos?"

"Yes, it is. We had tents on the lawn and a Dixieland band. That day was so perfect and then..."

Justine's mother twisted the large diamond encrusted band on her left hand.

"When was the engagement party, late summer?" Jamie pushed ahead with easy questions.

"You have a good eye. Are you a photographer?"

"An amateur at best. The photos were beautiful. I noticed a southern theme?" She looked at Justine's father for an answer.

"Blythe can probably answer that better; it's her side of the family that's Southern." He nodded to Justine's mother.

Blythe's large square diamond ring caught the slight bit of sun that filtered through the tall oak trees and flashed blue and red as she patted her husband's hand and smiled. As she held his hand, she narrated the story of her Southern ancestors.

"My roots go back to the 1700s in Savannah, Georgia. Many generations ago, my family, cousins to James Edward Oglethorpe, owned and operated a large rice and live oak timber plantation just outside of Savannah."

The lilt in her words lulled Jamie into imagining that far off time.

"Our land ran along the Savannah River just north of where the old cotton markets resided, along the lower river. My family grew cotton and did well until the Civil War." She moved her hands to her lap and looked off into the distance. "We all know what happened during Sherman's march to the sea, don't we." Her words became clipped, tinged with anger. "He closed off the River—the plantations couldn't ship their crops. Many families, ruined, had to leave their land." She exhaled, forcing a smile, looking directly at Jamie and Jack. "So there you have the history of my Southern roots."

"Does your family still own the land, if I'm not being too personal?" Jamie asked.

"Oh yes. We would never sell it, it's our heritage. My family lived there until the early 1920's when the cotton market collapsed, then moved to other areas of the South. We have maintained the house to some degree, but no one lives there fulltime anymore. We rent the land to local farmers."

"What a wonderful lineage to pass down to your daughter. Was your ancestor's named Oglethorpe as well?" Jamie was careful not to push too hard, but more information was needed on the family background.

"No, my family name is McKenzie. We are Scots. Our land lies below the Abercorn Creek area where it joins the Savannah River. It is a beautiful spot with rolling meadows." She waved her hand toward the water. "Similar to what we have here, isn't it, darling?" she asked, touching her husband's arm, not waiting for his answer. "In its day, the plantation produced much cotton."

Jamie looked to Jack. A slight nod of his head without looking up from his notes was her signal to continue.

"Dr. Colbert, you have a slight accent but it's not a Southern accent like your wife's. Could I ask how you two met, if that's not too personal?" She looked at Mrs. Colbert as she started to answer. "I'd love to hear the man's rendition of the meeting, wouldn't you?" Jamie smiled, encouraging him.

"Please, call me Paul." His green eyes flashed an acceptance of Jamie's knowledge of his wife's ability to dominate the conversation. "I grew up in Texas, outside of Austin, but attended medical school in Boston."

"He's a Harvard Medical School graduate," Mrs. Colbert added, moving the napkins back into a straight pile in the center of the table.

Jamie nodded and continued.

"After you graduated Dr. Colbert—Paul—you did your residency in Boston?"

"He was a resident at Massachusetts General Hospital where he trained with some world renowned doctors," Mrs. Colbert injected into the conversation again.

Jamie's look at Jack said, "How do I stop her from doing all the talking?"

Jack coughed to camouflage his amusement. "Mrs. Colbert?" Jack asked without looking at Jamie. "Is there any more of this delicious lemonade?"

"There surely is Detective, Chief Hereford."

Blythe carefully addressed him by his proper title and in a slightly exaggerated Southern accent, Jamie noticed. After she disappeared through the door, Jamie continued her questions. "Can you tell me how you met Mrs. Colbert?"

"It's pretty simple really. I attended a conference in Atlanta and had been selected to speak on a panel on heart bypass surgery as the representative for the younger doctors. Blythe's father was one of the older doctors on the panel, actually he was barely fifty at the time, but that seemed old to me." His smile revealed his genuine love for Blythe's father. "After the panel session finished, he and I discussed different aspects of our work as we walked to the next session. Throughout the day we kept bumping into each other and after the last session, he asked me to his home for dinner. I accepted. We sat in the living room talking when Blythe came through the door. She smiled, said hello, and took my breath away." He rose and helped his wife with the tray that she was carrying. "She still does," he added, placing a kiss on her cheek.

Jamie looked at Jack. His eyes, dark and enigmatic, held her look.

"What did I miss?" Mrs. Colbert asked as she refreshed everyone's lemonade.

"Nothing that you don't already know, my dear." Paul turned to Jamie to complete his story. "Blythe attended nursing school in Atlanta at the time, so we saw each other when I could get away or when she had vacations. When an offer came for a position in Boston, we married and moved there." He touched her hand. "It was hard for her to move so far from family, but she made that choice willingly and I love her all the more for it. We had Justine and she was a gift. We had tried for many years to have children with no success. When Blythe became pregnant with Justine, we felt truly blessed."

Mrs. Colbert's eyes teared up as she listened to her husband.

"Can you tell me how Justine met her fiancé, Thomas?"

Paul answered, knowing that Blythe couldn't talk at this point. "Thomas is the son of one of my associates. From the time he was very young, he was always around the house, almost like a son. One Christmas when he was home for a few days, we had his whole family for dinner." He looked to Blythe for confirmation and she nodded. "They had much in common, both well educated, athletic, loved to ski, skate, and run. We hoped that if they met in a more formal setting, a dating atmosphere, something might happen between them. As the months went by, they came to dinner often when they were home together. Before we knew it, they were engaged."

"She worked in Boston and he in New York during their courtship and engagement?" Jamie kept moving the story forward, wanting Paul to continue. She had chosen the word "courtship" because Justine's parents appeared so proper.

"Yes, but it seemed to work for them. He travelled to Boston and she took the train to New York."

"Did she have a boyfriend before Thomas?" There was a long pause as Jamie looked to Paul and then to Blythe for an answer.

"She did, a local boy, Daniel. She dated him in high school and then, off and on through college." Mrs. Colbert jumped in to answer. Her use of the term "local boy" suggested that this young man wasn't considered good enough for Justine.

"Do you remember what happened to them?"

"Not really. Justine stopped talking about him and we just assumed they broke up. She worked in Boston after graduation and dated a lot, but no one special, at least no one she talked about or brought home to meet us." Mrs. Colbert looked out to the water. "She finally realized that she had nothing in common with Daniel, not like she did with Thomas."

"Do you remember his last name?" The use of the word "finally" was very interesting, as though the parents knew he was wrong all along, but Justine didn't agree.

"Daniel, Daniel Roth." Mrs. Colbert had no trouble remembering his name, her tone harsh as she straightened the napkins once again. She disliked him.

"Do you know what happened to him?" Jack asked.

"I don't. I think he was teaching school at some point. History, wasn't it, dear?"

Paul looked down, crossing his legs as he nodded.

"Please, try these pastries. Louise just took them out of the oven."

Their body language said there was more to the story of Justine and Daniel, but they had told them all they wanted them to know today.

"Thank you, Mrs. Colbert."

The conversation turned to the weather and the view. They rose and Mrs. Colbert walked them to the door, saying she hoped that their discussion would help find Justine.

Jamie shook both of their hands. She knew exactly what happened to Justine.

Chapter Forty-Five

"So? What's your take?" Jack asked Jamie as he maneuvered the car down the Colbert's long oak lined driveway.

Jamie watched for traffic as they pulled out onto the shore road.

"Daniel Roth, he's the key. She's with him."

"What?" He pulled the car over to the side of the road where they had a clear view of the river.

Unhooking her seatbelt, she turned to him. "Look, he has to be the missing link. Mrs. Colbert didn't like him. Paul said nothing about him. He didn't even look at us when she asked him about Daniel teaching school. She said they were from two different worlds. He's a local boy, not worthy of her daughter."

"Okay. So they didn't like Daniel or his background. They wanted more for their daughter. Your parents probably wouldn't be happy with you right now, taking up with a cop. But it still doesn't tell me why you think they're together?"

"First, I think my parents would love you, especially my Dad." She leaned in and kissed him.

"Thanks, even if it isn't true." He kissed her on the forehead.

"She never gave him up. When her parents fixed her up with Thomas, she played along because she didn't have to answer their questions about who she was seeing. They assumed she was falling in love with him. She used Thomas as a cover while still seeing Daniel. When the engagement came up, she continued to weave the web of deceit. She sunk deeper and deeper into the charade. She knew Thomas would be hurt, unless.... " She paused.

"Unless he knew. Unless Thomas knew," she whispered. "That's it." Her voice rose as she folded her legs under her.

"Unless who knew what?" Jack played with the piece of hair that rested on Jamie's cheek.

"What if Thomas knew he was Justine's cover? Or even better, maybe she was his cover as well."

"Are you serious? You think they played both sets of parents?"

"Why not? What better way to keep your parents out of your love life? It makes perfect sense. If Thomas knew, it would explain the non-descript messages between them. Maybe he had a woman in his life that his parents didn't approve of. If Justine and Thomas came home together, celebrated holidays and weekends here occasionally, both sets of parents must have been thrilled. It worked until the wedding date couldn't be put off any longer. The courtship had gone on long enough and both parents pushed for a wedding."

Jack kissed her gently on the lips.

"What's that for?" She wiped her lipstick off his lips with her fingertips.

"For your devious bizarre mind."

"Well, isn't it possible?"

"It's so bizarre, it could be except when we checked the family property in Georgia, it was empty."

Jack checked the rearview mirror where a dark colored car backed up into the Colbert's driveway.

Chapter Forty-Six

Jack knocked, hearing a male and a female voice inside Thomas' apartment. The voices stopped. Jack tapped again. A disheveled man opened the door as he righted his t-shirt, pulling it down over lightweight khaki pants.

"Thomas?"

The man's face paled. "Yes. Detective Hereford, isn't it?"

"Good memory. Please, call me Jack. May I come in for a minute?"

"Ummm… sure."

"Inconvenient?" Jack asked, knowing Thomas hesitated because of the female inside.

"No, please come in."

The living room, with lots of dark wood and a massive fireplace, lived up to the usual fare of the old brownstones in this part of New York.

"The room looks different." Jack commented, admiring the view of the Hudson River.

"I had it redecorated after Justine—after Justine disappeared." Thomas looked away.

"Nice. Looks like it's had a woman's touch, the flowers, paintings, and the colors. A decorator's choices or…?"

Thomas's furtive look through the open double doors to the right caused Jack to follow his gaze. A shadow skimmed across the dark oak floor. A ladies' black silk robe lay across the bottom of a four poster bed. Cat green eyes locked on Jack as a woman lifted the wrap off the bed and donned the robe that clung to every curve of her wet, naked body. Knowing that she had his full attention, she leaned forward to fluff her curly, damp, black hair, providing him a perfect view of her ample breasts. In a much practiced move, she secured the tie so that the robe fell open in all the right places. She smiled a knowing smile, winked at Jack, and disappeared from sight.

Without pulling his gaze away from the open doors, Jack asked, "Did I interrupt something?"

"No, please sit down." Thomas slammed the bedroom doors closed. "Have you found something new about Justine?" Thomas asked, ignoring the provocative interruption.

Jamie's take of this situation was right on. Thomas waited too long to ask about Justine. "Not really. But I thought I'd run some ideas by you. I visited Justine's parents this week to review her case with them. I wanted to make sure I hadn't overlooked anything. Somehow our conversation turned to a Daniel Roth?"

When Jack mentioned Daniel's name, Thomas looked down. He wouldn't make a very good poker player.

"How are her parents doing? I haven't talked to them in a while. I try to call or stop by when I can." His voice trailed off while he tried to come up with a valid excuse for not keeping in touch with his fiancée's parents.

"They aren't doing well, as you can imagine. They miss Justine, especially Mrs. Colbert, which is why I decided to stop by. Thomas, can you tell me anything about Daniel? Did you ever meet him?"

"Daniel? Meet him? Why would I ever meet him? Justine told me about him. She dated him when they were young." Thomas walked to the window, his back facing Jack.

"Thomas, please don't lie. You know that eventually I'll figure everything out."

"I don't want to lie." Thomas turned to face him.

"Then don't. Tell me what happened."

"Am I in some kind of trouble?"

"We'll see when you finish your story." Jack sat on the couch, crossed his legs, and waited.

***

"I was right," Jamie exclaimed, slipping her paintbrushes into a bucket of water. "And who was the femme fatale in the bedroom?" she asked, sitting on the stool by her easel, keenly aware that she owned nothing remotely close to a black silk robe. "You were probably waiting for her to give an encore performance?" Jack's voice had a soothing effect on her. She missed him. "So, what are you going to do now?" She listened to his plans.

"Do you want me to go with you? Are you sure?" She hoped that he would say yes, but he was correct, it was a one day trip and he was halfway there already. "I'll see you when you come back." He'd try to be home tonight.

"Good luck and be safe. See you in a few hours."

They had never said the "I love you" words. The phrase conveyed a permanency that they both knew from experience didn't exist in life.

"Just like I thought," she said, picking up her brushes again and swiping a rich blue arc across the paper. "I'm getting pretty good at this detective stuff, right Max?"

Max opened one eye and then turned over.

Chapter Forty-Seven

The soft pitter-patter of shoes echoed through the house. Bouquets of fresh flowers adorned the tables in the large, light filled foyer. Justine shook her wide skirt to remove any wrinkles and smoothed her hair up at the back of her neck. Taking a deep breath, she opened the large wooden front door.

"Good morning, or is it afternoon already?" Justine cooed with a smooth, practiced Southern cadence. "Hard to tell here, the days drift by so slowly." She swiped non-existent hairs into her chignon. She recited the well-rehearsed opening, then turned her interest to the lawn behind him.

"I'm Jack Ford. I called earlier this morning to set up an appointment about an article I'm writing?" He used another last name so she wouldn't run at this point.

"Anna told me."

Filling her in with the information he had gathered from the meeting with her parents, he continued with the charade. "I'm researching historic pre-Civil War southern plantations that have remained in the hands of the same families for many years." He noticed that she wore her hair, dyed red, in a pulled back older style. Her polished Southern accent, her less cosmopolitan manner of dress, made her appear older, but he knew that he stood face to face with Justine.

"Why did you pick this home?" She stepped out onto the large white wooden veranda with a painted sky blue ceiling, closing the door behind her. She was hiding something.

"My investigation showed that this house is one of the few Georgian plantations that still remain in the possession of the original family. I'm interested in how and why the family chose to retain it through the years."

She stared at the river meandering past the edge of the green lawn. As though becoming aware that he still stood there, she said, "Please sit down, I've forgotten my manners." Justine's hands moved like her mother's as she waved at the chairs to the left of them. "How much history have you accumulated?"

"Enough," Jack stated, looking straight at her.

"Where would you like me to start?" She returned his stare.

"Wherever you would like to start." She was gutsy to stare him down.

The door to the house opened and a plump white-haired woman emerged, holding a tow haired child. "I wouldn't normally interrupt Mrs. McKenzie, except baby Paul is tired and needs his nap. I wasn't sure how long you would be. Would you like me to put him down?"

Justine's smile softened. "Please, Anna, that would be perfect. Thank you."

"Yes Ma'am." Anna retired into the house.

Turning back to Jack, Justine asked, "Did you know about that part of our history?"

"I have to admit I didn't." He hesitated and then added, "Mrs. McKenzie."

"I didn't think so, Detective Hereford. Shall I bring out some coffee for us? Sweet tea just isn't the same for us Northerners, is it? And you can call me Justine," she voiced over her shoulder as she entered the house.

"It's Chief Hereford now," he called after her, knowing that she was her mother's daughter and would want to address him by his proper title.

Chapter Forty-Eight

A lone male sat in a dark automobile hidden in the trees at the end of Jamie's road. He waited for her cottage lights to go out. His blood boiled as he recalled Jack strutting out of the cottage this morning with his arm around Jamie's waist. He had stroked her hair, her cheek and then, as though to spite him, Jack had kissed her, a long lingering kiss. As he drove away, he announced that he would be back tomorrow.

"Don't hurry, good Chief. She won't be here. Jamie will leave you a note saying she found a better lover," he smirked. What he wouldn't give to see Jack's face when he read those words. His laughter filled the automobile.

He bit down on the remainder of his Italian submarine sandwich. The oil oozed down his chin and on to his jacket. A piece of purple onion hung from his mouth as he chewed a wad of bread and salami. He slurped the onion slice through his pursed lips.

"Damn, no more napkins." He fumbled around in a gym bag behind his car seat looking for something to wipe his hands and face with. He pulled out a piece of soft blue silk. Fingering the thong, he remembered the beauty who had owned the underwear. She was tall, with long legs that wrapped around him, blonde hair that tickled his face as he lost himself in her smothering breasts.

Rubbing the silk panties along his stubbly chin, he inhaled her scent. She had proven to be sexually inventive, energetic, and athletic. But, after a while, she bored him; her voice grated on him when she complained about not being taken out to dinner. He smiled as he remembered her whiney words that last night. "Take me some place where I can wear clothes." Like he was going to be seen with a whore, a substitute. That's what she was, a Jamie lookalike.

"But," he said, "she's not you, Jamie, she's not you."

"Let's go for a swim first, over at the island where we can be alone. We can skinny dip, ride each other, and then I'll treat you to a nice dinner," he'd lied to her.

Stupid bitch that she was, she had agreed, excited like a little child. She enjoyed making love on the beach. He pushed the small rowboat that he kept anchored in the shallows out across the low water inlet, and rowed to the deserted beach. Laying her at the water's edge, he slowly stripped her, feeling her eagerness. He moved her into the water so they could ride the waves together, giving him his rhythm. She giggled as he toyed with her large breasts. She strained against him, moaning. When he had satisfied himself, he held her under the waves until her thrashing stopped.

He threw her nude body into the boat, her green eyes open in disbelief. Rowing out a short distance from the beach into the bay, he arranged her pink top, pocketed the blue silk panties, wrapped a rope around her ankle, and threw her over the side. He hid the boat back in the reeds. The tide brought her to shore. The Chief and that stupid wimp of a coroner said that she had tripped and drowned. How many so-called accidents could he get away with?

So far, so good. And these women, substitutes, stupid, unsatisfying look-alikes, the things he did to them, he had been forced to do. He felt sorry afterwards, but he couldn't be blamed for it. *It was Jack's fault*, he thought, fingering the blue silk material.

"If I had Jamie, they would all still be alive," he whispered. He had been obsessed with Jamie from the first time that he laid eyes on her as she stood framed in a doorway, the black dress hugging her everywhere. Her hair, pulled up with soft pieces escaping, created a halo effect around her stunning face. He closed his eyes, picturing her expression, a slight pout on her lips, her eyes narrowing as she searched the room for someone she knew, and then, that smile as she recognized a familiar face. She lit up the room as she moved through the crowd. Every woman envied her; every man undressed her.

A tap on his car window caused him to jump. He had lost focus, forgetting where he sat. He jammed the panties into the brown paper sandwich bag on the seat next to him. He rolled down the window, the rain splashing in. A police officer stood there, mouthing off about him sitting in the trees at the end of her road. He hid his face in the shadows of the car.

"Move the car, please. This is private property," the rain-soaked idiot told him.

"I'm sorry. I didn't know. I'm waiting for my girl, but she's late." Not a lie, he thought, she was his girl. He started to explain about his made-up girlfriend, a hot waitress. As he described her, he thought about that sexy number, Bev. She might be worth a try.

The officer acted disgusted, cutting him off, and ordering him to move the car, and then walked away. He fought the urge to put the car in reverse and run the idiot down. Instead, he waved and yelled an apology. Apologize for what, a chance to be with his woman?

He parked on a deserted street up the hill and hurried down to the wharf as the rain and wind picked up.

Chapter Forty-Nine

A thunderous roar rolled across the harbor, shaking the little cottage from the ground up. A flash of lightning ignited Jamie's bedroom, startling her. Holding her breath, she counted the seconds between the lightning strike and the rumble of thunder to see how close the storm was. Three seconds. This one was close.

For some reason, tonight's summer storm's crackling skidded across her nerves. The outside noises seemed magnified—the wind ripping through the trees, the pelting rain against the skylight, the squeak of the swing on the deck, even a human laugh. She had locked the doors and windows before going to bed. The rain pounded hard on the skylight. Voices floated through the window that was open a crack next to her bed. Her heart raced. A flash of lightning lit up the room, followed immediately by a crack of thunder that shook the tiny house. The squall hung right overhead. Jack's small alarm clock read 4:00 a.m. The digits flashed on and off.

"Please, don't let the electricity go off," she prayed out loud. Pita's voice whispered in her head, "Your magic number is four."

Glass broke in the kitchen, followed by a huge thud. Jamie sat straight up in bed. "Your magic number is four," echoed in her head.

"Max, is that you?" she whispered, sliding off the bed, grabbing the flashlight off the night table. Another loud crash followed by a groan. Someone had broken the glass in the kitchen door. Where was her phone? Why wasn't Max barking?

The blood pounded in Jamie's ears. Her phone was on the night stand, but where? Her hands swept across knocking over a half full glass of water. It rattled across the nightstand and then rolled onto the scatter rug beside the bed making a soft thump. She held her breath. No response.

Her hands fumbled with things on the table, glasses, extra change, a watch, her opal necklace. No phone, damn it. Where was it? Her heart beat faster. No, how stupid, she had left it on the living room table after she'd spoken with Jack.

A streak of lightening highlighted a man sprawled outside her bedroom door on the living room floor. Then, darkness covered him. She knew where he was, advantage to her. She analyzed her options—jump out the bedroom window, hide under the bed and hope he didn't find her, or just confront him. The bedroom window would take too long with the screen and under the bed she would be cornered. Only one option remained.

"If you move another muscle, I'll shoot you." Her words sliced through the stormy night air, sharp and steady, belying the panic that rose in her throat. "I've called 911." She waited for his response as she stood on the cold wet scatter rug.

His laugh echoed off the walls, surprising her. "If you shoot me, you'll kill the kindest, gentlest, most thoughtful lover you have ever had. And, please, call off the police."

Another bolt of lightning revealed Jack pushing himself to his knees with a wince.

"Oh my God. You scared the life out of me. I thought someone broke in."

"Please call Scott back and tell him it's a false alarm. I'd rather Scott didn't find me on your couch at 4 a.m. nursing a bruised knee with glass all around. Especially not with you in that cute little T-shirt and hair all mussed. That would make quite a story around the station." Jack rubbed his knee, wincing.

"I never called the police. My phone's in there." She pointed the flashlight to the table next to him.

"And the gun?"

"That was in here," she laughed, pointing to her head. "I had to say something."

"You are unbelievable. If someone had broken in, what do you think all that make-believe stuff would have done? He could have done anything to you," said Jack, always the voice of reason.

"I did have the flashlight to beat him with." She flipped the light around and gasped as she saw the glass scattered across the floor in all directions.

"I'm sorry. I opened the door and with Max sprawled there, I lost my balance, grabbed the table, and it tipped. Max of course just turned over and fell back to sleep. I didn't want to wake you up by turning on the lights."

"Well, that ship has sailed." Jamie picked up a few large pieces of glass. "Did you cut your knee?"

"No, banged it against something hard, maybe the book case? What a klutz I am. And I'm very tired." Jack rubbed his eyes. "I'll clean up the mess. Please stay away from the glass with your bare feet. Was that a special vase? I'll replace it if I can." He rambled while starting to laugh.

"All I have is a bag of frozen broccoli." She picked her way through the glass to the freezer.

"Great, my favorite vegetable." His laughing continued.

Jamie handed him the bag of frozen vegetables wrapped in a dishtowel as he moved to the couch. "Put it on your knee so it doesn't swell and I'll get a broom and sweep up this mess. No, the vase wasn't anything special," she lied. Pita had always filled it with fresh flowers from her garden. "How did you get back so early?" she asked as she pulled a broom out of the pantry and grabbed her flip-flops beside the front door. "I didn't expect you until later."

Jack grabbed her waist, pulling her down next to him. Her T-shirt rose.

"Taking advantage of the cleaning lady?" she managed to squeeze out between his quick kisses. She dropped everything and began tickling him. She enjoyed seeing him relaxed, tired, and ticklish. He rarely lost control.

"More like you are taking advantage of a tired, wounded cop." He pulled her closer, tickling her under the arms. As she squirmed, she could feel the heat of his body under her hands. His hands inched higher and higher up her thighs.

"I missed you." Her words came out breathless, surprising even her.

"I missed you too. I'm so used to being around you that I couldn't stay away even a night. Thus, what you see." He pointed to the glass on the floor. "I'm really sorry. I can tell that the vase was special." He continued to caress her thighs.

"No, it wasn't really." She lied again. "Tell me about the trip. Profitable?" She knew he felt guilty about the vase. Her concentration became blurry as he moved his hands along her body. "Four is your lucky number," echoed through her mind.

"Very lucky" was her last thought as Jack leaned over and turned off the light.

Chapter Fifty

Huddled behind the bandstand at the end of the wharf, the stranger wiped the rain from his binoculars with the lining of his jacket as the rain dripped down the back of his neck. This was not at all what he had imagined for tonight— sitting here alone in the rain. Using his binoculars, he spotted the living room light on. He focused in as Jamie materialized at the glass sliders dressed in a short blue t-shirt. Her hair hung loosely over her shoulders. He wiped his mouth, took off his baseball cap, and wiped his forehead with the sleeve of his jacket. The rain continued to pelt him.

She waited for him, he assured himself. But how could he get to her? Would that stupid cop be watching her cottage all night?

Jamie bent over to pick something up from the floor.

He shifted to catch a better view of those long legs, but by the time he reached the other side of the bandstand, she had moved behind a table. He scurried back to his original position. Removing his camera from his backpack, he focused in on her.

She rose, brushing her hair back off her face, lifting the edge of her t-shirt even higher. The camera clicked, echoing through the heavy air. She excited him like no other woman ever had.

So close, he thought. She was so close he could almost touch her. He extended his fingers in the air, tracing her face, her hair, and then slowly travelling down her breasts to her flat stomach and finally her legs, those long legs that would wrap themselves around him. He closed his eyes and could smell her, feel her loose hair skimming over his skin as she slithered along his naked body. His blood started to simmer. He couldn't wait to show her tonight how a real man could make her happy.

When he opened his eyes, she was gone. He held his breath, hoping she would finish what she started. His need to have her was building. As if on cue, Jamie reappeared with something in her hands, tantalizing him, tempting him to come to her. His camera clicked continuously.

He rose, placing the camera back in his bag. He followed her, using the binoculars as he rounded the bandstand. She leaned over the couch, placing what looked like a towel down on a pillow. He halted in mid-stride, his heart rate accelerated and his blood pounded in his ears like the thunder that rolled across the sky. Jack sat there, right in front of her.

He swung around and banged his head against the back of the wooden bandstand, his whole body shaking. Lightening zapped across the sky, but he saw nothing except the vision of Jamie leaning over Jack. The thunder sent a shudder along the entire length of the wharf as the lightning cracked above. The wind picked up, driving the rain into his white, enraged face.

He turned back. She carried a broom in one hand and something else in the other. He slinked closer to the edge of the wharf, focusing in on both of them. Jack placed his hands on Jamie's waist, pulling her down on top of him. With her hands full, she couldn't fight him. She wriggled, trying to get away from him. His hands touched her everywhere. She continued to struggle.

As he continued to peer through the binoculars, he realized that Jamie wasn't struggling at all. She touched Jack's face with her long tapered fingers and then kissed him with those soft pouty lips. Jack took advantage of her and slipped his hands up under her T-shirt. She vanished from sight. All he could see was Jack's back and his hand placing Jamie's nightshirt on the floor. Then the room went black.

The rain soaked through the stranger's hat, slid down his face, off his long dark eyelashes onto his cheeks as the stormy gray eyes stared into the darkened room. His hands tightened around the binoculars as he lowered them to his chest. Jack was using her as his whore. The sweet talking, handsome son-of-a-bitch was taking advantage of a young, innocent beauty. He had to end this, to rescue her. He might even have to get rid of the Chief. That wouldn't be so bad, maybe a little boating accident? He smiled, envisioning Jack's body washing up on shore, the coroner leaning over him, declaring it an accident. He laughed. How incompetent they were. He pulled up his collar and tucked his binoculars into his soggy jacket. The wind driven rain continued to soak him as he skulked across the wharf muttering, formulating his plan to rescue Jamie and rid himself of Jack.

A dark form inched its way from behind a parked car and followed the stranger up the hill.

Chapter Fifty-One

"I bet the nanny surprised you when she appeared with the baby," Jamie commented, folding the afghan over the couch. "Boy, what I would have given to see the look on your face. How old did you say he was?"

"Oh, like you would have guessed that?" Jack felt relaxed today, even though he didn't have much sleep last night after he stumbled into the cottage. "I think she said nine months. Little Paul, named after her father. He wore a pair of jeans with no shoes and his fat little feet hanging out. His huge brown eyes lit up when he spotted his mother. His smile and dimples definitely belong to his mother and grandmother."

"You like kids." It was a statement, not a question.

"I love kids. Don't you?" He hoped she did. Funny, he'd never asked Lizz that question, maybe because he already knew the answer. Lizz, after seeing his sister Jess in her eighth month, said she would never get pregnant and mess up her figure like that.

"Tons of kids would be great. I hated being an only child, especially after my parents died. I would spend my entire day playing with a baby if I had one."

As he waited for her to continue, he realized that she spoke of her parents now without breaking down. "Tons, huh? Well, I better take you to visit my sister one of these days. You can meet her two kids. I call them spirited," he added. "She calls them hellions. A slightly different point of view, I guess."

"Pick a day and we'll go. I'd love to meet your sister and her hellions."

She surprised him with her positive answer. "When I go into the office today, I'll check my calendar, then co-ordinate with you and Jess."

"My calendar is pretty much open except for work meetings that can be moved if I know far enough in advance. So, tell me more about the plantation?" She yawned as she poured Jack a cup of coffee. He knew that she probably hadn't slept at all before he stumbled in at 4 a.m. And after that, neither of them got much sleep. He stretched, his mood greatly improved today—he had solved a missing person's case and had received a sexy welcome home from Jamie. He still had to replace the vase.... He smiled. And the broccoli.

He stirred two sugars into his coffee, watching the whirlpool in his cup as he told her about a trust set up years ago that maintains the McKenzie plantation house and the property surrounding it. The remaining land, overgrown now, still shows troughs where a horse drawn plow turned the soil, where cotton once grew, twigs and branches jut up. Piles of decrepit wood and crushed shells lay in a circle where shacks had housed the workers. Justine had given him a tour.

"You'd love the place. Daniel spends his time off taking caring for the house and gardens. Those flowers you love? The droopy ones that climb up the back trellis? They hang all over the front of the house and the porch."

"Wisteria? They smell divine. Does the plantation have a name? Was there a long driveway with huge oaks lining it?" Jamie jotted notes on the edges of the newspaper spread in front of her on the table. Jack knew she would be on the computer researching everything about the plantation before he drove down the road to work.

"A long dirt drive canopied with huge live oaks led to an enormous white house with columns. Justine called it 'Riverview.' Remember the Colbert's back yard rolling toward the water? Well, the plantation is exactly the same, just as Mrs. Colbert described it, with the back lawn running to the river."

"What a painting that would make," she joked with him. "Did you meet Daniel?"

"Poor guy, when he saw me, he looked like his life just blew up. They must have lived every day in fear of being found out."

"Well, you really don't look like a reporter," she kidded. Jack, muscular and tough looking, not a desk-job kind of guy and with the sunglasses, he surely was a cop. "I wonder why she didn't refuse to see you. Interesting." She continued with her notetaking. "Did they ask what you're going to do now that you know about them? Doctor Colbert, Paul, knows about all this? Are you sure?"

"Absolutely. Justine said she had talked to him right before I arrived and he had warned her that we were still looking for her. I told them both that I had to think about what to do about this one, especially since her father knows the truth. What would you do?" He avoided referring to her ability to close her eyes and see. "You have a good feel for this stuff."

"Well, I'm not sure what I'd do." She sipped her coffee as Jack created a vortex in his second cup. "Should I pull out the Ouija board?" she asked, making one of her box doodles on the corner of the newspaper, laying her glasses on the table.

"If the board helps us, please do," he quipped.

"Paul knows about baby Paul?"

"He does, but he hasn't told his wife. He must have done some soul searching to keep a secret like that. I don't think I could do it, could you?"

"No, yet I'm not sure that we, well, not me for sure, have the right to destroy that confidence and the relationship between Paul and Mrs. Colbert." For some reason, Jamie couldn't call Mrs. Colbert by her first name. "Does she hate Daniel so much that Paul couldn't tell her about the baby? Wouldn't her heart soften toward Daniel if she knew about the marriage and a grandchild? Does status mean that much to her?"

Jamie cut right to the heart of the issue in a few seconds and put a personal face on it. His pager went off. "I better head to the office. Scott's paging me. We'll talk more about this when I come home?" He hated to leave.

She was so cute sitting at the kitchen table with her feet wrapped around the edge of the chair and her T-shirt pulled over her knees, writing her notes. She pushed her hair back and sipped her coffee, flipping the newspaper page. There was no white space left on the previous page.

"Anything special on tap today?" he asked as he bent to kiss her forehead. Funny how normal this felt.

"A shower, a little research on Riverview, maybe a walk up to the Historical Society and if the mood hits me, some painting." She reached up to cradle his face as she kissed him. "Hopefully that will hold you until you come home. What's your day like?"

"Don't know yet. Never know until I'm in the office. I'll call as soon as I talk to Scott, how's that?"

"Perfect."

"Please don't roam too far from home?"

"You know, I think Justine wanted to be found." She powered up her computer. "She used the family name, lived in the family home. She wanted them to find her," she mused as Jack closed the door behind him and left her to her research.

Chapter Fifty-Two

"What's up Scott?" Jack asked, picking up a pile of yellow post-its from his secretary's desk. He scanned the notes looking for a smiley face in the corner, Martha's way of telling him what needed his immediate attention. Only a few notes had her mark.

"Well Chief, something weird happened that I thought might be important. I tried your pager and cell last night, but they were off." Scott looked away, brushing an imaginary speck from his shirt.

"I returned late last night, was tired and shut them off." He could tell that Scott knew exactly where he was, but Jack didn't feel like confirming it.

"Close the door and sit, Scott. What happened?"

Scott followed orders well. He shut the door and sat his lanky body on the edge of a table beside Jack's desk. He pulled out a notebook from his back pocket. It amused Jack that Scott copied almost everything he did. He flipped pages, looking for the notes that he wanted to relate and began.

"Well Boss – ah, Chief."

Jack put his feet up on the desk. Scott knew that he hated being called 'Boss.'

"That's fine, Scott. Hard to break a habit. Don't worry about it. So?"

"I was checking on Miss Jamie like you asked me to do and about..." He hesitated as he doublechecked his notes, then continued. "...About 3:30 this morning I came across a guy sitting in a car tucked in the trees where he had a perfect view of her cottage."

"And?" Jack straightened in his chair, dropping his feet to the floor with a thud.

"When I asked him why he was parked there, he had this story about waiting for his girlfriend who waitressed and was hot."

"Get to the point, Scott," he interrupted, his gut telling him there was something significant here.

"I told him to move on, that he was parked on private property. He drove away and I had Teddy check on him. Teddy said the guy parked his car on Holbrook and walked in the pouring rain to the wharf. As the guy moved down the road, Teddy said he ducked behind the bushes every time a car came by. He had binoculars, a camera case and we think he was spying on Miss Jamie from behind the bandstand." It was amusing how Scott always referred to her as "Miss Jamie." He must have gotten the habit from his Southern mother.

"Are you sure?"

"Not much else to look at from there. At one point, when the light was on in her cottage, Teddy said he moved closer to the edge of the wharf so he could get a better view. Kept switching between his camera and binoculars."

How much did his deputies see? The back of his neck felt warm.

"What else happened?" He needed to know every move this guy made.

"At one point, Teddy said the guy ran to the back of the bandstand and hit his head against the wood. Then, he leaned against it like whatever he saw upset him."

"Who was he?" Jack's voice was flat.

"We tracked the license plate. No surprise there. It was rented out of Boston and paid for with cash."

"Any description of the guy?"

"Not much. The guy who rented him the car remembered nothing specific. Said the man was tall, light brown or blond hair, he couldn't remember. Said he had a hoody on and sunglasses so he couldn't tell us much more." Scott licked his forefinger and flipped a page.

"Teddy saw him dressed in rain gear, a baseball cap, crouched in the dark. Said he thought he was tall, maybe 6' 2", or so. When I saw him, he had on a baseball cap, Yankees." Scott's face showed what he thought of that.

"He kept his face in the shadows and turned away as though looking for something on the seat when I used my flashlight. His hair was light brown or maybe dark blonde and curled around the back of his cap, no hoody. I stood behind the front window so all-in-all, I didn't get a good look at him. At the time, I thought his story might be true, he could be waiting for Bev or one of the other waitresses in town. I don't remember ever seeing him before though. Figured he was a tourist making a move on one of our local gals."

"Great." Jack needed something to follow up on, but what?

"I'm sorry, Chief. I had nothing on him. All I could do was tell him to move."

"Not your fault, Scott. You and Teddy did great getting the information you did. I appreciate that and I'm sure Jamie will too. We have to be a little more careful now that we know this guy is spying on her. Did Teddy follow him when he left?"

"Started to, then we received an emergency call over at Atwood's and Teddy headed over there and by the time I drove back up Holbrook, the guy had vanished."

"Figures. When we do get a call, it's when we're busy."

"You think he might have something to do with the drownings? Anything you need me to do, Chief?"

"I don't know, Scott. I can't think of anything right now. We have to watch Jamie and the cottage every minute now. This guy's trouble, I know it. What happened at Atwood's?"

"Mr. Atwood thought his dog had gone missing. Teddy found him lying behind the shed trying to keep dry." Scott laughed. "We do have some strange emergencies down here."

"Glad there was no real difficulty. Atwood's a nice guy. Thanks Scott, that's all."

Scott slid off the table and quietly closed the office door behind him. Jack tapped his pencil on the desk. He couldn't worry about what his guys had seen; they were discreet.

But this guy? Why was he watching Jamie in the pouring rain? And could he be the serial killer, now after her? She was his type. How could he trap him before he harmed her or someone else? He leaned back in his chair, putting his feet up on the desk again.

Jack hated this guy. The pencil in his fingers snapped in two. He would catch him and make him pay for frightening Jamie.

He started to formulate a plan. The pencil pieces clanged in the wastebasket.

Chapter Fifty-Three

"What brings you here in the middle of the day?" Jamie reached up to return a plate from the dishwasher to the cabinet. "What happened? A problem?" she asked over her shoulder.

Jack had mulled over what Scott said about the guy on the wharf. Jamie needed to know, but he didn't want to frighten her any more than he had already.

"You're awfully quiet. You better fess up or I'll have to resort to the tickle mode of interrogation." She reached across him to pick out the last dish, clipping him on the chin with her forefinger.

Leaning back against the sink, Jack pulled her close. He rested his head on hers, inhaling the sweet fresh smell of her hair, rubbing her back with his hands. His life was perfect, but only because she was in it. He couldn't think of something happening to her.

"You know how much you mean to me, don't you?" he asked. Why couldn't he tell her that he couldn't live without her, that he loved her?

"I do. And you know how I feel about you." She pulled back from him, placing her hands on his cheeks. "What's bothering you? You're starting to scare me. It's not Justine; it's something else, isn't it?"

"I can't tell you how much you mean to me, how much you have changed my life. And, you should know that." He wrapped his arms tighter around her. "I don't know what I'd do without you."

"I'm not going anywhere, at least not until the fall," she attempted to joked with him. He didn't smile. "Oh my God. It's something terrible, isn't't?" She stared at him. When he didn't answer immediately, she asked, "Someone

shot at you, didn't they? Did they hit you? Say no, please."
Her voice wavered.

"No, nothing like that. Boy, you can go from one extreme to another in a split second. You can't worry about that. Promise me?" He didn't want her to turn into Lizz.

"I'll try not to."

"That's not a promise, but probably the best I can get right now." He had to lead up to the stalker carefully. "Let's talk about Justine first. The other thing can wait. What do you think? We never finished our conversation this morning."

She led him out to the deck. "So, what are you thinking?" she asked once they sat on the swing.

"I thought about what you said about not acting like a bull in a china shop. I agree. Things caused Justine to run and hide. I'll have a little heart to heart with Paul."

"Do you know why he chose not to tell Mrs. Colbert? What if he asks you to tell her so he won't break a promise he made to Justine? It's really messy, isn't it? However it works out, the case is solved. That's good, right? Why are you smiling?"

"Nothing. Just thinking we do have a happy ending, thanks to you."

"I'm not sure Mrs. Colbert will share your enthusiasm. She'll be thrilled to know that Justine is alive. And it's a family affair at this point, correct?" She expected no comment as she thought out loud. "Paul should handle this situation. But then, what will happen to his relationship with Mrs. Colbert when she finds out he knew all this? Do you think that Justine will talk to her mother?" She stopped for a second. "You have to tell Paul what you know."

"Yup. Lots of questions and not many answers. I'll call him and recommend he convene a family meeting. I can be there if he wants, we can be there together if you like. I'll wait to contact the Boston guys until I talk with him. I don't want this story to somehow blow up in the press before Paul or Justine has a chance to talk to Mrs. Colbert."

Now that they finished with the Justine discussion, he knew he had to tell to her about last night.

"Were you okay last night, before I fell into the living room and scared you half to death?" he called as walked to the kitchen and poured them both a cup of coffee.

"You know how I love thunderstorms." She followed him into the kitchen. "But…" she hesitated. "But this one was different somehow. I can't explain why. The thunder exploded and rumbled across the water, shaking the bed so much I couldn't fall asleep. Every time I thought about drifting off, a menacing clap woke me up. At one point, in between the roars, I thought I heard voices outside."

"Voices?" Jack handed her the cup of coffee.

"Probably weren't voices, but sounded like it." She shrugged. "I left my bedroom window open a crack. I can't sleep in a stuffy room." She sipped her coffee. "The noise could have been a car radio on the wharf. Why?"

"Anything else happen?" He tried to sound nonchalant, stirring sugar into the coffee.

"Something happened last night, didn't it? Tell me. Another woman on the beach?"

"No, God, no. Humor me. Tell me what went on before I arrived."

"After the voices, I looked at the clock. It was four o'clock, exactly. In my head, now this is going to sound really weird, I swear I heard Pita's voice say, 'Four is your lucky number.' Why would she say that?"

"Yup, why would she say that?" Jack hesitated a few seconds, figuring Pat's words meant that he would fall into the house at 4 a.m. and she would be safe. "Trust me, there's always something buried in what you experience, it just takes us awhile to figure it out." He cleared his throat, thinking how to begin.

"Scott told me about something that happened last night. I'm not sure what it means, but I think we need to be careful." He recounted the events that Scott and Teddy had been involved in. Jamie looked confused.

"Who is he? What does he want?" She placed her coffee cup on the counter. "He watched enough to know you were gone and that I was alone. Do you think he has something to do with Justine? No, he couldn't, could he?" Her speech accelerated as she eliminated possibilities. "Do you think he's the killer?"

"I don't know who he is... yet. When Scott spoke to him in the car, it was dark. He had longish light brown or blond hair that curled up at the back of his Yankees baseball cap. He looked away when Scott put the flashlight on him. Teddy said he stood about six feet two inches." He saw recognition on her face. "What?"

"Doesn't that sound like Matt to you?"

Jack knew that it hurt her to even ask that question. The thought had crossed his mind. Thinking it was Matt wasn't proving it. He hugged Jamie close. "I don't know. That description could fit a hundred men down here. Too early to tell, but I'm working on it." He kissed her gently on the lips. "You have to be careful, that's all. Promise?"

"I promise."

This time, although he managed a promise out of her, he didn't feel any better.

Chapter Fifty-Four

Jamie paced the floor waiting for an answer from Andrew, her computer security guru. She had called him after Jack told her about the stalker. "I have a favor to ask you, Drew. You can say no if you feel uncomfortable with it." She condensed her story down to someone shadowing her in Oyster Point and the description of the man that she suspected—Matt.

"Have you told the police down there?" Drew asked.

Jamie pictured Jack's razor in her bathroom cabinet. "I have and they're watching the cottage. But I'd like to be proactive about this. I don't want to feel like a victim. I was hoping you might be able to investigate Matt's digital traffic, maybe his cell phone usage, figure out his locations? I can give you dates and times."

If she could piece together where Matt had been last night, she'd know if he had been the one on the wharf watching her or worse, was around the nights the women had been found on the beach. Drew, a wizard at digging out information, had a large number of sources who could do background searches without being detected.

"I can look, but it might take a little time," Drew stated. Jamie heard the clicking of the computer keys as she provided Matt's information.

"Whenever and whatever you can find. Thanks Drew. I owe you."

"No. I just hope I find something. I'm not happy with you being in danger. Be in touch."

She heard the click as he hung up.

She faced the painting sitting on the easel. What if it wasn't Matt? Then what? That could make him anyone, a nameless, faceless stranger. The undefined male stared out at her. "Just like you," she said.

And why would Matt frighten her? What's his motive, as Jack would say? Matt had always been a total gentleman, opening the car door for her, ordering the wine. She had trusted him. Why would he change? Why would he be stalking her, hiding in bushes and peering at her from the wharf? It wasn't Matt's style, not the Matt she had known in Boston.

She felt so cold inside, like the night her parents had died. That night, she feared what would become of her, where she would live, and who would take care of her. Now, she feared this unknown man, what he wanted of her. She was terrified she knew him, frightened that she didn't.

Chapter Fifty-Five

"Okay Miss Jamie, I have a road trip for us today." Jack came through the cottage door and picked her up off the floor.

"I thought you had a very busy day?" she asked, securing her arms around his neck. "I'm glad you're here,'" she whispered against his cheek, knowing he had saved her from those inviting dark places that she was prone to go.

"What's going on? Something happen after I left?" He pushed her away so he could see her face.

"No. I just tend to go into overdrive sometimes."

"About what?"

"Nothing really. I stood looking at that damn painting," she said, pointing to the easel, "trying to solve the mystery man's identity."

"Well, how about you run away with me?" He slid her body along his until her feet touched the floor.

"That's the best offer I've had all day."

He pulled on her ponytail. "And, how many offers have you had?" he asked, his senses aroused.

"Let's see there was—" he tickled her before she could continue. Catching her breath, she asked, "So where are we off to?"

"Guess."

"Oh God, we aren't going to play this game again, are we?" She threw out, "Billings Island?"

"Is that the only place you've ever been?" he chided her.

"Down here, sure. Okay, I'll widen my horizons. Somewhere in Oyster Point?"

"No."

"No, huh. P'town?"

"No."

"Do we have to use your boat to get there?"

"Well, we could, but I think I'll drive."

"I give up. I have no idea. Have we gone there before?"

"Nope. And, you know the penalty for giving up." He smugly picked up her chin and kissed her lips as he tugged on the scrunchie holding up her ponytail. Her hair tumbled down over her shoulders as he threaded his fingers through the strands to find the tie that held the halter top straps around her neck.

He swept the ties off her shoulders, gliding them slowly down her arms. Pulling away to catch her breath, he watched her, his eyes, half closed, peering down at her, his breathing erratic. She touched his cheeks and kissed the tip of his nose.

"How do you do this?" he asked, kissing her eyes, cheeks, and then her lips.

"I'm glad you came back early." She snuggled her body against his.

"Not half as glad as I am." He rubbed his hands down her bare back, until they reached the other set of ties that held her halter top on. Pulling the loose ends of the bow, he continued to massage his way down to her waist.

She wrapped her arms around his neck and stroked the back of his neck, her fingers moving through his hair. He wanted to go for a haircut yesterday, but she persuaded him not to. She said that she loved his hair a tad too long.

"Well, where are we going?" her words sounded hushed.

"Right now?"

"When you came in?" she gave his hair a slight tug.

"My sister's." He swung her up into his arms, and carried her into the bedroom, her halter top drifting softly to the floor. "In a while."

Chapter Fifty-Six

Jack parked his SUV at the end of the long sandy driveway behind Jessica's dark blue Honda minivan. The front door of the house flew open and a petite, curly haired woman rushed down the stairs, the screen door slamming behind her.

"Finally," she threw out, almost knocking Jack over as she planted a kiss on his cheek. "I thought you would be here earlier."

"Got busy," he answered as he opened Jamie's car door.

"Oh, really? Doing what?" Jess smirked.

"Jamie, this is my busybody sister, Jessica. I'm already regretting bringing you here to meet her."

"It's nice to meet you, Jamie. Please, call me Jess, everyone does except, of course, for my big lug of a brother." Hugging her, Jess kicked Jack in his shin with her pink flip-flops.

"Ouch. You know, you always did that when we were kids. I should know better than to stand behind you." He jumped away as she kicked out at him again. "But then, I thought you were a mature, old married lady these days. Sorry, my mistake."

"I'm really pleased to meet you too, Jess." Jamie felt a small twinge of envy watching the easy interplay between the siblings, things she had never experienced as an only child.

"Come on in if you can stand the mess. Jack, Terry and the kids are out on the boat checking traps and should be home soon."

"The house is adorable," Jamie commented, walking up to the two story cedar shake Cape style house.

It resembled a fairy tale cottage with bright white wooden flower boxes below each window overflowing with brilliant pink petunias, cool blue lobelias, and silver leafed ivy.

"Thanks. It was in tough shape when we bought it."

"Tough shape is being kind," Jack said, tapping Jess on the top of her head. "I would have torn it down, but Jess and Terry thought it had good bones and they were correct. What they didn't expect was the long view to the ocean that appeared after we topped some trees and cut down others on the back hill. Wait till you see it."

Jack curled his hand around the back of Jamie's neck as they followed Jess through a bright yellow, high tech kitchen and out the French doors to a screened-in area. The porch, with a long wooden picnic table, a yellow and green flowered wicker couch, led to a deck beyond. The sweet smell of the petunias blooming in the hanging planters wafted over the entire deck. Jamie stood admiring the endless view of the Atlantic Ocean as it met a cloudless sky.

"You're so right," she said to Jack. "It's spectacular. You did a great job clearing the land, Jess."

"The yard resembled a jungle. As we hacked away at the undergrowth, we saw a tiny peek of water here and there. Terry and Jack figured out which trees had to come down. We still have a huge pile of firewood. Jamie, remind me later to show you the photos I took last fall of Terry and Jack, the woodsmen. I was sure the trees would land right on the house." Jess touched Jack's arm. "Yet, the house still stands, the view is awesome and the kids have a super back yard. Come, let's sit and talk until Terry gets back. Once he returns with the gremlins, there will be bedlam to deal with. Can I get anyone something to drink? Jack? Jamie?"

"Not for me right now, but thanks Jess. Jack, is the car unlocked? I left my camera in the console."

"I'll go." Jack started to get up.

She placed her hand on his arm. "You spend time with Jess and I'll be right back."

Walking to the car, Jamie thought about how she would give anything to have a sister like Jess, someone to talk with, confide in, and joke with. She had spent most of her young life talking with imaginary friends, like the stars, and then she found Kate.

No camera in the console. She reached under the front seat and found nothing but crumbs and a used napkin, the remainders of one of Jack's quick breakfasts. When was the last time he had vacuumed the inside of this car? She must have thrown the camera on the back seat when she left the cottage still feeling the afterglow. She smiled.

As she closed the front door, she heard a sound behind her, the cracking of a branch followed by what sounded like the click of a camera. She froze. An animal? She bit her lip to keep from calling for Jack.

Whoever this guy was, he was not forcing her to live in fear. Jack's key ring had his office keys on it. She placed them between her fingers. She'd gouge his eyes out if he came anywhere near her. She had used this technique when walking in the city at night.

She scanned the trees from behind her sunglasses, keeping her movements calm and natural. Nothing, she saw no one. If he was there, he was well hidden. Somehow that thought didn't make her feel any better.

Opening the back door, she grabbed her camera, flicked it on, and shot some photos toward the trees. The click of her camera sounded like a gun shot in the silence. She fumbled with the camera's lens cap and it dropped to the ground.

"Damn it," she mumbled, bending to retrieve the black dot on the sand. Why hadn't she hooked the damn cap to the camera? The back door swung into her, knocking her against the back seat.

The crackling sound of brush underfoot was loud and close. *Click, click, click....*

***

"Jamie seems really nice. You failed to mention, of course, that she was tall and drop-dead gorgeous," Jess kidded Jack as they both sipped lemonade on the back deck. She had offered him a beer, but he had passed on it, taking a glass of her homemade lemonade instead.

His baseball cap hid his eyes as he sat on the Adirondack chair, hands folded on his lap, looking out at the water. "She's a handful," he conceded, "even for me."

"Looks to me like you don't mind having your hands full. It's been a long time since you brought a woman to meet the family." Jess watched as Jack pushed his cap back.

"Yup, it has been."

"That's it? That's all you're going to say to me, your dear darlin' sister?" Jess leaned over and punched Jack on the bicep. He seemed relaxed today, enjoying himself. He had brought Lizz here and that didn't go exactly swimmingly.

"You didn't ask me anything," he teased.

"Okay then, tell me what's going on. Is this serious? You seem pretty hung up on her. Do I need to buy a new dress? Lose weight? Give me time, Jack."

"Pretty hung up on her? Yes. And lose weight if you want, but don't buy a new dress unless you have some place to wear it."

"Oh boy, this is going to be a long afternoon, I can tell."

"I don't know what you want me to say." He shrugged. "I like her. I like her a lot, okay? She's fun, thoughtful, smart, easygoing, and unpredictable. She's well-travelled, has a career of her own, and is a very talented artist like Pat was. Pat left her the Oyster Point cottage. She came down from Boston to clean it out and sell it in the fall."

Jess didn't like the sound of this. If Jamie left, Jack would be nursing his wounds like he did years ago after the Lizz breakup.

"Do you think she'll actually go back... leave you behind?"

"Don't know. She had a life before me. We've only known each other a short time. I hope not, but..." He hesitated. "You know as well as I do that she has to make that decision herself." His tone became flat as he stared at the ocean. "I can't make her stay, I'm not sure I can even ask her to stay."

"You have to give her a reason to stay." Jess could hear the pain in his voice. This gal had touched something inside him that Jess thought had died years ago. Her brother, the confirmed bachelor, the man who hadn't given any woman the right time of day in years, had allowed this one to slip under his skin. She could hear it in his voice, see it in his actions, her big brother was actually in love. Jess never believed that Lizz was right for him. She never liked her and guessed the feeling was mutual.

"I don't know how she feels. And, to tell you the truth, I'm afraid to ask. Maybe the answer won't be what I want to hear." He looked at Jess. "She's a tough cookie, has overcome a lot of difficulties in her life, the latest being the death of Pat. Both her parents died in an auto accident when she was a kid. She's an only child. Pat was a mother figure as well as her guardian." He stopped, taking his baseball cap off, adjusting the strap in the back and placing it back on his head. "She's fragile sometimes, yet tough. She's been on her own a long time and guards her feelings well. Who knows," he leaned over and grabbed Jess's curls. "Someday maybe I'll actually understand what's going on in her head. You women make it mighty tough on us poor guys." He tried to lighten the conversation.

"How did a young girl ever survive losing both of her parents? I thought it was bad when we lost Dad. But we had each other." The pain that she felt back then still existed sometimes. "She seems genuine, Jack. You have to let her know how you feel."

Before he could respond, he checked his watch. "Do you think she's been gone a long time?"

"A few minutes?"

"Too long. Why did I let her go alone? Son-of-a-bitch, if he does anything...." Jack was up and running through the porch into the house.

"Jack? What's the matter?" Jess called, as she ran through the kitchen trying to catch up with him.

Chapter Fifty-Seven

"How goddamn stupid am I?" Jack berated himself. "Please God, don't let me be too late," he prayed, jumping over the coffee table in the living room as Jess' voice faded behind him. He had no time to explain, he had to get to Jamie. He flung open the front screen door, reached the top step, and froze. His car sat in the driveway right where he had left it. She had sat up front, so why was the rear door ajar? He didn't have a good feeling about this.

"Jamie!" he yelled, placing his hand where his shoulder holster should be. "Damn." He had locked his Glock in Jamie's closet because he never wore it around Jess' kids.

Jess appeared behind him at the screen door. He signaled for her to stay inside and be quiet. He recognized the helpless, fearful look in her eyes. Again, he gestured for her to remain where she was. He crept down the stairs, scanning the trees along the drive. No sounds, no movement, no one. The pain in his chest took his breath away.

"If he hurts her, I'll tear him apart. I'll kill him," he whispered, his words jolting him. When he had killed in the past, he did it in self-defense or to protect the life of someone else. Yet today, right now, if this guy had laid one hand on Jamie, he would cause him pain, great pain. He was sweating even though it wasn't hot. He shoved his cap back and rubbed his sweaty face on his t-shirt sleeve.

Clear your mind, damn it. Jack took a deep breath. He crouched in front of the SUV, making his way around to the open door. The blood pounded in his ears.

A thud, the sound of feet hitting the ground was followed by, "Ouch."

Jack rounded the car door, coming face to face with Jamie fiddling with the cap on her camera lens.

She looked up in surprise. "Hi."

"Christ Almighty, I thought he had gotten you," he whispered, squeezing her so hard he thought he would break her in two.

"Hello to you, too. What are you talking about? Did you see him?"

"You were gone a long time." He backed her away from the car so he could shut the door. Stroking her hair, he leaned against the SUV so he faced the woods, his arms still around her. A quick flash—he saw it up behind the rocks.

She started to turn. "It's him, isn't it?"

"Shush... yes." His eye caught the sunlight playing off something in the distance, a glass, a mirror, or binoculars? His eyes kept searching the trees.

She started to speak when Jack clamped his hand across her mouth.

"Quiet... I think he's still here." He ran his fingers over her cheeks, "Listen to me carefully. I need you to walk up to the house, as though nothing is wrong, go inside with Jess, and lock the doors. Do you understand me?"

"I heard a noise," she started. He interrupted her again, this time by kissing her, which didn't deter her from continuing. "I took some photos of the woods. I couldn't see anything, but I could feel him near." Her words flowed faster and faster.

"I was frantic. How stupid was I to let you go out here alone? And don't answer that." He had to see her eyes while he spoke. "Please look at me. If anything had happened to you, I don't know what I would do." Leaning his forehead against hers, he said, "Well, in this case, I know exactly what I would do. I would hunt the bastard down and when I caught him ..."

This time, she placed her fingers across his lips. "Please find him and then we will figure out what to do with him."

He looked up to the pile of rocks where the flash had come. He saw nothing. He had to say these things, just in case. "This is not how I had hoped to say this, but I have to say it now." His heart rate accelerated as his words did. "I love you." He had no idea what she would say, but the words were out there.

When she stared at him and said nothing, he continued on. "I know it as sure as I'm standing here, holding you in my arms. When you didn't answer when I called, and by the way, why the hell didn't you answer me when I yelled?"

"I didn't hear you. I fell on the back seat when the car door hit me and then you arrived." She twirled her fingers through his hair. "Can you repeat what you just said, please?"

"I never felt fear like that. My chest tightened, I felt rage, blinding rage. You have to know how I feel, just in case. I love you very much, more than I ever thought possible, much more than I wanted to. I've fallen in love with you, Jamison Janson." He waited.

She brought his face down to meet hers. "Please don't keep saying 'just in case'—you frighten me when you say that. I love you too, Shane John Hereford. I didn't expect to fall in love with you either, not that there's anything wrong with you. I just didn't need any complications in my life." She caught her breath and continued. "I didn't want to be hurt again, you know that. I couldn't help it. I fell in love with you."

"When you didn't say anything and looked at me like I had three heads, I wondered if you were going to run." He kissed her nose and tapped her on the backside, like a little kid he was sending off. "Please, go to the house now. We will definitely finish this conversation later."

"What are you going to do? You don't have your gun."

"He's not after me—he wants you."

"He might go after you to get to me. He's sick, remember?"

"No kidding." He tried to lighten the mood. "I think I might know where he squatted to watch you. Please, go back to the house and wait. And don't tell my nosey sister anything until I get back."

"Just be careful. Now I can tell you that I do worry about you."

"I love you too," he whispered, releasing her hand as she walked toward the house.

Chapter Fifty-Eight

Jess reached for the screen door handle just as Jack turned to wave her off. She knew better than to cross him. Something was going on and she hadn't the foggiest idea what it was. She watched him slide the side of his t-shirt up, reaching for his holstered gun. It wasn't there. He looked back at her as if to say, "It's okay. Just stay where you are so I don't have to worry about you."

He called Jamie's name. No reply came back. He moved stealthily down the driveway, low to the ground. In an instant, he rounded the open door and had someone in his hands. Jess reached for the door handle, but remembered Jack's warning. The car door blocked her view. Then, as the door closed, Jack stood with his arms around Jamie.

"Oh, bro," Jess whispered, "you're in deep this time, very deep." She watched her brother caress Jamie's face and then she wrapped her arms around his neck. Her smile grew. "You are both in very deep. Hooray." She felt embarrassed watching the interplay and affection between them. *Wait till Terry gets wind of this.*

Jamie strolled up the driveway toward the house, leaving Jack leaning on the car. She looked back as he called to her. All Jess could hear was something about Jamie's camera. He strolled to the other side of the car, opened the front door and the next thing Jess knew, he disappeared. She pushed the screen door open for Jamie.

"What's going on? I've never seen Jack run that fast since he was a kid. And why is he looking for your camera when you have it?"

"He told me to tell you to wait until he returns and we'll talk about all this. Do you see him? Where did he go? He doesn't have his gun with him."

Jess heard the fear in Jamie's voice. "Where's he going? Should I call Terry and see if he can make it back to help him?" If anything happened to Jack, Jess knew she would carry the guilt. "It's my fault, you know, that he doesn't have his gun. I asked him not to wear it around the kids. Now, what if he needs it?"

"Please don't, Jess. You know Jack—he doesn't do anything he doesn't want to. He would never wear his gun here. Actually, he rarely puts it on when he is off duty."

"I don't have the slightest idea what's going on."

"He asked that we lock all the doors, so that's what we're going to do. And, about calling Terry, he couldn't find Jack now. He might even hinder him. Jack does his best work when he has no one to worry about."

"Except himself," Jess added, as she closed and locked the front door.

Chapter Fifty-Nine

Jamie's perfume wafted up to him as he moved from behind one tree to the rear of another, drawing closer and closer to her. He shifted his body around a scrub pine trunk, crouching low in the shade.

Only a few yards away, he focused his binoculars on her. He knew for sure that God had never created a more beautiful creature. She invaded his thoughts day and night. And, soon, with a little luck, all of his dreams would come true because he was running out of patience. His previous rescue plan had been washed away with the rain on the wharf.

How poetic of him, he smirked. She didn't belong with Mr. Detective. She belonged to him. He didn't want another lookalike. He loved her.

As Jamie leaned into the back seat of the car, his gaze travelled up the muscular calves, to the athletic thighs, and then across her shorts, pulled tight across her backside. She stretched forward and, much to his pleasure, raised her leg, resting her knee on the seat. His blood coursed through his veins, causing his head to spin, and his hearing to go dim. He could take her now, on the back seat of the Chief's car.

How perfect would it be if the arrogant jerk came out and found her writhing with pleasure under him on the back seat of his car? He caught himself about to laugh out loud. As much as he wanted to taunt the Chief, she deserved better than that. His Jamie should be made love to on a large, soft bed where they could roll on top of each other, her hair spilling over him, her breasts tantalizing him, her legs wrapped around him. His discomfort reminded him that he had to take her from that bastard's clutches first.

He refocused the binoculars, admiring the outline of what looked like blue flowered underpants under her white shorts. They hugged her hips. His thumb and forefinger moved together as though feeling the soft, silky panty in his hand. He imagined sliding them down those long tanned legs to her ankles, her kicking them to the side so she could move over him. He needed a release. He needed her. Standing, he stepped forward on the soft pine needles.

Crack.

The noise resounded through the silent pine grove. A hidden branch. He slithered back behind the tree. Using a mirror from his pocket, he watched her slide slowly out of the car and turn towards him. He raised his camera, clicking away. Maybe she hadn't heard the crack of the branch? She seemed more interested in her camera. *Click – click - click.* Had she heard him? Wanted to photograph him? He would let her take photos of him all day when they were together.

She dropped something small and black on the ground. As she bent over to pick it up, he leaned out and adjusted the camera so he could see into the gaping neckline of her sagging t-shirt. *Click, click.* Matching blue silk bra, she's that type, perfect in every way. The cheap pick-ups who stripped for him wore ragtag underwear, if they had any on at all. Except that last one, she had been classy, a silk thong and no bra and those glorious breasts. He'd been sorry to lose her. On the beach that last night, she had pleased him over and over again. But, then, they always wanted more.

The screen door clanged and Jack appeared on the top step.

Crap, that's what he got for daydreaming again. Jack called to her, like a dog. His hatred for Jack bubbled up in the back of his throat as he snuck back up the hill, one tree at a time as Jack approached the car. His mirror reflected the image of Jack caressing and kissing her. He had missed his chance—again. Jack, always there, watching and touching her. His anger rose by the second as he retreated up the hill farther and farther away from his Jamie.

Looking back using the mirror, he caught his foot on a hidden branch, cracking the glass against a small protruding rock as he fell. He sat for a moment on the pine needles, ensuring that his fall hadn't been heard. Jack, too enamored with Jamie, hadn't heard a thing. He checked his binoculars. They were unbroken, but where was the cap? He checked where he had fallen. Not there. He couldn't take the chance of retracing his steps now. He would have to return after Jack and Jamie left.

The mirror could be replaced. No big loss. And his hand only had a minor cut. He wiped the blood on his jacket sleeve and struggled up the hill until he reached the large rock where his backpack sat. Fumbling inside, he pulled out his favorite keepsake, a pair of Jamie's silk panties. He had managed to steal them off the drying rack on the deck when she was away from the cottage. He brought them to his nose. Too bad she had washed them. He folded them carefully, placing them back inside the backpack. Taking out a piece of paper towel, he wiped the lens of his camera and binoculars and packed them inside his bag, throwing the towel away.

Lifting the pack from the ground, he stole one last glance at Jamie. Then, crawling up the hill, he disappeared into the dense scrub pine forest.

Chapter Sixty

Jack circled around the back of Jess' house. Staying low, he sought coverage in bushes and behind trees as he attempted to retrace the path the stalker had taken to spy on them. Maybe he was still lurking around. Trying not to disturb any debris, he made his way to the hill where he thought that he had had seen the glints of light. Using his car as a starting point, he swept the ground around the trees, hoping to see evidence of the stalker. Nothing.

He could have grabbed her, damn it. He must have followed them, but he hadn't seen him. Jack picked up a rock and hurled it into the trees. The flutter of wings broke the silence as frightened birds took to the sky.

Didn't he work? Jack slammed his hand against a tree, frustrated because this guy seemingly came and went without anyone spotting him. He's not stupid. Jack bent down to pick up a broken branch. How could he find where he stood with hundreds of trees all over this damn hill? He sniffed the cracked wood. A new break. He fingered the branch. His car sat no more than twenty feet away. The stalker stood here watching her.

Jack grabbed a roll of yellow crime tape and gloves from the glove compartment of his SUV. Marking the trees with trunks large enough to hide a man, he climbed higher and higher up the slope, checking around each of the chosen trees. All he had found was the broken branch which proved nothing, he thought, as something shiny caught his eye. Smiling, he took out his phone and called Phil.

***

Sitting on deck chair, Jack pushed his baseball cap back, removed his sunglasses, and rubbed his eyes. "I called Phil. He should be here soon." He focused on Jamie.

"What did you find?" Her voice sounded hoarse.

"I'm not sure, some broken branches, a smashed mirror, and something that looked like a red liquid, blood maybe. With any luck, the bastard is bleeding to death somewhere."

"Oh my God, he was that close," she inhaled, handing Jack her camera. "I took a couple of photos. Maybe I caught him in one."

Jack clicked through the pictures. A shadowy figure or was it just a tree? He moved to the next one. A man? Hard to tell.

"Okay, I've been sitting here quietly listening to you both talk in code. I don't understand what the hell's going on. Whose blood? Jack, please tell me what's going on?" Jess begged.

Looking up from the camera, Jack sought Jamie's approval to share her story. She nodded. And so, Jack recounted the main episodes that led up to today's fiasco, leaving out any discussion of Jamie's nightmares.

Jess sat frozen, listening to the encounters, the stalking, and the bodies. "Oh my good God, I can't believe this. I have chills," Jess hugged herself. "Who is he, do you know?" She glanced at Jamie, then Jack.

"We have some ideas, but nothing definite."

"You think he killed those women on the beach?" Fear coated Jess' words.

"I wish I knew, trust me. So far Phil doesn't have any evidence that those women were murdered, although he suspects that they all had sex before the ..." Jack hesitated, seeing horror and disgust on Jess' face, "the accidents. The bodies floated in salt water for a while, compromising the evidence. They all looked alike, tall and blonde, in their thirties." Jack hadn't told Jamie the details of the most recent body they found. "Last week, a nude woman washed up with a rope around her ankle." Jamie turned to him with fear in her eyes, and then it turned to anger.

"It's me, isn't it? These women are dying because of me. He's killing lookalikes. If only I hadn't come down here this summer, those women might still be alive." She stood and began to pace. "I've done all this, three deaths, maybe more."

"We don't know that." Jack's blood froze as he watched and listened to Jamie, her voice flat and monotone. "We don't know how long he's been stalking you... maybe you're just his type." It was a lame response, he knew. "So far, Phil has listed the deaths as accidental and I can't prove him wrong. And, if you hadn't come down this summer..." the look in his eyes finished the sentence.

"We have to find him and stop him. He's sick, vicious, and he'll kill more women. We have to give him what he wants."

"We will do nothing until Phil completes his analysis on what I found today. Do I make myself clear?" Jack tried to look stern as he shifted his gaze from Jess to Jamie. "Do I have agreement from you two? You will do nothing until I've talked to Phil?"

"I can't do anything because I don't understand what's going on," Jess acquiesced.

"I'll wait to hear Phil's take on today." Jamie didn't look at Jack.

"What does that mean? You won't do anything today, but maybe tomorrow you will? Or you'll wait until we have all the evidence?" He had to know that she wouldn't do anything foolish.

"I won't do anything stupid, if that's what you're worried about. I've done enough of that lately." Jamie looked Jack into his eyes, "But we have to end this. I can't sit by and let innocent women die because of me."

Phil interrupted the conversation, walking onto the deck unexpectedly, the screen door slamming behind him.

"Sorry, I rang the bell, but no one answered, so I let myself in. Let's get to it, Jack. What've you got for me?"

As Phil followed Jack outside, he turned the piece of broken mirror over in his gloved hands, testing the red smudge. "It's definitely blood."

"Can we use it?" Jack questioned. "All I want to know is can you get DNA from it?"

"Well," Phil walked around the rock picking up shards of glass and bagging them, "I think we have DNA and even a fingerprint or two, but unless I have something to compare them with, none of this will help. If he's in the system for some reason, we'll be lucky. If not," Phil shrugged.

Jack acknowledged his statement. His attention turned back toward Jess' house where Jamie stood on the stairs, shading her eyes from the sun, watching them. He had to find this guy. One of these days, if he didn't stop him, he would take her. He had to protect her because it was his job, but most of all, because he loved her.

"Jack?"

"What?" Jack snapped. He realized that Phil had asked him a question. "I'm sorry Phil. I was trying to figure out how I could catch this guy. What did you ask me?"

"I know you want to protect her, but you have to stay focused. How would you catch him if he wasn't after her?" Phil nodded in Jamie's direction as he continued selecting debris from around the broken mirror. "I asked if you had any idea who he was."

"We can only guess who he might be and no DNA."

"I need it, Jack." Phil insisted, frustration showing in his tone.

"I know. We both know what I have to do to catch him. It's harder for me this time because I have more at stake." Jack watched Jamie disappear into the house.

"I know it's difficult, but remember, you're the best at catching guys like this." Phil collected his bags. "You need to get into his head, figure out what he'll do next based on his previous actions. I'll do what I can with this stuff, but call me with any other information you gather. You can never tell what piece may make this story complete. And DNA, I need DNA."

"Thanks Phil." Jack patted him on the back, then headed to the house.

Chapter Sixty-One

Jamie pushed her eyeglasses to the top of her head. Tilting her chair back, she stared at the blank computer screen, willing something to appear. It had been almost a week since she'd talked to Drew. She had to do something, but what?

In the bedroom, Jack slept, his arm across his eyes blocking out the sunlight. When they returned last night, he had removed the baby Glock that he had given her out of the locked box on the floor of the closet and placed it in the top drawer of her night table, next to her side of the bed.

"Use it if you have too," he said, "except not on me." He had strapped his own gun under his shirt and left for the office.

Jamie hated guns, detested having one near her, and the thought that she might have to use it made her nauseous. Jack taught her how to handle this gun at the police shooting range. It was small and fit easily into her hand.

As much as she wanted to lock it up again after he left, she had to admit, she felt better with it next to her and she had fallen asleep immediately. One of Jack's men had been not far from her front door, keeping watch until Jack had returned around dawn. He managed to tiptoe into the bedroom without breaking everything in his path. She felt his kiss as he wrapped his arms around her and, fully clothed, had fallen into a deep, sound sleep. He slept quietly, his breathing regular.

Looking down at him, she wondered how, in just a few months, her entire world had been turned upside down. One moment, she was totally in charge of her life and the next minute, two men interrupted her life's rhythm; this man, asleep in her bed, who brought sunshine into her heart and made her feel safe, and an unknown man who occupied the shadows of her existence, made her fearful and hesitant. Her heart accelerated when either of them was near.

Jack took a deep breath and turned over on his side.

Yesterday had been wonderful, except for the fright filled middle hours. She touched his hair. After Phil left Jess' house with his baggies, Jack and Terry fired up the grill. Jack cooked the fresh cod that Terry and the boys had brought back and he teased Terry about how scrawny the five steaming lobsters looked. Terry, in turn, ragged on Jack about Jamie, asking him how tight the leash around his neck felt. Jack glanced at Jamie, mimicking a choking motion with a hand around his neck, saying, "I hope it's tightening, I still have room to breathe." Terry gave him a brotherly hug.

Jack had a wonderful connection to them. The kids adored him, jumping all over him, Jess was the protective older sister, and Terry was like his brother. How lucky he was to have a family who loved him and accepted him no matter what.

"And I stupidly put them all in danger," she whispered. She picked up the coverlet from the chair and placed it over Jack's shoulders.

After dinner, the four adults had relaxed on the deck, stomachs full, watching the colors of the sunset bounce off the eastern clouds and the distant water. She leaned against Jack as they sat on the glider, his arm around her. No one said anything until Jess couldn't contain herself anymore and stated, in no uncertain terms, "What the hell are we going to do about this guy?"

Terry, angry when he heard the story, volunteered to help Jack catch "the creep." "Shit Jack, I'm with you all the way."

"Will you please watch your language Terry? I don't want you to forget and talk like that in front of the kids," Jess scolded.

"Well, I'm still with you, Jack. What can I do to help," Terry winked at Jamie, "I'm a Navy SEAL, well, was years ago. Not sure that's a help, but I can shoot a fly off the back fence from…."

"Terry?" Jess hugged him. "No gun talk, please?"

"Yes, ma'am." Terry grabbed Jess, tilted her back, and placed a big wet kiss on her lips. "Can the kids see this?" He tickled her until she collapsed on the floor laughing.

"Mimicking the photo of the Navy sailor in Times Square?" Jack grinned and grabbed Jamie, lifting her right off the swing, swung her around, and planted a long sexy kiss on her. "How's that, Terry?" as Jamie feigned a fainting spell, her hand to her head.

"Not bad, not bad at all. You're catching on quick, bro." Terry slapped him on the back, as he grabbed Jess off the floor.

She hadn't laughed so hard in a long time. When it was time to leave, Jess and Terry gave her a hug, saying how glad they were to have her there and "come back with or without the big lug." She heard the whispers to Jack that they would do anything they could to keep her safe from this "crazy," as Jess called him. For those few hours, she felt like she was part of a family again.

Her computer interrupted her thoughts. Back in the living room, she turned on the computer camera and Drew appeared on the screen. Jamie watched and listened.

"Are you sure?"

"Positive. I'm sorry if it's not what you wanted to hear."

"I'm sorry too." She sunk back in her chair. "Thanks Drew. I'll be in touch."

"I'm here if you need more help. Again, I'm sorry. Be safe."

"Talk later. Thanks." She turned off the camera, closed the lid of her computer, and walked to the deck. Matt's phone had made no calls during the times that she had provided to Drew. So she had no idea where he had been.

"I heard what he said." Jack came up behind her, wrapping his arms around her. "It will be okay, I promise. We'll get him."

Jack's words, well meant, chilled her. "You can't promise," she whispered, as she held on to him. "No one can promise that."

Chapter Sixty-Two

"I'm not happy with this visit," Jack repeated for what seemed like the hundredth time as he pulled into the parking garage under Matt's office building.

"I know, but we need his DNA and I'm the only one who can get it." She pulled down the mirror on her visor, fluffed her hair, and added a bit more lipstick. "Wish me luck." She kissed Jack on the cheek, opened the car door, and walked to the elevator, wearing her Jimmy Choo beige patent strapped heels that Jack loved, a royal blue Chanel suit, a matching beige leather Choo bag slung over her shoulder. She knew Matt's clientele well and she would blend right in.

Knowing that Jack was watching her every move, she turned, blew him a kiss, and entered the elevator.

***

Arriving on the seventeenth floor, Jack still hadn't decided what he was going to do. The office listings showed Hollings and Son in Suite 1721. Dressed casually, a dark brown polo shirt with a collar, a lightweight beige jacket, khaki slacks, and brown loafers, he had hoped Jamie would ask him to go to Matt's office with her. He knew better. She would handle this alone because she was angry and wanted her life back. By habit, he patted his jacket for his gun. She made it perfectly clear that she would acquire Matt's DNA, one way or another and he was not to interfere.

He paced in front of the elevator. He admired her tenacity; Jamie knew what had to be done to nail this guy and she would do it. Fear never kept her from anything.

A door opened and two men walked out of an office, exchanging papers. He recognized Matt. If only he could grab him and pull some of that dirty blond hair out of his head. Instead, he froze. Jack knew that if Matt recognized him, he might blow the whole thing for Jamie. And boy oh boy, would she be angry.

Facing the stainless steel elevator doors, Jack had a perfect view of Matt's reflection as he passed by. Matt never looked up from the papers in his hand. He and his fellow lawyer entered through a set of frosted glass doors at the end of the corridor where Jack made out a blue blur—Jamie. Then the doors closed.

Chapter Sixty-Three

Jamie chatted with Matt's secretary, Carla. A single woman in her forties, Carla had worked for Matt's father's law firm since she was twenty-two. When Jamie first met Matt, she couldn't figure out which of the two men, Matt or his father, Carla had her hooks out for. Both men were single; Matt's father, Edward, a charming, handsome man in his late fifties, had invited Jamie out to dinner a number of times, to the consternation of his son. Edward had divorced Matt's mother, Yvonne, years ago, and never remarried, although he always managed to have an attractive woman on his arm. He had stayed with Yvonne as she died in the hospice. Jamie figured that he loved her, just couldn't live with her.

Carla, a petite, hard looking redhead, dressed expensively. Jamie remembered Carla as a blonde the last time she saw her.

"You look wonderful as a redhead," she remarked to Carla.

"It's a wig. You can change your appearance with just a tweak here and there, can't you?" Carla gave her a cold icy stare that stopped her from responding for a moment.

What was she saying? "Well, the color goes wonderfully with your skin. You are a natural redhead." She controlled her emotions. "Carla, can I use the ladies room? It was a long drive up."

"Of course. Use our private one. You know where it is."

"I do. Thanks," Jamie answered as she entered the bathroom off the waiting room. Once inside, she twisted the lock, leaned against the door, and held out her trembling hands. Fearing the nausea she felt might cause her to vomit, she leaned over the sink.

All this time, they assumed that the stalker was a loner who looked like Matt. But what if he had help – a woman? Carla? Or maybe it was Carla alone? Using a wig? Except, Carla was not six feet tall. Jamie splashed cold water on her cheeks. As she toweled her face, she saw Carla's lipstick sitting on the counter. Using a plastic bag from her pocket, she scooped up the tube. Turning it over, it read "Frosty Melons." She almost laughed out loud. How appropriate, she thought, placing the bagged tube in her pocket. There was nothing of Matt's in sight. He used his private bathroom off his office. That's where she had to go next.

A knock on the door made her jump. Carla voiced, "Jamie, Matt just called and he's on his way back. Are you okay?"

Jamie swung the door open, hoping to catch Carla leaning against it. She wasn't. "I'm fine, thanks, Carla. Shall I just go into Matt's office and wait?"

"Why don't you just wait here?" Carla's question was really a statement. She turned and sauntered back to her desk, adjusting her tight fitting red silk blouse over her ample hips.

Jamie sat down and the door opened. Matt strode in, looking as handsome as ever. Deep in conversation with the other lawyer, he didn't notice her until he looked up from the document in his hand. He passed the papers to the other lawyer and dismissed him with, "I'll catch you later, Tom. I have to take care of this now," pointing to where she sat, legs crossed.

Tom's gaze took in Jamie's pink polished toe nails, travelled up her long, tanned, bare legs to her unbuttoned jacket and matching blue silk chemise. She watched his eyes move up to her pink glossed lips, at which time she bestowed her sexiest smile. She had him.

Without taking his eyes off her, he said to Matt, "I can see you are going to have your hands full. I'll make a few phone calls about this matter and get back to you later, if you're here." He nodded toward Jamie, smirking.

Tom's smugness annoyed her. Surprising that Matt and his father would tolerate such openly chauvinistic behavior from one of their lawyers, especially since he had no idea who she was. She played along, uncrossing and crossing her legs. She needed Matt on her side right now.

Matt extended his hand, helping her out of the soft beige leather chair. He gave her a hug and whispered, "Boy, have I missed you." He kissed her on the cheek. "You look gorgeous. Looks like Oyster Point really agrees with you." He opened the door to his office and held it for her. "Come in and we can talk. You have to forgive Tom. He's a great lawyer, but a bit of a jerk sometimes. What brings you up here? Everything okay?"

Turning, Jamie caught Carla on her cell phone speaking Spanish. "Everything's fine. I had a business meeting," she lied, "and thought I would stop and check on the status of Patrice's estate. I'd like to have a clear title to the cottage so I can sell it." She walked to the window. She had always loved Matt's view, a panorama that included a full view of Boston Harbor and the Custom House, her favorite building.

"Surprises me. The last time we talked, you seemed pretty happy down there. Trouble in paradise with the Chief?"

"What? Oh no, why?" She watched his face, but there was no indication of him mocking her.

"Well, you're talking about selling. I thought you two were close, that's all. I actually didn't think you would sell Pat's cottage." He hesitated. "Do you need money? I can lend you some to tide you over."

"God, no. I don't need money." He was being so solicitous, like the old Matt.

"Then why are you thinking of selling the cottage? You love that place." His smile was warm and genuine. "Are you moving in with him?"

"Oh my Lord, no. You sure are jumping to conclusions today." Shaking her head, she continued, "Have you seen where he lives?" She tried to act as natural as she could. "I'm not sure I'll sell, but I want to be able to if I want to, that's all. How far away are we from the probate being complete? "

"It's on the Judge's desk. I'm waiting for him to review it and sign off. Are you sure you're okay?"

"I had a long meeting. You know how that is. Can I use your bathroom to freshen up?" She pointed to Matt's private bathroom.

"Absolutely. Would you like a coffee or cold drink?"

"Coffee would be terrific, thanks," she answered as she closed and locked the door behind her. Matt's hairbrush rested on the counter and his toothbrush stood in a clear stand by the faucet. Either one of these items would be missed if she took them. She quietly opened the cabinet over the sink and saw a treasure trove of razors and combs.

Chapter Sixty-Four

"Are you sure you're okay?" Matt questioned again. "You seem on edge." Standing in the parking garage, he placed his hands on her shoulders. "Something's wrong, I can tell."

It took all of Jamie's strength to keep from pulling away from him. Instead, she placed her cold hand over his. "I'm fine, really I am. I'm juggling a lot of things right now." She hated using her great-aunt's death as an excuse, but she was desperate. "It's hard going through Patrice's belongings." She hoped that he would be satisfied with that excuse.

"Your hands are so cold." He rubbed her hands in his. "Can I help? I could rent a truck and make runs to the dump for you."

The image of Matt tossing rubbish into the back of a pickup truck, dressed in his Armani suit, wingtip shoes, and his eyes shaded by Versace sunglasses made her laugh. In all the time she had known him, she had never seen him in a pair of jeans. Casual for Matt meant his jacket off and his tie loosened.

"I appreciate the offer, but I'm good right now. Maybe later, when I have things more organized inside the cottage. I promise I'll call if I need help."

"You know, I've really missed you." He continued to rub her cold hand in his and then pressed them to his lips. "I had forgotten what a beautiful woman you are."

The nausea started again. If she pulled away, he would suspect something. "I've missed our talks too." Her words sounded hollow and forced.

"Come back to Boston. You don't have to live down there. You have an apartment here. We can meet like we used to do, talk, and have dinner."

"Have you met anyone this summer?" Jamie forced the conversation away from herself, hoping to pick up information about what he did this summer.

"That's one of the things I wanted to talk to you about. Her name is Sidney. She's a lawyer. We met in the courtroom, the Reisien murder trial? Remember how that was dragging on last year and my father wanted nothing to do with it? After he handed it over to me, I knew why he didn't want to represent this client. He had nothing to present to the jury to prove his innocence except for a few circumstantial items that could be blown away in court." He pushed a stray strand of hair off her forehead. "To make a long story short, I lost the case to Sidney. When I left the courtroom, she was waiting for me and asked if we could have drinks some night. She's like you, interesting, bright and beautiful. We met for dinner and found we had a lot in common. You know my father," his smile disappeared. "Her Dad is a carbon copy. He owns Hadley and Hadley. Sidney is the second Hadley."

Standing there, Matt seemed his old self, animated, interesting, and talkative. He talked as though everything was normal and that was the dangerous part of him.

"... and so that's why I'd love you to meet her, have your opinion on us. You know I've always valued your opinion on everything," Matt concluded.

"I'd love to meet her. Not sure when since I'm in Oyster Point for most of the summer." The more she considered it, the more she thought this meeting might work out well. It would give Jack a chance to exercise that gut feeling of his that he's always touting.

He kissed her cheek. "Let me know when you'll be back up and we'll meet."

"I'm happy for you Matt. Call you as soon as I have a date." She waved as she walked toward the car where Jack sat watching the entire episode.

Chapter Sixty-Five

On a beautiful, warm, late August night, Jack and Jamie strolled hand in hand down Charles Street in Boston to the Liberty Hotel, the old home of the Charles Street Jail, to meet Matt and his girlfriend, Sidney.

"This is the craziest thing I've ever done, meeting a suspected serial killer in an old jailhouse for drinks." He took her elbow as they neared the pub. "I don't like this anymore than I liked him kissing you in his garage."

"You've become very possessive lately, Chief," she kidded him. "You know as well as I do that we can gather information this way. As long as he's sitting with us, we know exactly where he is."

Jack opened the door. "You are much too logical, my lady," he whispered in her ear. "If DNA results were in, I'd be arresting him tonight, instead of socializing with him."

"Shhhhhh," she warned as she glanced around the room. "They're over there in the corner booth. Please behave as though you don't suspect anything." She snatched his hand. "Act cozy. We might generate a jealous reaction from him."

"I can do lover boy." He kissed the top of her head. "Here we go," he whispered, extending his right hand to Matt, keeping his left hand in the small of Jamie's back. "Matt."

"Chief." Matt shook Jack's hand. He leaned in and kissed Jamie on the cheek.

"I'd like you both to meet Sidney Hadley. Sidney, this is Jamie Janson and Chief Hereford, Jack." Putting his arm around Sidney, Matt continued, "I told you about Jamie, my long-time friend and confidant. She inherited her grandaunt's cottage in Oyster Point on the Cape and I'm handling the probate for her." Sidney nodded. "Jack was a Boston Police Detective before he became the Chief of Police in Oyster Point. I guess that's a quick summary." He held the chair out for Sidney. "Shall we all sit? I don't know about anyone else but I'm starving."

"So nice to meet you, Sidney." Jamie clasped Sidney's hand and sat down across from her, apologizing for her cold hands. "I'm cold sometimes, even in the summer."

"She's not lying. When she visited me in the office a few weeks ago, her hands felt like ice," Matt added.

"I've been to Oyster Point and love it there. Such a quaint little town," Sidney added.

Jamie nodded. Looking across the table, she felt as though she was looking in a mirror. Sidney sat with the same hair, same height, even the same color eyes. Grasping Jack's hand under the table, she listened to Sidney describe how she and Matt battled in the court room. Jack rubbed her hand. He saw the same thing: Matt's next victim.

Sidney asked her how she and Jack had met and how long they had been in a relationship.

A relationship? The term sounded so serious, so long term, and so alien to her. She who avoided permanency of any kind, rented her apartment, dated most men no more than five times, and worked for herself, didn't want an anchor, attachments, or more hurt.

She turned to Jack, "We've been seeing each other a few months." She rubbed Jack's fingers. "I met him the day I opened up Pita's cottage in April. I was running and crashed into him on the beach," she joked, trying to act natural.

"Four months and sixteen days ago," Jack added, placing his arm around Jamie's back, his hand rubbing the back of her neck. "Not that I'm counting."

Why did he have that number at his fingertips? He smiled at her and her heart warmed. She felt safe with him; he wouldn't hurt her... would he?

"Well, there's such a thing as love at first sight you know." Sidney cuddled closer to Matt, kissing him on the cheek, "Even when you're standing in a courtroom looking across the table at the opposition."

"I certainly agree." Jack drew Jamie closer. He mouthed, "I love you," as his eyes turned to watch Matt's reaction.

She squeezed his hand.

"I guessed right about you two," Matt remarked as he watched the interplay between them. "Jack, you seem to make her happy. I'm glad. Jamie and I have been floundering around, adrift for a while without anchors. I think we may both have found that perfect someone." He kissed Sidney's hand.

"Well, before you embarrass Jack and me anymore, I'm going to the powder room. Jamie, are you with me?" Sidney adjusted her cocoa brown fitted jacket as she slid out from behind the table. Tall, she wore sling back spike heels that showcased her well-muscled legs.

"I'm right behind you." Jamie rose, but not before squeezing Jack's knee and whispering in his ear, as Matt spoke to Sidney, "Be a good boy while I'm gone. I'll see what she knows. You work on him. His anchor metaphor was creepy."

Chapter Sixty-Six

Jack checked his watch. Jamie and Sidney had been gone for over fifteen minutes. Any time she was out of his sight, he felt uneasy these days. Matt sat in front of him, so what could go wrong? Yet, his gut told him that something wasn't right. Matt rattled on about his recently finished case, describing his sleazy male client, declaring how commanding Sidney had been in the courtroom. Jack couldn't say why, but he found it real hard to associate this man in front of him with the guy on the wharf or in the woods near Jess' house. He didn't even seem to be the same guy who was pawing Jamie at the cottage.

Matt was a prominent lawyer. Could this guy be a cold hearted murderer, a peeping Tom? It didn't make any sense. Jack had yet to fit the pieces of these murders together. And the bits concerning Matt certainly didn't add up.

Something sparkled on the floor—Jamie's opal. It must have fallen off when she stood up. It flashed red as he picked it up. Patrice's belief that the opal had magic and could keep Jamie safe always had him laughing. He looked over at Matt. The necklace felt warm in his palm as he slipped it into his jacket pocket.

Matt finished his sentence and waited for Jack's response.

"I'm sorry Matt, my mind wandered off. I was wondering where our gals are."

"You know women when they go into a ladies' room together. They're probably comparing notes on us," Matt joked.

"I'm going to the men's room. I'll be right back."
As Jack approached the men's room door, a young woman
rushed out of the ladies' room, smacking into him.

"Oh, I'm terribly sorry," she apologized.

"No harm. I wasn't really looking. Ah...," Jack
pointed to the ladies' room exit, "Could you do me a favor
and ask a woman named Jamie to come out when she can?"

"I don't think there was any one in there but me,"
the young woman answered.

"Are you sure?" Jack's words became louder,
clipped. "There should be two women in there." He heard a
swishing sound in his ears.

"I'm pretty sure. I'll check again if you want me
to," the young woman replied, heading through the door.

Matt joined him. "What's up?"

"We'll see in a second."

"Sorry, no one." The young woman shook her
head. "But I have to find the manager, the window fell out.
Not sure how that happened."

"Fell out?" Jack pressed her. "What do you mean?"

"The window's gone. Bugs are flying in
everywhere. I'm sure if it stays that way, people from the
alley might come into the ladies' room. The owner should
close off the room until that window is fixed." The woman
headed to the front of the restaurant.

"You bastard." Jack turned so abruptly that Matt
bumped his head against the wall. "How'd you do it?" Jack
clutched Matt by the jacket lapels. "You hired someone to
grab them while you had me feeling safe, sitting there,
chatting with you, didn't you?"

Matt coughed as Jack tightened his collar. "What
the hell's the matter with you?" Matt wound his hands
around Jack's, yanking on them, trying to loosen Jack's
grip.

"Where's Jamie?" Jack's face was inches away
from Matt's.

"Have you gone berserk? What the hell are you talking about?"

A passerby moved away from both of them as Jack pressed his knuckles into Matt's neck. "If you hurt her, I'll kill you, do you hear me?" His words came quietly. "As God is my witness, I will kill you."

Matt gasped, thrusting Jack back against the Men's room door. "You're crazy; you know that, you're crazy."

Jack's phone rang. "This better be her." It wasn't. "Hi Phil. Did you get the results? What?" He loosened his hold on Matt's neck.

"Are you sure?" Jack glowered at Matt, blocking him from moving anywhere. "What does that mean?" Jack listened for a few seconds and then added, "She's gone, Phil." Jack released Matt, pushing him to the side. "So where does that leave us? A what? You're breaking up." He listened to Phil, responding." "Yup, got it. Thanks, I'll call you back."

"What do you mean Jamie's gone? Gone where? She's with Sidney."

"Did you hear that woman? There's no one in there. The window's gone. They're gone." Jack pointed around the vicinity.

"What the hell's happening? Gone where?" Matt grabbed Jack's arm as Jack tried to push him aside, walking to the front door of the restaurant.

"They're gone and you know where they are." Jack shoved Matt out the door. "That, my friend, is what's happening."

Matt turned, causing Jack to stop short. "Where are we going? Why are we leaving without them?" He placed his hand on Jack's chest, pushing him back. He matched Jack physically, in height and weight, but not in strength.

"I don't know how you did it or what game you're playing, but if you don't tell me now, I'll do something I'm might regret later. I know you'll regret it."

"Tell you what?"

"How you got Jamie out of the bar. Who helped you?"

"I still don't have any idea what you're talking about." Matt started back into the bar. "They're still in there, they have to be."

"No, they aren't. Somehow Jamie and Sidney disappeared right under my nose, out that window."

"You know how insane that sounds. Why would they do that? You've been watching too many TV shows."

"Really? Too much TV? What about the guy who's been frightening the life out of her, following her, watching her? Like you don't know?" Jack hit the wall with his fist. "If she's hurt..."

"Excuse me, guys. Can you take this disagreement down the street, please? You're scaring our customers," the pub manager approached Jack and Matt.

"Sorry. Are you going in to check the ladies' room window?" Jack asked.

"I'm heading there now."

"I'm an off duty Boston detective. Maybe I can help." Jack didn't have the time to explain the entire sequence of events to the manager. A little white lie wouldn't hurt and he needed to see the window area, check for clues. "This is my associate, Matt."

After the walkthrough of the ladies' room, Matt asked, "Someone's been stalking her?" He leaned against the outside wall of the bar. "Why didn't she tell me? Call me? Maybe I could have done something." He grabbed Jack's arm. "Where's Sidney? Are you telling me someone took both of them? Out through that window? That's impossible. How does someone abduct two women against their will and lug them through that opening?"

"You tell me." Jack patted the piece of glass he had rescued from the floor in the ladies' room. He had wrapped it in a piece of toilet paper. He wasn't sure, but it appeared to have a red smudge on it, possibly blood. Phil could test it.

"You're proposing to help her now? After you scared the bejeezes out of her all summer?" Jack secured Matt's arm and forced him up the street. "I was so sure it was you. Now, I find out that there's only a family DNA match. Where's your father? And where's your car?"

"My father? You think my father had something to do with this?" He stopped and shoved Jack's hand away. "Hold it. Let's straighten this out here and now. Before Jamie came to my office a few weeks ago, I hadn't seen her since April."

"I talked to you in Oyster Point, at the cottage. She took you to the club. You waited for her at the beach."

"Me? Are you crazy? I never met you until tonight." Matt hesitated, his voice cracking as he seized Jack's arm. "Oh my God, run. I know who it is. Let's go."

Chapter Sixty-Seven

The room smelled musty. Jamie shivered on the cold, wet dirt. She had no idea how long she had been unconscious. She remembered standing in the ladies' room chatting with Sidney. There was a noise, glass shattered, she turned to see what happened and then, nothing. When she came to, she found herself tied up and stuffed into the back of a van. Sidney sat next to her moaning, her head thudding against the wall with every bump. The world swirled again and she remembered nothing more.

"Sidney?" she whispered through the dark, heavy air. She felt dizzy, disoriented, and alone. "Sidney, are you there?" She extended her hands, tied at the wrist in front, and watched them be sucked into the black void. A moan?

"Sidney, is that you? Are you okay?" she whispered again. Forcing herself up on her knees, she attempted to stand. Without the use of her hands and a rope secured around her ankles, she tumbled back against the wall, knocking her head against jagged, jutting hunks of rock, scraping her elbows as she slid down.

"Ouch. Goddamn it, I'll kill myself before he has a chance to do it." She lifted her hands up and massaged the lump forming on the back of her head. Jamie recognized the rope around her ankles, the killer's signature. The other women probably started here, like this. She felt woozy. How did he manage to kidnap them both? Chloroform? Out of Jack's sight for a few minutes and somehow the weirdo caught her and Sidney as well. He could've left her behind, but instead he took her too. Why? Maybe she saw him?

"Sidney? Sidney, are you there? We have to get out of here." She was pretty sure the stalker would kill them both.

As the door creaked opened, the last rays of sunlight blinded Jamie. A man's silhouette filled the doorway. The darkness disguised his features.

"Who are you?" she demanded. "Why are you doing this? Don't hurt Jack. He has nothing to do with this. You have me."

His cold, hollow laugh echoed off the stone walls as he disappeared out of the doorway and into the pitch dark chamber. The door slammed shut behind him.

"He has everything to do with this Jamie, and you know that. He's the only one you care about these days, right my love?" His coughing overtook him for a few seconds. "We'll see. You'll change your mind. I'll make you forget him." His words came from a spot across the room from her. The crunching footsteps stopped.

"Get up, Miss Sidney. Let's see how close you come to the real thing." His voice sounded the same as Matt's, but there was something different, something about the way he pronounced his words.

"Matt, is that you?" She fiddled with the ropes.

Suddenly, Sidney's joy filled the room. "It's you, isn't it? I could tell from your aftershave. Thank God, some madman kidnapped us." Jamie heard a scuffle in the blackness.

"What are you doing?" Sidney questioned. "Please stop, you're hurting me." Her words echoed off the stone walls, followed by a whacking sound and then, a curse.

"You're a feisty one, huh? I like a little fight in my women." Silence followed, then, "You bit me, you bitch." A slap was followed by a scream.

"Please don't hurt her, whoever you are. You wanted me, not her." Jamie begged. "I'm here. Let her go."

"I'll get to you, don't worry. I'm just warming up with Miss Sidney here."

Jamie heard him struggling for air. Asthma. Matt didn't have asthma, but he had used an inhaler at the restaurant. Said he had a cold. Jack was with him... where's Jack now? "Oh God, no. God if you're there, keep Jack alive, please. Don't take him too, please," she whispered. "I don't know if I could take it."

"I've waited a long time for you, Jamie, and the anticipation is almost as good as the act. First, we'll see what your twin can do. I might keep her around too. Nice to have a twin, isn't it?"

"I don't understand. You had Sidney." She heard nothing. "Wait. Come back. She's not my twin," she screamed as the outside door of the cellar slammed, leaving her alone.

Chapter Sixty-Eight

"Why the hell are we driving to the Cape?" Jack growled. "What does this have to do with the abduction? Tell me now or I'll have us stopped on the highway." Jack reached for his phone.

"Tell me what the DNA test said first," Matt responded, heading toward Route 3.

"Phil said that you weren't an exact match, but close. If it's not you, it must be your father. Jamie said he had a thing for her."

"It's not my father, damn it. And how did you get my DNA anyway? Don't answer that. I guess that's the only reason she came to see me." Matt slammed his hand against the steering wheel. "It's my twin brother, Luke, that son of a bitch."

"You have a twin? Why the hell didn't you tell someone?"

"When? Did you bother to ask me? No, you and Jamie just assumed I was the guy." He was angry. "You never told me what's happening." He turned to look at Jack. "I care for her, maybe not like you, but I do care for her. I could have helped, maybe stopped this from happening if I knew what was going on."

Jack waited for Matt to work through his shock.

After a few seconds, Matt continued, "I know where he might have taken them, to my family's cottage. Father allows Luke to stay there when he isn't working, which is most of the time. He always wanted everything I had, but wasn't willing to put in the time to get it."

"Tell me everything about this genius brother of yours," Jack broke in. "If I had known about him months ago, maybe I could have stopped him and the women would still be alive."

Matt stared straight ahead while summarizing Luke's life for Jack. In a monotone voice, his words framed a picture of a sickly young boy who suffered from asthma, bronchitis, and allergies; a boy who was coddled by his mother and disregarded by his father. His mother excused Luke's character flaws as outgrowths from his illnesses. She relinquished the care of Matt to his stern father, while she spent her time pandering to Luke.

Jack allowed Matt to ramble on because he was exposing as much about himself and his relationship with his parents as he was about his twin.

As Matt swerved in and out of traffic on the Sagamore Bridge, he continued his story. Luke, a talented musician, craved the accolades that Matt had won through his athletics—trophies, school letters, and of course, the cheerleader's adoration, not a standing ovation for his piano sonatas from an auditorium filled with fur wrapped women and cigar smoking gentlemen.

At first Matt felt sorry for him, but that ended abruptly when a young coed accused Matt of breaking into her dorm room, attacking her, forcing himself on her, and then threatening her with death if she told anyone. Matt's mother beseeched his father to intervene, and of course, "good ole Dad" made the entire incident go away for Luke. He assumed his father paid off the family so that they wouldn't press charges.

"That was just the beginning of a long trail of incidents where my father stepped in and fixed things for Luke. Obviously, my father thought he was taking care of him, but instead, he encouraged him to continue down his destructive path to today." Matt's red Arden Jaguar XKR convertible hugged the road as he pressed the gas pedal. "Now, quickly update me on what's been going on with Jamie."

Matt stared at the road as he downshifted approaching the mid-Cape rotary. He checked his watch. Keeping to Route 6, he increased his speed once again.

"You better be correct about this." Jack hesitated before asking, "What did Jamie know about your twin?"

"I might have mentioned him once when we were discussing our families. Not sure I told her he was a twin. She probably never even remembered I had a brother. She didn't talk about her family because it hurt too much, and I never talked about Luke because he had been such a disappointment. Luke rebelled against everything, my parents, me, and always against going to school and working. He felt our parents were wealthy; I fulfilled their dreams of a perfect son, so why did he have to make money or do anything but spend theirs? And yes, our parents expected much from their sons—well, from me."

"We don't have time for a wild goose chase. We'll lose them, he'll kill them. Are you sure he's here? Are you sure it's him?" Jack was throwing darts, knowing he was just as responsible for this situation as Matt was. When Scott did a background check on Matt, he said that Matt had a brother, a musician. He should have pushed for more information on him, but he didn't. Was he getting soft in Oyster Point, losing his instincts?

"Who else?" Matt interrupted Jack's berating of himself. "You said it was me and I'm telling you it wasn't. So, who looks like me? Luke. Yes, I'm sure. And he shouldn't be that much ahead of us."

"All I know is that some guy stalked her all summer. Then, you appear at the beach and, later that day, at the house frightening her. Weird things like that happened over and over all summer—a man on the wharf in the night rain spying on her, you taking her to the club, then someone following us to my sister's. That's where I finally picked up some DNA. Hurry, can't you get this damn car to go faster? I called ahead so we won't be stopped."

Matt took his eyes off the road to look at Jack for a split second. "I'm trying, Jack. I'm pushing as fast as I can. And stop accusing me. You think Luke murdered those other women?"

"I do. Three maybe? Maybe more back in Boston." Jack grabbed the car door handle as Matt took the corner, the car almost shifting to two wheels as Matt sped down a dirt road, rocks, and shells flying in their wake.

"I followed you, your brother to this road the night Jamie asked him to leave." Jack felt a tingle up his neck.

If he lost her.... He couldn't go there, couldn't look in that dark corner.

Chapter Sixty-Nine

Luke yanked on Sidney's hair, pulling her head back. He wheezed after dragging her down the sand dune to the water's edge.

"My, my, don't we smell sexy." He cupped her chin in his hand, planting a wet kiss on her lips. He moved his nose all around her skin, her ear, and into her hair. He inhaled her essence, his breathing shallow.

"Matt, stop it." Sidney tried to pull away from him. "Why are you doing this? Where are we?" The darkness engulfed everything. As he let her go, she fell backwards and tripped, hitting her head on the ground. He had tied her ankles.

"Oooowww. This is not funny. Take the rope off. I can't stand."

"You'd like that, wouldn't you?" His cough overtook his words. "But, I can't. Know why?" He gasped for air. "Because you would run. And today, I couldn't catch you." His coughing continued.

Finally, he straddled her on the damp sand, his breath rattling like a wild animal. He ran his fingers through her hair catching his watch band in the back. He yanked it free.

Sidney's scream filled the darkness, bouncing off the outgoing tide.

"You are beautiful, you know that? I have to say, you are the closest to Jamie so far. Leave it to Matt to locate a perfect replacement when he couldn't have her." He let out a low, growly laugh followed by a raspy cough. "But tonight, thanks to him, I have two of his trophies. Too bad, dear brother."

"Get off me." Sidney broke into his thoughts. She shoved him, trying to move her legs away from him. "Trophies? Where's Matt?"

"You'll be one of my trophies." With one hand, he grabbed her wrists and held them over her head while he ran his other hand over every piece of her upper body until he reached the edge of her skirt and ripped at it.

"Stop, you're hurting me. Don't do this please. I can give you money or jewelry, whatever you want."

"There's only one thing I want." He ran his hand up the inside of her legs. She had long bare legs and maybe no underwear. Then, he felt the panties, silky little things for his collection. One yank and they were off. He passed them by his nose and then placed them in his pocket. Her blouse was next. He yanked her bra down, breaking the front fastener as he fondled and sucked on her breasts.

Sidney screamed, her hands straining to get loose. She wiggled under him, trying to knee him. Instead, her movements excited him more.

He needed the ocean to give him rhythm. He grabbed Sidney's arms and dragged her half naked body into the water and untied the rope from one of her legs.

Chapter Seventy

"He'll drown her if I don't get out there," Jamie muttered as she hitched herself along the dirt floor. Something sharp cut her hand.

"Ouch. Damn it. That's all I need to do, bleed to death in this God forsaken place." Her voice became louder and angrier. She touched the ground feeling scads of broken shells.

"You bastard. Just in case we make it this far, we can cut ourselves to pieces by the door. You're so smart." She picked up a large broken shell with sharp edges and rubbed it against the rope around her ankles. "No one's that smart."

She heard Sidney scream outside.

"If I catch you off guard...." Her hand ached from grasping the shell so tightly. "Maybe, just maybe...." She pulled her ankles apart as she rubbed the shell against the rope. Her mother would be horrified to see her in this un-lady like pose. "Ankles crossed, please Jamison," her mother would say as she slumped on the couch, knees spread wide open, reading her book. The thought made her smile. Then she heard a snap as the rope collapsed at her feet.

"I'll be damned." Her ankles, raw and sore, bled. She patted the ground around her and found only slivers for as far as she could reach. No wonder he had ripped their shoes off in the van. And those were expensive shoes too. The sharp shell edges pushed against her hands, feet, and knees as she stood. Picking the shards from her palms, she tried to find her bearings in the darkness.

Her hands ran along the wall to where the door should be. Taking a step, she banged her foot against the cement stairs. Stifling a cry, she rubbed her big toe and wiped the blood and shell fragments from the bottom of her foot. She hated to do it, but she wiped her hands on the blood orange Carolina Herrera shift that had cost her two months' salary.

"I hope the blood comes out—otherwise, you creep, you'll buy me a new dress. Now you owe me shoes and a dress." She felt for the door. "Where's the damn doorknob? A handle, something?"

The old, rough, wooden door generated splinters as she slid her hand down the planks, finally grasping a pull-up latch. As she lifted it, the door swung open with a squeak. Frozen in place, she waited. Nothing.

Hands on the door jamb, she tapped her big toe in front of her looking for a step or a drop. She found it, a slight drop down, and more shells.

Damn him. She stepped to the left and bit her lip as the shredded shells cut into her foot. After the pain subsided, she shifted to her right foot, the shells tearing into her skin once more. Hiking up her skirt, she stepped as far as she could until she reached sand and fewer shell fragments. She exhaled, wiping her face with her forearm and pulling her hair back out of her face. Somewhere along the way, she had lost the orange scrunchie.

Okay, where's the bastard? She listened for a few seconds and heard nothing. Then, she heard a splash, followed by a muffled scream—Sidney.

Jamie crept ahead, her eyes adjusting to the darkness. As she reached the edge of a dune, she noticed a shadowy form at the edge of the water below her. Finding a small sandy path between the beach grass and small shrub pines, she set off down the hill. The razor sharp edges of the beach grass slashed her already cut and bleeding feet. She couldn't think about the pain; she had to reach Sidney. Losing her balance, she slid on her fanny for a short distance, the sand invading her shift and underpants. She froze. A dark monster lifted its head, looked around, and then returned to his rocking movement in the water.

Jamie felt nauseous. He held the women under the water while he raped them. She gagged. Her anger surged as her hand felt an object next to her, a rock.

"I have to stop him," she repeated over and over in her mind as she ran down the hill, torn and bleeding.

Chapter Seventy-One

Matt slid the car to a stop in heavy sand. Trees and darkness surrounded them.

"Why are you stopping here? Where the hell are we?"

"Shhhh. Get out of the car and leave the door open. Don't slam it. I don't want to alert him. Grab the flashlight under your seat." Matt slipped from the driver's seat, his Berluti brown leather shoes sinking to the rims in the soft sand. He swore under his breath and continued down the road disappearing into the darkness.

Jack stepped out of the car, flashlight in hand, following Matt's direction into the shadows. He pushed his jacket back from his gun holster. As he approached Matt, he spotted the tail end of a white van parked in the overgrown driveway next to the house. He motioned to Matt that he was going to check it out.

Using his flashlight through the back windows, he could see rumpled blankets, old coffee cups, and a towel with a stain. Blood? He moved the light around. Something sparkled, something small, round, and orange caught his eye. His heart stopped. It was Jamie's scrunchie, as she called it, the one she had on her wrist at dinner tonight.

"He used the van. There looks like blood in the back. Jamie's hair tie's in there," Jack whispered as he met Matt at the end of a path.

"Let's do it." Matt pointed up the walk and motioned to Jack to be quiet.

Against his better judgment, Jack motioned for Matt to follow behind him. He took his jacket off, folded it and laid it on the front step, and pulled out his gun, letting it hang by his side. His eyes darted from shadow to shadow.

Now that he knew that this was where Sidney and Jamie were, he didn't have to trust Matt's intuition.

He should have called Jess today, she'll worry. His mind always ran through a series of random thoughts when he found himself in danger. Jack pointed to the door, checking with Matt behind him. Matt signaled for him to enter the house.

Jack pressed down on the latch and opened the door slowly.

Matt clicked on a high intensity flashlight. The beam travelled down a long dark corridor to a kitchen at the back of the house. Jack fingered his gun, clicked on his flashlight, and scanned each of the two rooms on either side of the corridor. He shook his head, nothing.

He strained to hear Jamie or Sidney's voice. He heard only his own breathing. The fluorescent light over the kitchen sink cast a deadly blue light at the end of the hallway. Turning to Matt, he whispered, "I don't think they're up here. Is there a cellar?"

"Through the kitchen to the right, there's a door. Watch out for the stairs." Matt's words were clipped, hushed. "Quickly." He rushed past Jack down the corridor, causing sheets of paper to dislodge from the wall and float to the floor.

Jack paused in front of the papers. Photographs of Jamie. The pervert had taken pictures of her everywhere, in her Boston apartment, through the cottage windows, painting on the beach, dressed and undressed. He ripped a handful of them off the wall and shredded them. Luke would pay for this. Jack caught up with Matt who waited for him at the end of the corridor. He grabbed him by the shoulder, pushing him against the wall, causing more photographs to drop to the floor.

"I'll kill him for this." He pointed to the hundreds of images of Jamie.

Matt's eyes flashed with momentary anger as he looked at the shredded photos. "Protect our girls. If you can take him alive." His words hung in the musty air. "Let's go. Down to the cellar, his favorite spot." Matt unbolted the door, pulled it open, and disappeared into the shadows.

"Where the hell are the lights?" Jack whispered. His hands moved along the side wall at the top of the stairs. Spider webs enveloped his hand. "Ouch, you bastard." Jack had grabbed on to an exposed hot water pipe. He hit the light switch.

"Look at this place, it's a cave, dirt and shells everywhere. And the steps, how quaint." He took them two at a time, skipping the cracks and missing boards. He lost his balance on the last step as the board lifted up on one end, his momentum taking him crashing into the cellar wall. Picking himself up, he spotted red smudges on a rocks.

"Blood over here." His throat started to close. "Where are they? I thought you said they would be here?"

"Out here," Matt opened the bulkhead door to the back yard.

"What's out there?"

"The water, his boat, and with luck, Jamie and Sidney."

Chapter Seventy-Two

A kiss, like a butterfly, touched her lips. A far off male voice murmured, "Are you waking up, my beauty?" Jamie fought to open her eyes, a rocking motion making her nauseous.

"Dad?" she croaked. "Where are we?" A black void stretched in front of her, moisture coating her face, and the taste of salt water permeating her lips. She shivered.

"You're safe, my love, with me."

She felt his breath on her ear, smelled the sourness of it. Her head ached, the voice distorted by the swooshing noise in her ears. *Not Jack*, her mind said, *not Jack and not Dad*—Jack's breath smelled of Spearmint gum and Dad's of cigarettes. She tried to sit up, but the darkness swirled around her, throwing her back into something hard. She grabbed for the sides of the boat to steady herself. *Oh God, no*, her mind screamed as she remembered what had happened. *Keep calm.* She could do this she told herself. She twitched her foot, attempting to move, but her feet were tied together again. The bile from her empty stomach rose into the back of her throat. A hand from behind clamped across her mouth, allowing her to make only strange animal-like noises.

Bastard. She wasn't going down without a fight. She bit down hard on a long slender finger.

He howled, hitting her on the side of the head with the back of his hand. The world spun around, her stomach heaved. She fought to hang onto consciousness. Closing her eyes, she played possum on the bottom of the boat.

Remember, your dream and reality are mixed up.

"I'm sorry I struck you, but you bit me." He sucked on his finger. "Come, my sweet. No one will bother us

273 • She's Not You

here, even the arrogant Chief," he murmured, lifting her out of the boat.

If Jack's alive, he will find you, you scumbag, she screamed in her head.

He splashed through water, carrying her limp body in his arms.

She squinted, seeing her friends above in the dark night sky.

He placed her down on damp sand, untied one leg and tugged on her other ankle rope. After a loud clanking noise, he was gone. She fought to stay awake, but fell into the darkness.

She awoke cold and reached for her blanket. She rubbed her eyes. Sand on her hands made them feel worse. "Where am I?" she asked, pushing herself up. The world swirled, her head throbbed and her body ached. Slowly memories flashed back—Matt, Sidney, the boat, the darkness... her dream.

"Son of a bitch, Matt. Where are you, you bastard?" Her raspy voice received no answer. The old lighthouse base on Billings Island encompassed her. A stake driven into the sand secured the rope tied around her ankle.

"Oh my God. It was me in the dream. Oh my God... you bastard, what have you done?" Her croaking became louder and louder. "I won't die here—do you hear me? You can't make me die on this island."

The tide rose. She yanked on the stake, then the rope. Neither budged. Her heart raced. Something, there had to be something. She remembered her head had been resting on something soft, a man's jacket. She shook it and rifled through the pockets—nothing. She wiped the sleeve of the jacket across her face. Was that her blood or his? It better be his, the bastard. If it wasn't, it soon would be. She would find him or Jack would. She rubbed the egg on the back of her head.

"Oh Lord, I have to get away. Where's the shell?"

She threw the jacket to the ground and riffled through her shift pocket. The shell hid in the corner. Could she cut through this thick rope? She dug her fingers into the sand searching... nothing.

"Please let this work. Jack, where are you?" she whispered, scanning the horizon. No lights on the water. The tide inched up on her. She reached for her opal. Gone. Her good luck charm, lost.

"Well, JJ, you're on your own. No one's here to help, not even your magic opal." Her fingers, bloodied and raw, continued to rub the shell against the rope.

Chapter Seventy-Three

Jack struggled to hear sounds as he paused on the top of the dune. Pitch blackness stretched out in front of him, a blackness that crept into his heart. Where was she? He heard nothing but the lapping of the waves.

She was gone. He had shadowed Jamie all summer, and then, this one night, when he thought that he had the stalker in front of him, Luke took her. He should never have let her out of his sight. Maybe he could've waited outside the ladies' room. He would have heard the glass break, caught the guy before he took them. Would've, should've... could've....

"Oh God, what if this guy hurts her or worse?" he whispered. He had to put away his guilt while he concentrated on finding her. But she wasn't just another missing person, she was his... love.

"Do you see anything, Jack?" Matt uttered, bringing him back to the moment.

"Shhhhh. Did you hear that?" They stood like statues, hardly breathing.

"There, did you hear it? A groan?" Jack tumbled down the hill heading for the water.

Matt ran to the edge of the water and grabbed up Sidney. She moaned as she lay in his arms. "I'm fine," she sputtered. "Go find Jamie. He took her." Her coughing cut off the rest of her sentence. "Get your hands off me," she cried, striking Matt in the face. "Jack, help me."

"It's okay, this is the real Matt. The other guy is his twin, Luke. Sid, I need you to help me. Do you know where Jamie is?" Jack asked as he knelt across from Matt, the waves soaking his tan slacks and seeping into his loafers.

"I don't know." She fought to sit up leaning against Matt. "How can that monster be your brother?" She clutched Matt's arm. "What's wrong with him? Why did he do this?"

"He's sick."

"Let's focus on getting Jamie back. I'll deal with Luke when I find him. Trust me." Jack gave Matt a withering stare. "Tell us what happened."

"Jamie came out of nowhere screaming and jumped on him, trying to pull him off me. She swung a rock and hit him as he tried to rape me. This is his blood, not mine." She rubbed at the stain on her shirt as though she could erase his memory by eliminating the blood.

"Son of a bitch," Matt muttered as he pulled her blouse together.

"It's okay, Sid. We can wash that off later. What happened next?" Jack struggled to remain calm. He knew that every minute counted.

"Jamie thought she had knocked him out and had my hand, pulling me from the waves when he grabbed her from the back, pulling her hair, and then hit her with something." Sidney coughed, still expelling salt water from her lungs.

Jack turned away, vowing that when he found Luke, he would twist him in two like a pretzel for what he had done to Jamie and Sidney.

"What happened then?" Although he didn't want to hear the details, he needed to if he had any hope of finding her.

"He tossed her to the ground," Sidney continued. "She tried to crawl away, but he dragged her back by the leg. She kicked him, clawed his face, slapped him." She stopped for a few seconds, her breath coming hard.

The two men exchanged looks, waiting for her to continue.

"I know this is hard Sidney, but you have to help us," Jack pleaded.

"He's so strong. I couldn't help her." She coughed up more salt water. "I was exhausted from trying to keep my face out of the water." She adjusted her skirt.

"What else, Sid, keep going." Matt encouraged her.

"A boat, I heard a boat. He took her away in a boat." She tried to stand, but fell backwards on Matt. "Matt, I couldn't stop him." Her tears turned into deep sobs. "Oh my God, Jack, what will he do to her?"

"Matt, your car keys please. You stay here with Sidney. Call 911 and have her checked out. I'm going after Jamie."

Matt tossed his keys. "Where?"

"I think I know where he might have gone, Billings. When's high tide?"

Matt shook his head, cradling Sidney and dialing his cell phone. "I have no idea. If you wait until the ambulance comes, I'll go with you."

"No time. You stay with Sidney. She's hurt and frightened. Don't leave her now. I'm almost certain it's Billings. I'll explain later. Call my brother-in-law and tell him to take his boat and meet me at the island." He rattled off Jess' telephone number.

Jack crawled back up the sand dune, hearing Matt talking to the 911 operator. He prayed for God to keep Jamie safe, something he didn't do often enough lately.

Reaching Matt's car, he tore down the street, shifting into a lower gear as he entered Route 6 at the end of the dirt road.

"What if I don't get there in time? What happens if she's hurt or even worse? Then what? Your fault, this is your fault."

He ran through every possibility as he burned up Route 6 careening on to Main Street. His cell phone almost slipped out of his sweaty hands.

"Dan? Jack, the Chief, here. I'm taking my boat out. Police business. I'll be heading out to Billings. Just don't stop me. Thanks."

Chapter Seventy-Four

Jamie submerged the rope burns on her wrists and ankles in the salt water. The open gashes on her feet stung so much she wanted to scream. At least the wounds had stopped bleeding.

What if he didn't come back? What if Jack caught him and he didn't say where she was? The tide inched higher and higher. Could she swim back to the wharf? Maybe a boat would see her. Should she go now? Panic rose inside her. She had to be prepared for everything, even the worst case, rape and death at his hand. He wouldn't kill her; he had wanted her for too long. As she made her way back to the stake, she found a loose brick. She retied the rope lightly around her ankle and wrists and waited.

The sound of a boat cut through the stillness of the night. She prayed that it was Jack. Would he remember her dream? She hid the shell in her pocket and pushed the brick under her, covering it over with sand. She lay down and played possum.

"Hello, my sweet thing. Did you miss me? I had to get a few more things to make us comfy while we make love." His hand on her face was icy cold. He ran it down her neck to her breasts. She had to endure his pawing and not move.

"I've waited so long for us to be together." He cradled her breast, reached down to kiss it. "You don't know how much I've wanted you and now, finally, you are mine. I don't want you to be jealous of those other women. Yes, I made love to them, but only because I didn't have you." His cold hands reached under her shirt. "I thought only of you as I made love to them."

She struggled to keep from pushing his hand away.

"I had to get rid of them, they knew too much and would have run to the Chief. We didn't want that now, did we? And they weren't like you, strong and beautiful. None took my breath away like you do." His hand continued to move up her leg. "They whined all the time, just kept whining. They wanted more, all of them. But you…."

Jamie controlled her urge to gouge out his eyes.

"I made a mistake with your twin. You interrupted my rhythm, I hadn't finished." He moved his hand still further up her leg, pulling on her underpants. "I know you were jealous seeing me with her, but when I was finished, I would have disposed of her, too. I only want you, to make love to you forever." His fingers moved inside her underpants. "I left her alive and now she will tell the Chief everything." He coughed and coughed. "But he'll never find us here, our special place."

He killed those women. He touched her and her stomach lurched. Why was he doing this now? They had been friends for years. He had many chances to seduce her. What made him such a monster?

Her hand inched under her body, searching for the brick. He leaned in to kiss her breast. She swung as hard as she could. He pitched forward with unbelieving eyes wide open and flopped on top of her.

She stayed still. He didn't move. His dead weight suffocated her. She pushed and shoved until he landed on his back with a thud. She wiped his blood off her face and neck with the back of her hand. She untied the ropes around her ankles and as she rose to her feet, his hand grabbed her calf.

"You bastard, get your hands off of me." She turned with such fury that he rolled away, but not before the brick connected with the other side of his head. She felt like bashing him over and over again as rage filled her. Instead, she dropped the brick, ran to the encroaching waves, gulping for air. Diving in, she submerged until she thought her lungs would burst. She surfaced. The darkness hid him. Had he moved? She couldn't tell. She should have killed him. Swimming to the boat, she thrust herself through high waves, finally sinking under the water. She floated up to the top, next to the boat. Using every ounce of energy, she hauled her waterlogged body into the boat. She lay on the bottom catching her breath. Exhausted, she leaned over the side, yanking on the anchor's rope.

"Oh my God." She tugged on the rope again. When it didn't budge, she jumped into the water, held her breath and located the rope fastened to a solid block on the bottom. Untying one knot, she surfaced for air. She started to dive back down when a yank on her hair caused her to fly out of the water, slamming her back against the boat.

"Let go, you're hurting me," She spit out, coughing up salt water.

"Why are you trying to escape?" His face, covered with blood and his hair matted against the side of his head, made him look like the monster that he was. "Why did you do that?" He yanked her from the water. "I love you. Don't you understand? I'll protect you against harm, against Jack. We can be together now. No one will find us or separate us. I promise." He kissed her cheek.

His words chilled her to the bone. "You frightened me by tying me up. Why did you do that?" She knew that if he took her from this island, Jack would never find her. "I love you too. Let me catch my breath for a minute. Please don't tie me up again. My wrists and ankles are bleeding." She sat coughing up salt water, regaining her breath.

"I'll take you back to rest."

Jamie had to stay on Billings as long as she could. She pushed her hair back, stood, and dove under the water, swimming for shore, scraping her knees on shells as she reached the beach. She knelt, chest heaving, trying to inhale fresh air. There was a splash behind her. He fell to his knees beside her. What now? Run from him, attack him, or play along with him? As exhausted as she was, she stood and stumbled ahead toward the base of the lighthouse and the stake where he had tied her up. Picking up the brick and hiding it behind her, she waited.

He stopped about ten feet from her, his mouth seemingly moving. But she heard nothing but a pulsating flow of rage in her ears. Let him come, let him come closer. She had to do this, no one was coming to rescue her.

He swayed and fell to the sand. He lay still.

Did he pass out or was he playing possum? The tide rose. She stood, shifted to his left, closer to the water as his hand shot out. Backing up, falling back over the lighthouse base, she yanked her leg away from him, but not before he was up on his knees and thrusting his body over her. She raised the brick and swung. Something hit her in the stomach just as she made contact with his head.

Her world swirled and went black.

Chapter Seventy-Five

Once into the channel, Jack switched on the boat's running lights, hit the throttle, and roared out of the harbor at full speed heading to Billings. The red and blue police lights flashed.

There was no way to know if the blackness would help or hinder him. It wasn't the darkness that he worried about, but the rising tide. He had maybe an hour left before the island would be submerged. Once the water rolled over the island, there'd be no place for Jamie to go. The waves covered the sand in minutes.

He shook his head… could she swim? She had worn a life vest in the boat.

"Stay alive Jamie, please, for me," he kept repeating over and over. What would he do if he was too late? "She's tough. She'll be there when I get there."

He shut off the lights and circled the island, attempting to see any movement. Finally, he spotted the outline of a small boat. Luke had taken her here. He drifted in as close to the little boat as he could. Dropping anchor, he slid, without a splash, into the water.

The sky was the darkest right before dawn.

Chapter Seventy-Six

Jamie moaned as she pushed herself up on her elbows. Her head, hands, and feet, even her stomach hurt. Water covered her fingers and stung her open wounds.

The tide was coming fast. If she was to escape, she had to go now. She struggled to regain her bearings. Which way was she facing? No lights, just the stars, her friends.

The North Star, where was it? What had she seen through her skylight at night when she was small? Her head throbbed. The star should be at the end of the handle. But which handle, Big or Little Dipper?

"Concentrate JJ. Where are you, my friend?" There it was, at the end of the Little Dipper. She faced north. Jack will be impressed. If she moved a quarter of a turn, the harbor should be straight ahead and the boat as well.

Jamie rose and fell backwards with a splash. She felt the tug, the rope around her ankle. A heartbreaking cry rose from deep inside her, "No, oh no, nooooooo you bastard. Jack," she shrieked, her words echoing off the waves breaking over the island.

Then there was silence.

***

A piecing cry. Jack heard his name, he was sure of it. Treading water, he strained to hear her voice again. He heard nothing but the thrashing of the waves on the island. He pushed through the water on foot, rising and falling as the surf knocked him around. His eyes burned as he searched the darkness. Nothing moved. The tide had covered most of the island— new moon, higher tide.

285 • She's Not You

"Jamie," he shouted, slashing through the surf. "Jamie, where the hell are you?" He hesitated, trying to think where the lighthouse would be. To his right?

"Jamie?" The water felt like weights attached to his ankles and slowed him down. "Luke, you son of a bitch. Jamie, let me see you," he whispered, his eyes adjusting to the darkness. Cracked and broken shells sliced into his feet as he headed for shore. Ahead, a form, floating. He pushed harder through the water. "No, God no." His voice rose above the sound of the crashing waves.

He clutched the dark body, turned it over, heard a splash, and then felt a searing pain in his side.

Chapter Seventy-Seven

Jamie floated through a quiet, black world. Slowly, it became lighter and finally, her eyes fluttered open. He stood outlined by the predawn sky with his back toward her. He pulled the cord time and time again trying to start the engine. He was leaving the island.

Her head rested on a wooden seat. All that mattered was finding Jack. She had heard his voice, but where was he? He wouldn't leave her with this monster unless... there was no unless. Concentrate on the task at hand—escape and find Jack.

"Shit." He held up his hand, sucked on his thumb, and then, tugged at the rope again.

Her hand inched into the space below her. She touched something woven, a wicker basket? He probably stole the boat, or was planning a romantic dinner with someone? She pulled the latch up and slipped her hand through the tight opening.

Ugh, soft stuff. A rotten apple maybe? A wrapped plastic sandwich? Squeezing her hand further into the basket, she felt something cold, smooth, and solid, a wine bottle. Perfect. Sliding her fingers to the neck, she lifted the bottle, gliding it through the crack, making a slight squeaking noise. She froze. She had to reach him before he sensed her movement behind him. Her timing had to be perfect.

Jamie rose inch by inch, first to her knees and then to her feet, coordinating her movements with his. She made herself small as she approached him. The boat swayed. She froze. His thrashing with the engine cord continued. Lifting each leg up over the seat, she stood so close that she feared that he could feel her breath on his neck, hear her heart beat. She wiped her wet palm on her tattered damp shift.

Grabbing the bottle with both hands, she shut her eyes and swung it with all the force she could muster. She let out a cry as the thud reverberated up her arm, causing such a pain in her shoulder that she thought she had dislocated it. The motion carried her arm back, connecting with the other side of his head. He pivoted with a startled look on his face, crumpling to the bottom of the boat.

Grabbing the rope from the seat behind her, she tied his hands using the nautical knot Jack had taught her. Then she secured his ankles as well. As she stood, she spotted Jack's boat silhouetted against a lightening sky.

"Oh God, where are you?" she whispered, combing the water that covered the island looking for something, anything. "Jack, Jack, where are you?" she screamed. When no answer came back, she knew what she had to do.

Jamie jumped into the cold, dark water.

Chapter Seventy-Eight

"Stop fighting me, Jack. I can't wrestle with you, we'll both drown. I'm not letting go." Jack had been floating on his back near his boat when she found him.

"Who..." his voice cracked. He floated off somewhere.

"Jack, it's Jamie."

"I'm sorry I couldn't save—couldn't help." His tiredness overwhelmed him. Sleep, he just needed to close his eyes and sleep.

"Stay with me, Jack, stay with me. Wake up." Her pleading words echoed off the water. "You have to help me. Grab the iron bar. We can do this, we're a team, remember? You said that." He felt his arm being lifted. "Please, you promised me you wouldn't leave me, you wouldn't hurt me. You promised. Help me, goddamn it. Someone help me!" she yelled.

Jack stretched for the bar, cold in his hand. He struggled to pull himself out of the water. So hard, too hard. Her hand pressed his side, causing pain.

"Ah," he mumbled. He remembered now. He thought it was Jamie floating, but as he moved closer, Luke had lunged from the water catching him off guard and striking him in his side with something sharp.

"He won't win, you know that. Luke won't win, I won't let him." He inched himself up using every bit of energy he had. He heard a noise, a boat's motor. "Honey, are you still there?" He swung an arm out. "Are you hurt?"

She planted his hand back onto the bar. He felt her push him from behind.

"You can't get rid of me that easily. A homicidal maniac is no match for me." He heard her gasping for breath as she encouraged him up the ladder. "Keep going, you're doing great."

"Is that a boat?" A light flashed in his eyes as Jack turned toward the noise.

"Here, we're over here!" she yelled, waving her sore arm, holding Jack with the other.

Jack heard a splash and then felt someone's hands grab and lift him up into the boat.

"Stop Matt, get away from him!" Jamie swatted, punched, and wrapped her arms around Matt's legs as he climbed the ladder with Jack. All of a sudden, Terry appeared beside her in the water.

"Stop, Jamie, let him go. Matt's twin brother, Luke, killed the women. Where's the bastard?" Terry grabbed her by the arms.

"Luke? Oh my God. That's why Jack used his name, not Matt's. He's in the boat. I hit him with a wine bottle and tied him up. I thought he had gotten free." She hung on to Terry, sucking huge breaths.

"Hot damn, you're something," Terry chuckled as he helped Matt climb into the boat and pull an exhausted Jamie to safety. "I thought you smelled like you had been partying." Terry gave her a little hug, trying to relax her with his jokes.

"Oh my God, thank you. How did you know where we were?" She knelt down and cradled Jack's head.

"Jack had some idea about this island, thought Luke would take you here for some reason. Not sure why."

"When Jack took off after you, he told me to call Terry and tell him what was going on. Terry showed up in a flash," Matt added. "Jess stayed with Sid."

"He's okay, Terry? It isn't bad, is it?" she asked.

Terry gave her a thumb up as he wrapped Jack's wound. "Bro, I think you are going to live to tell this great fish tale."

"Thank God. Matt, I'm so sorry. I just thought...."
Jamie reached for his hand.

"Don't be sorry. How could you know?"

"How's Sidney? I tried to help her but...." Jamie
had to take a breath.

"Sidney's okay. You helped a lot. When he took
you, he left her for dead. She's tough—like you." Matt
gave her a bear hug. "God, if Jack and I had lost the two of
you." His voice cracked. "I left her with Jess at the clinic
once I knew she wasn't in danger. I still can't believe this
night."

"Jack, you're one lucky guy, the wound isn't deep.
You lost a ton of blood though." Terry used the boat's first
aid kit and taped Jack's wound closed. "Can you drive this
boat Matt?"

"I don't have a choice? Where to?" Matt replied.

"We're taking these guys back into safe harbor.
Radio Jack's deputy to send someone out here to secure
Luke before he takes off. Also have an ambulance waiting
for us on the wharf. Wait for me while I check on Luke."
Terry jumped back into the black water.

"Be careful of him," Matt called out after Terry.
"Jamie, can you radio Jack's guys?"

She nodded. Matt started up the boat.

*　*　*

Jamie huddled in the back of the ambulance wrapped in a
white cotton blanket, her hand resting on Jack's chest, as
they sped to Cape Cod Hospital. His hand moved, grasping
hers tightly.

"Are you okay?" he asked, his voice barely audible.

She kissed his cold fingers. "Don't you ever, ever
scare me like that again, do you hear me?"

"Yes ma'am. And you? God, I thought you were
dead." His frigid hand tried to reach her face. She leaned
forward. "Did he hurt you?" Jack continued.

"He made a valiant try. We had a few tussles, but in the end, he got the worse of it." She shook her wet hair. "Boy, do I need a hot shower, I smell like wine. And look at this dress. It's brand new and cost me a small fortune." She prattled on, trying to relax him.

"I'll buy you a new one and shoes to match," he tried to laugh, but winced. "What did he do to me, by the way?"

"Oh sure, on your salary." She rubbed his hand in hers, letting the blanket slip off her shoulders. "He stabbed you in the side with something, but the EMT said, luckily, he must have been weak because he missed his mark. He didn't hit anything vital. You did lose a lot of blood."

"Will you stay with me?"

"They want to check me out as well so I'll be there with you. We'll need to give statements. I'm too tired to think about any of this."

"I didn't mean now. I mean will you stay with me in Oyster Point, not go back to Boston? After all this is over?"

"Are you afraid to stay alone now?" she joked, the coldness in her heart slowly evaporating.

He smiled at her. "I love you, Jamison Janson. I don't want you to leave."

"I won't leave you," she whispered as the ambulance swung into the hospital emergency entrance and Jack closed his eyes. "I promise."

Chapter Seventy-Nine

Blue Crane Creek meandered along the base of the amethyst colored Grand Teton Mountains with their deep glacial pockets of white. It was October. The autumn reflections of the aspen and cottonwood trees ran like streams of liquid gold through the rich lapis blue creek. The first snowfall gently rested on the trees and covered the bright rust-colored grass with a soft dusting of white.

"It's so beautiful here. How could you ever leave?" Jamie questioned Jack.

"Ah, seen through the eyes of an artist," he joked with a slight wince.

She watched him straighten in the saddle, touching his healing wound.

"Even I'd forgotten how gorgeous it is." He stared at the mountains, his tall black and white tobiano stallion, Tornado, shifting under him. "I haven't been back to the ranch for over a year."

"Why?" It was hard for her to understand why he would stay away from a place like this. "I'd spend as much time here as I could." A rancher's role fit Jack perfectly, living outdoors, riding, and roping. He seemed to be made for this type of life.

"It's hard to explain." Choosing his words carefully, he continued. "I work with the ranch hands all day, checking fences and moving the herds around. The physical work is great, but at night, there are a lot of memories."

"Not happy ones?" She tried to read his face, but it was shadowed by his hat and sunglasses.

"You know more than anyone else that being alone with happy memories is sometimes harder than being alone with sad ones." Jack pulled on the reins, moving Tornado closer to Jamie. "I built a wing onto the house thinking I'd have a place of my own, a life of my own." He shrugged. "I brought Lizz here once without telling her that I owned it. She thought I had rented it. She stayed two days, packed up and flew back to New York City declaring she hated this God-forsaken place, that she had never been so bored in her entire life. From that point on, my visits consisted of a week or two a couple of times a year to check the books, catch up with the guys, and help move the herds. Bobby, my foreman, works the ranch like it's his own. I'm lucky to have him. When I'm sure that the ranch is in good shape, I fly back to Boston. My life, what there is of it, is in Oyster Point." His statement hung in the frosty air for a minute. He wasn't feeling sorry for himself, just stating facts.

"Why didn't you ever mention this place to me?" she asked as Tornado edged closer to her palomino filly, Beauty, for warmth.

Jack's breath billowed out and then floated off with the clouds. Removing his hat, he rerolled the edges and flicked at an imaginary speck with his fingers before sliding the hat back on, low over his eyes. He was the epitome of the perfect cowboy, the Stetson, suede jacket, horse and the unshaven jaw. She had fallen in love with him somehow along this strange journey that they had taken together, and it hurt her to see him tortured by his past.

"I won't be upset by your answer, you know."

He touched her hand. "I hope you won't. It has nothing to do with you. After Lizz's reaction, I buried my personal information. When I looked up and saw you on the beach that day, you touched something in me." Tornado pawed at the ground. "I couldn't even talk straight." He watched a hawk circle above them. "I couldn't get you out of my head, no matter where I was or what I was doing. I couldn't read you. There never seemed to be a right time to tell you about my past and all this." He hesitated as though wondering how to phrase the next sentence. "I saw your reaction about the boat, a flash of doubt about my past." His statement hung in the air waiting for her to destroy it.

"I won't lie. I did wonder how you could afford a boat like that on your town salary. Matt...Luke brought up the corruption charges against your partner." She shook the snow off the soft beige Stetson that Jack had given her when they arrived. "I never really doubted you. I knew you were a pretty solid man."

"Well, that's not the most ringing endorsement I've ever gotten, but I'll take it for now. Everyone should be loved or hated for who he is, not for what he owns. It's that simple. You know that I'm not good at talking about myself, about my background, education, possessions. It makes me uneasy. None of this stuff makes any difference to me."

That statement made her laugh. "I know that for a fact. All I have to do is look at where you live; your boat is worth more than your house." She laughed even harder.

"You said you liked my place, that it had potential."

"It does." She put a gloved hand across her mouth trying to camouflage her laugher with a fake cough. "I'm sorry. I didn't mean to interrupt you."

"Well, if you are going to make fun of my home." The words hung in the cold, as he leaned on the horn of the saddle.

"I'm sorry. No more mocking."

"Yea, that's about to happen." He squeezed her hand. "Anyway, this is all my great-great-grandfather's doing." He looked across the valley with a slight smile creeping across on his face. "He found this place, loved it, and stayed here. It has always passed to the oldest male in the family so, here I sit with much more than I need or want." He took a deep breath, again creating large frosty billows as he exhaled. "I've never told anyone about this place."

"What happened with Lizz? Did you two break up after the episode here?" Jamie tried to keep the unfamiliar feel of jealousy out of her tone. She hated the thought of him being in love with someone else. It was silly and once the questions left her mouth, she was sorry. "I apologize. That's none of my business. I don't know why I asked that, really."

"I'll tell you anything you want to know. I assume Jess mentioned Lizz? She talks a lot." He smiled, shaking his head. He quieted Tornado with a pat and a soft word. "Jess never liked Lizz, and I couldn't blame her. Lizz had no use for the Cape, for Jess, for the boat or the kids, for that matter. She wanted to marry someone else, not me. I was never going to be who she wanted. I guess I was a novelty in the beginning, a puppy she thought she could train, but it didn't turn out that way. I'm not sure why she wasted so much time trying to change me. The longer it went on, the bigger the fights became until the gap between us was so huge that I had to leave," he paused. "Jess called Lizz a cold fish, and Jess is always right. She's actually a real good judge of people. Don't tell her I said that though."

"You sound like you had nothing in common with her." She didn't know how far to go with the questioning, but he would change the subject when he had enough of her prying.

"I guess I didn't. But I had to figure that out myself after some very painful years. You know, after a while, a relationship is something you both have even if it's not working anymore." He looked toward the mountains. "I know there have been men in your life, and no, I don't want to hear about them." He pushed the brim of her hat down over her eyes. "All I'm saying is that you know how hard it is to be the one to walk away. I wanted her to leave, but she wouldn't—she really thought she would break me, like one of my wild ponies. Anyway, Jess was good; she listened when I had to get stuff off my chest."

"You and Jess are so lucky. I'm jealous. That sounds awful, doesn't it? But I never had anyone like her, never had that closeness with a sister or a brother. Well, Kate would be angry with that comment, but even with her, somethings were best left unsaid."

"You have family now." He leaned over and planted a kiss on her cheek.

"Yes, I do." She stroked his three day old beard.

"And how many guys were there before me?" He laughed, with a wince. "Nah.... Don't tell me. Let's finish this conversation tonight in front of the fire. By the way, you look great with those rosy cheeks and that hat. This place agrees with you. Let's see the rest of the ranch. You ready?"

"After you, cowboy." She tugged on the reigns, turning Beauty away from the edge of the bluff, pulling up beside Jack. Tornado, like his master, was intimidating, muscular, sure footed, spirited, and yet, gentle. He stood stoically, pawing at the snow covered ground, awaiting Jack's command. He patted Tornado's neck and the four of them trotted off as a light snow started to fall.

***

Jack stepped through the dark wooden carved door, a coating of snow on his hair and shoulders. He kicked the door closed behind him.

"You shouldn't be carrying logs with your side still healing. I could have brought them in, I'm pretty tough you know," she teased. She continued to look at him without saying anything.

"What?"

"I was thinking that's how you'll look when you're old and gray."

He dropped the hefty load of logs next to the fieldstone fireplace that he had built with stones from the ranch. He shook the snow from his coat and hair onto her as she knelt starting the fire. "You plan on being around that long?" he raised an eyebrow.

Jamie brushed off the melting slush he had thrown her way. She caught his stare. "Maybe."

"Maybe, huh? Let's sit and talk about this. If you have conditions, you better state them now." He threw his jacket on the couch, ran his fingers through his wet hair, piled three large logs on the fire, and joined her on the rug in front of the fireplace. "Just remember what you promised a dying man." They sat, their backs against the couch, as the fire caught sending a wave of warmth out into the room.

"You weren't dying." She wiggled her toes inside her socks. "Doesn't that heat feel good?"

"You didn't know I wasn't dying." He put his arm around her and pulled her against his chest. "And here I thought you loved it out there today."

She could feel his strong heartbeat. She rubbed his cold hands in hers. "I did love it. When you went outside, I thought how beautiful it must be here at Christmas. You could place a tree right there in front of that window." She pointed to a spot to the left of the fieldstone fireplace that looked out onto the snow covered mountains.

"Did you cut down your own tree when you were young?" she blurted out before she realized how hurtful it might be for him to go back to that time. "I'm sorry. I seem to be saying that a lot lately."

"Don't be sorry. Those are great memories with my Dad." He circled her palm with his fingers.

"We'd tie on snow shoes, plod through the woods creating a trail through the deep snow. Finally, we would come upon an open meadow. My father stood in the middle of the field and looked back at all the trees along the edge. 'Well, Tyke,' he'd say, 'which one do you think your mother would like?' I'd looked at hundreds." He laughed. "At least it felt like that. I'd wander back and forth along the trees, measuring the height, smelling the needles, narrowing down my choice. When I pointed to one, my Dad would say, 'Just the one I was looking at.' I'd feel so proud."

His memories engulfed her as they swirled around the room.

"We'd chop it down, tie it to the sled, and pull it back to the house, the tree overflowing the sled so much that it looked like the tree was moving on its own." His tone told her how much he had loved his father.

"Many times I'd think we'd never find our way back, but later, when I was older, I realized that my Dad took the same way out to the meadow and back every year. I never told him I knew." His laugh lit up his eyes. "My mother waited for us with hot chocolate and warm cookies. When we brought the tree in, we always had to trim a bit from the top." He had lost himself in the glow of those days. "Sometimes more than a little. But my Mom would always say it was perfect, the best one yet." He squeezed her hand.

"You know, I've never spent the holidays in this part of the house since I built it." He pulled away from her. "You're right, that would be a perfect spot for a tree." Thinking for a minute, he continued, "How about we spend Christmas here this year?"

"What? Here? Us?" He jolted her out of his Christmas story.

"Why not. We can stay through New Year's. Would you like that?" He sounded excited. "It's gorgeous here. The town and the ranches are decorated; the neighbors have gatherings, at least they used to. We could have an open house, just like the old days. Maybe even go to midnight Mass?"

"You're serious, aren't you? What about your job? Can you afford to take the time off?"

He stared at her.

"I didn't mean afford like that." She gave him a gentle nudge. "I mean can you be away from the job for two weeks? After all, what would Oyster Point do without you there to protect it? And we have all those other cold cases in the box to solve," she questioned.

"Please, don't you think we've solved enough mysteries this year? We both have earned some time off. And I haven't taken a real vacation since... I can't remember when. And this year, it would be perfect, spending my first Christmas in this house with you."

She sat stunned. She hadn't thought about celebrating the holidays in years. December made her think of her parent's deaths. Most times on Christmas, she'd go to Kate's and after dinner come home, fall asleep and wake up the next morning to her regular schedule. Spending holiday time with someone special, someone she loved? Her eyes started to sting.

"What about your family? What will they think? Won't they miss you?" she tried to make her voice sound normal.

"My family can come out here if they want. There's plenty of room. And they would be happy if we spent the holidays together, very happy. But, we don't have to if you don't want to. Maybe you have other plans. I just thought," he stammered. "Would Kate want you there? Her first Christmas with Logan?"

"No, she would be thrilled... and Logan will have plenty of family around him." She stared at him, her tears about to spill over. Her throat tightened. She kissed him hard, her hands clasping his unshaved cheeks. She snuggled back against his chest, wrapping his arms around her.

"Tomorrow, we will search for that perfect tree, and mark it with a ribbon so we can find it when we come back at Christmastime," she whispered, wiping the tears off her cheeks. "Do we need to buy ornaments and lights? Can we get them here or do we have to bring them with us?" Now she was getting excited.

"I'll take you up to the attic later and you can go through the family Christmas stuff to see if there's anything worth using, anything you like. We haven't touched those boxes in twenty years, I bet." His breath against her ear made her feel wobbly. "I'm sure we'll need new lights, but the ornaments should be okay, right?"

"They'll be perfect." She heard the childlike anticipation in his voice.

"We can drive to Jackson and buy whatever we need, whatever you want, go Christmas shopping together. You can help me find gifts for Jessica's kids, for everyone. But you can't peek at what I buy for you."

"Now I'll have a challenge buying a gift for the man who has everything." She folded her fingers through his.

"I will have everything this Christmas and for many more to come, I hope. Jamie, I love you more than life itself." His voice was soft in her ear.

"And you're mine." Her tears spilled over. "How did we ever get this lucky?" This time she spoke her thoughts out loud.

"Do you think all our angels had something to do with it?" He brushed the tears from her cheeks. "She's mine now and I'll watch over her. You can all rest," he said aloud to the powers that be, staring into her eyes.

"My 'gift' will drive you crazy," she reminded him.

"Your love?"

"That too," she teased him between kisses. "I can be quite jealous and possessive, you know."

"Please do." He grabbed a pillow from the couch and placed it on the floor.

The heat of the blazing fire spread through them both as they became lost in each other's arms, in their dreams of spending a Christmas together.

Jack and Jamie received an early Christmas gift, an unexpected meteor shower that lit up the skies over Jackson, Wyoming.

The End

About Judi Getch Brodman

Judi's software consulting work has taken her all over the world even out to the Marshall Islands where she flew to work each day. Her bookshelves are filled with photographs and journals that capture her experiences and feed her imagination as she writes. But her roots and true inspiration come from New England, in the mountains of Vermont and by her childhood beaches of Wellfleet on Cape Cod.

In 2011, she began her writing journey with three published travel articles on Ireland, The Many Faces of Ireland, followed by a short story, Safe Harbor, published in July 2012. Then, inspired by the death of her sister in 2015, Judi wrote and published two children's books, "Fiona - the Lighthouse Firefly" and "Fiona the Firefly - LOST!" both titles available on Amazon, the proceeds of which feed a scholarship fund that Judi set up in her sister's name. Scholarships are being awarded to students studying Business and Technology.

In her spare time, Judi is a professional watercolorist, reads, walks, gardens, and enjoys family and friends. But wherever she is, her characters and their magical worlds fill her mind.

Judi has been involved with writers' groups for years, has taken Creative Writing at FAU, and has worked with authors in workshops whenever possible. She's also an editor for Wiley's technical magazine, Journal of Software: Evolution and Process.

She's Not You is her first novel.

Social Media

Facebook: https://www.facebook.com/judigetchbrodman/

Blog: https://judigetchwriter2.blogspot.com

Website: https://judigetchbrodman.wordpress.com/

LinkedIn: https://www.linkedin.com/in/judigetchbrodman

Acknowledgements

To Steve, for his love and encouragement during this long process…

Review

"She's Not You is a taut, engaging mystery that plays out against the vividly observed beauty of Cape Cod. A perfect beach read." Heidi Jon Schmidt, author of The House on Oyster Creek.

Made in United States
Orlando, FL
12 March 2023

30966811R00166